COME APART

CRYSTAL KASWELL

Copyright

This is a work of fiction. Similarities to real people, places, or events are entirely coincidental.

Also by Crystal Kaswell

Come Undone Trilogy

Come Undone

Come Apart

Come To Me

Dirty Rich

Dirty Deal - Blake

Dirty Boss - Nick

Dirty Husband - Shep

Dirty Desires - Ian

Dirty Wedding - Ty

Dirty Secret - Cam

Pierce Family

Broken Beast - Adam

Playboy Prince - Liam

Ruthless Rival - Simon - coming soon

Inked Hearts

Tempting - Brendon

Hooking Up - Walker

Pretend You're Mine - Ryan

Hating You, Loving You - Dean

Breaking the Rules - Hunter

From the Author

Five years ago, I started writing my first novel. After stumbling a lot and revising even more, I finished the early incarnation of this book. I published it in 2014 under the title *Rouse Me*.

At the time, I was still writing screenplays, still hearing "no one wants romance" or "no one wants stories about women" constantly. The very act of writing about a damaged woman finding love felt revolutionary. I had no idea what a "romance novel" was, but I knew I wanted to write a story about love that was romantic—my idea of romantic.

Then I wrote a bunch more books (including this one, a third *Rouse Me* book, and a dirty Cinderella story). Somehow, I lucked into my niche with my fourth book *Sing Your Heart Out*. By the time I started work on book three in that series, I knew I had my path.

I started writing damaged rock stars. Then damaged bad boys of all types. I found my voice... even if it wavered from time to time.

Then, I decided *Rouse Me* didn't reflect what I write

anymore. I took it down, with plans to rewrite it to bring it "on brand." Only it refused to fit neatly into the "Crystal Kaswell brand."

Last year, I published it anyway. And people liked it. A lot more than I expected. It wasn't my next *Tempting*, but it found readers and those readers wanted the rest of the *Rouse Me* series.

So… I reworked those too. It took awhile (it's been nearly a year now), but the entire trilogy is now available.

This series is a love triangle. It's about the hard choices and difficult moments that come with a relationship. And it's about how falling in love sometimes means falling apart before you piece yourself back together.

That's why the entire series is called the *Come Undone Trilogy*. This is book two, *Come Apart*. Reading book one first is recommended, though it's not strictly necessary. Each of these books is a complete story, one trial and tribulation in the live of Alyssa and the man she chooses.

This book is a little different than what I usually write in terms of prose, subject matter, and hero. But it's the same, at its core. This book, like all my books, is about two damaged souls finding each other and helping each other heal.

This series still holds a special place in my heart as the books that started it all.

It's not for the faint of heart, but if you're ready to take the plunge, I promise to take you on a wild ride.

———

Please note this book contains material which may be triggering for some readers (including explicit descriptions of eating disorder behavior).

Chapter One

Laurie greets me with her usual goofy smile.

"Is it time for the daily booty call already?" She smirks as she motions for me to step inside, not bothering to wait for a response. "You can head on back—she's in the yard."

"Thanks," I return, stepping inside. "And if you're feeling jealous of our booty calls, maybe it's time to have a couple of your own," I tease.

She rolls her eyes, waving her hand in a dismissive gesture.

"Please—if I want a booty call, I can get one."

I grin, shaking my head as I walk through the house.

I don't doubt it.

The backyard—and God, is it a backyard—is huge and landscaped immaculately. The already lovely area is currently awash in the soft, orange glow of sunset.

And there's Alyssa, sitting on the couch, hoodie wrapped around her bare legs.

She's reading her Kindle, of course. Probably something English majors ignore in favor of Cliff Notes.

"Some lawyer here to see you," Laurie announces.

"I hope you're not in trouble," Alyssa mimics, her voice blending seamlessly with Laurie's.

She rolls her eyes, but the fond smile softens the teasing.

Laurie folds her arms over her chest, arching a brow. "You know I write comedy for a living."

"It eludes explanation." Alyssa looks up at me—a quick glance to register my presence—then back down to her book. Her lips curl into a warm, secretive smile. "I have a chapter to finish."

That smile could melt glaciers.

Of course, I might be a bit biased.

But just a bit.

She's definitely won over more than a few hearts with that smile on screen.

I wait the few seconds she takes to finish reading.

She likes to tease me like this sometimes, but it isn't difficult for me to take.

The view keeps me entertained.

And gives me time to plan out exactly how I'm going to fuck her next.

If she could hear my thoughts, I doubt she'd be able to read another word.

But she can't.

So she just finishes the chapter and sets her Kindle aside.

Her attention shifts to me.

I feel the heat of it immediately.

I'm clearly not the only one thinking ahead.

Her eyes pass over my body slowly, taking their time.

Lingering over her favorite places.

They eventually make their way back to mine, the heat in them clear.

I feel a renewed flash of it rush through me. She bites her lip.

God, I love that look—that look that screams *I'm thinking about touching you right now, and I like the thought of it.*

No one has ever looked at me quite the way Alyssa does.

I've had other girlfriends, fucked other women. But none of them ever stared at me with this kind of want.

This level of almost desperate lust.

Being so openly desired only intensifies my own response.

And it's intense enough as it is.

My cock throbs in interest, already rock hard.

And I haven't even touched her yet.

"Oh, get a room," Laurie quips, stepping back towards the door. "But, seriously--do you want a room? Because I'll make like a tree and get the hell out of here."

Alyssa shakes her head—Laurie really does make the worst jokes—and gets off the couch. "We'll be quiet."

"Uh-huh." It's Laurie's turn to roll her eyes. "As much as I appreciate the free porn show--even if it's more of a free porn podcast what with the lack of video--I'll just go grab a bite." She steps into the living room and yells back to us. "I'll be back in an hour! But give me five minutes to put on something presentable!"

The glass door slides shut with a click.

Leaving us alone.

Something that isn't lost on either of us.

"We should get dinner first," I suggest.

I don't mean it, obviously.

The only thing I'm hungry for is what's between her smooth thighs.

"You're funny." She takes another step towards me.

"Maybe I want a matcha latte before Peet's closes."

It's an empty protest.

And she totally calls me on it.

"There's a Peet's by your house."

"What if I like this one better?"

My eyes scan down her dangerous curves.

I'm already salivating.

She shakes her head.

"Your protests are pathetic."

She takes another step towards me.

Until she's close enough to touch.

My fingers curl into my palms.

God, she smells so good. Like oranges and honey.

I want to lick her until she screams.

I go still as her fingers skim my waist, sliding just under my T-shirt.

I try to stick to my plan.

I have to tease her, to get her wanting me so badly she thinks she might burst.

I can't give in so easily.

"I'm very convincing."

She shakes her head. "You're awful. Completely lacking belief." She presses her body against mine. I'm weakening rapidly. But I find I don't really care. This is far from a losing situation. "I could teach you a little about acting. You could use it." Her grin is bright and happy.

I almost want to stay like this just to keep that grin on her face.

Almost.

I want her taste on my tongue and my cock buried deep inside her more.

Luckily, she also has other ideas.

She closes her eyes and presses her lips to mine.

She's so soft and so hungry.

Just how I like her.

She moans the second my fingertips brush against her skin.

She's making this impossible.

"You only want me for my body," I try. A flimsy objection, but my blood is quickly rushing out of my brain.

"I can't help it. You're painfully hot." She takes another look at me as if to confirm. She nods. "Very painfully." She smiles, an irresistible mixture of joy and lust.

"Hmm. So it's my fault you're objectifying me?"

"Of course. If you had a better personality, I'd care about that too."

"Oh, really?"

"Really," she laughs.

I'm going to have to get her back for this teasing. I'm going to have to torture her until sweat slicks her skin and she's begging me for release.

She kisses me again with that laughing mouth, her nails digging into my skin. I love those fucking nails, like a blinking sign screaming *I want you.*

Her lips part and her tongue slides into my mouth.

She pulls me towards the couch.

"I shouldn't reward your insensitivity." I slide my hand over the curve of her waist.

"But you will." Her eyes flutter closed. She kisses me, her back arching, her body straining against mine.

I bring my hands to her chest, cupping her breasts over her dress. She groans softly, almost a beg. She's already desperate. She already wants this so badly.

I trace the neckline of her dress slowly, back and forth. She groans louder.

I slip my fingers into her bra.

She breaks our kiss, nearly panting. "Luke." She reaches for my jeans. "You better not... You better..."

"I better what?" I slide the strap of her dress off her shoulder.

Then the other.

She's wearing a hot pink bra, one that barely covers what it needs to. She'll look so much better without it.

"You know what," she warns.

I push the straps off her shoulders, pulling the cups off her breasts.

Damn.

The generous curves hang just right, unlike some of the hard domes surgeons install in this town.

Her nipples are already hard and tight.

Heat courses through my body.

I need to be inside her.

I rub my fingertips over those velvety points. "Maybe you should enlighten me."

She presses her body against mine again, her crotch grinding against me.

God, she feels so good. But I have to wait until she's begging.

I pull my shirt over my head. She relaxes, no doubt sure my protests are just for show.

"You're awful." She lifts her ass and slides out of her dress.

I stare as she peels off her bra and kicks off her panties.

Those hips, the smooth skin of her stomach, that ass, her perfect tits...

She's a fucking wet dream.

And she's looking at me like she wants to eat me alive.

I'm a lucky bastard.

Any blood left in my brain rushes downward.

I slide out of my shorts and shift onto the couch, on top of her.

She rocks her hips into mine, groaning as she rubs her wet pussy against me.

I can smell her desire.

I watch her changing expression, my ears tuned to the soft moans escaping her lips.

She wants me.

And I want her. All of her, all at once.

I want to slam myself into that wet heat, drive into her hard and fast, watch her perfect tits bounce as I come inside her.

She's in an agony of pleasure, groaning and shaking and digging those nails into my back again as she rubs against me.

I've tortured her enough.

I grip the base of my leaking cock and set it against her tight pussy.

Her entire body arches underneath me as I push inside in one go.

No more playing around.

———

Alyssa talks me into takeout at my place.

We sit on the floor, our plates on the low coffee table in the living room, a seemingly endless bottle of tequila between us.

She eats slowly, paying careful attention to every bite. I'm more obvious than I mean to be about watching her, and she looks at me with a weariness usually reserved for conversations about Ryan the asshole. "I'm not going to binge just because you aren't watching me."

"You're right. But I worry."

It's the reality of the situation.

How can I not worry about her recovery?

She shifts away from the table, frowning. "You're going to have to...get used to it."

She darts a glance at me.

"I know."

I do know.

It's just easier said than done.

She stabs another piece of her dinner and takes a bite.

She chews, slowly. Swallows, slowly.

I don't care how slow she does it, as long as she's eating.

She turns her eyes to the table and clears her throat. "Have you heard from Samantha?"

I see what she's doing.

Diverting my attention.

Samantha, my ex-fiancée, is one of my least favorite topics of conversation.

We met in elementary school.

She was a little more proper than me, a little more straight laced, but she was smart and cynical even at that age.

We became fast friends.

She didn't share the classic movie obsession I inherited from my mother, but she understood part of it stemmed just from the love I had for her.

And when Mom passed, she was there for me.

She helped me get through the hell of that time.

She was there through the knockout drag out fights I had with my father.

She was on the other end of the phone when I needed to call someone in the middle of the night.

When the ache in my chest got so bad I felt like it would swallow me whole.

We were so close, I never considered that it would ever be otherwise.

You don't have a whole lot of context at that age.

And that experience definitely tightened our bond even more.

But, like a lot of friends during that time, we ... drifted apart.

We went off to college, had separate experiences.

The phone call every few days turned into every few weeks.

And then tapered off into holiday calls.

Then to nothing.

There wasn't any dramatic break or anything. Life just happened, like it does.

We lived our own lives.

I'd think of her now and then, but that was about it.

Until law school.

By a twist of fate, we ended up going to the same one.

Only, this time, we were both very much adults, with all the corresponding parts.

And the time apart made us see each other differently.

Our friendship turned into more.

Maybe it wasn't the most passionate relationship. I didn't want to tear her clothes off and fuck her every time I saw her like I do with Alyssa.

But it was good.

We were compatible, we had so much in common, so much shared history.

We fit. But then I got her a job at my father's firm.

And my life imploded.

Though I don't know if that quite does it justice.

But there isn't really a word to encompass the bomb of finding out your dad was screwing your girl.

But it wasn't just physical.

She had a full blown affair with him.

Even when she knew how much I hated him, how much I hated how he treated my mother.

How I blamed him for her death.

As if that wasn't enough, she then fell madly in love with him. And then tried to leave me for him.

And I was the idiot that never saw it coming.

Unfortunately for her, my father was not on the same page.

She got a hefty dose of his asshole side.

She was devastated.

And I...I just couldn't let us go.

She knew me like nobody else did. Knew the child I was before my mom's death, the adult that I'd become.

But that wasn't enough.

Holding on was my mistake.

When he rejected her, I begged her to take me back, promised things would be like they were in the beginning.

When we were both happy.

When she would never have even thought of looking at another man, let alone my father.

She gave in.

I wore her down.

But then...I couldn't hold up my end of the bargain.

I ignored her at every turn, our relationship too damaged to salvage.

I didn't realize it until I had her back.

And then, I didn't know what to do.

So I took to avoiding the issue.

I looked away so much I didn't even register when her depression turned darker.

When it turned dangerous. Not until she tried to kill herself.

A harsh wakeup call that snapped me out of my wallowing, that forced me to grow a pair.

She survived.

But our romantic relationship was done well before that.

Now...we're friends.

I call every week or two. Visit her at her parents' place in San Diego every once in a while.

I owe her that much after our shitty history.

"Do you really want to talk about her?" I ask.

Alyssa shakes her head. "No, but it's better than wondering."

She looks at the floor.

"You're not jealous..."

"Cause you're never jealous?" She folds her arms, arching a brow at me.

"Never," I respond, half joking. "I've never been jealous in my life."

"Uh-huh."

I sigh.

"Okay, that's not true. I do get jealous of Jack McCoy from time to time." I move closer to her. "Have you seen his closing?"

"I've seen his eyebrows," she says, softening.

"Oh yeah?"

She looks me in the eyes. "They're amazing. So full and lush. I'd kill for those eyebrows."

"They're huge," I counter.

"They're gorgeous."

"But he's so old," I try.

She shakes her head.

"Age is just a number. He's distinguished. He's got the most beautiful, wrinkled face." She tilts her head thought-fully. "It's so full of character."

I slide my hands around her waist. "Now I'm getting jealous of him all over again."

"Shock of the century." Her voice is light again.

Good.

She brushes hair out of my eyes and presses her lips to mine.

It's such a sweet diversion.

I almost feel like we could dodge this topic forever.

But that wouldn't be right.

I try not to avoid things so much these days.

"I haven't heard from her in a few weeks," I admit. "I'm sure she's the same. Lonely, but okay."

She rests her head against my chest, sighing. "I'm worried about the loneliness."

I brush my fingers against my chin, tilting her head so our eyes connect. I don't like seeing her so worried. Especially not about something like this. "You know I'd never..."

"I know, but..."

Her gaze drifts to the pool in the backyard as she trails off.

The first place we kissed, though from the look on her face I really hope she's not reliving what I remember as the utter exhilaration of our lips meeting.

If she is, she must be thinking of what an ass I was to pursue her so aggressively. What with the small matter of her being engaged to my asshole business partner.

I don't regret it.

I reach for her hand, wanting the physical connection. The simple touch feels so good.

I rub the back of her hand with my thumb, considering my words.

I want her to feel secure.

"I want a life with you, Ally. I don't have a life with her anymore. A weekend a month maybe. That's it."

"Two most months," she corrects.

I nod.

She's not wrong.

"Still." I shake my head, leaning in, hoping she can see the sincerity in my eyes. "I don't want her." I cup the side of her face. "I don't want anyone but you."

"Are you sure?" A little spark returns to her eyes.

"Of course. I want you so badly it kills me. I'd drive to Las Vegas and marry you tonight if I thought you'd have me."

Her pink lips curve into a smile. "And you'd text Ryan a play by play."

I smirk at the thought.

Not a bad idea.

"He needs to know all the details of our newlywed sex."

She laughs, giving me a look.

"You're insane."

"You should see what I sent him when you were getting dressed."

"Please," she scoffs. "I know what it said—I'm an awful tease and I'm constantly torturing your poor, innocent ex-fiancée."

She's grinning now.

Is the room suddenly brighter or is it just me?

"Would you prefer if I didn't torture you?" I ask. "Say if I never sucked on your nipples?"

"Luke!" Her cheeks turn red. Beet red.

Fucking adorable.

"So you don't like that?" I push, enjoying watching her reaction.

"Of course I... You're awful. You know that?"

I move towards her until I feel the warmth of her body.

Her eyes still on mine, she wraps her arms around my neck.

"I think you like my particular brand of awful," I murmur. "I think it makes you wet."

And I kiss her. Hard.

Like I've been wanting to for the last fifteen minutes.

My hands slide up her sides and she arches into me, a soft moan escaping from her mouth to mine.

"Alyssa..."

"I like the sound of that 'Alyssa.'" Her hands slide down to my shoulders and I let her push me onto the carpet.

She shifts her body onto mine, straddling me.

I grip her hips.

"We're going to have this conversation eventually," I point out.

"Later is eventually." She lowers her body onto mine, her legs squeezing my own, her chest pressing against mine.

She kisses me hard.

I stifle a groan.

All I want is to be inside her again, until she's screaming my name and digging her nails into my back.

"After we talk," I force myself to say, breaking the kiss.

She huffs out a frustrated breath.

"Fine." She rolls off me and flops onto the carpet. "Okay. Talk."

"It's a good talk," I reassure her.

She narrows her eyes at me.

"Likely story."

"I love you."

"Okay, it's starting off good," she concedes.

I smile, but it fades as I speak.

This is important.

"I really do want a life with you. I want your face to be

the first thing I see every morning. The last thing I see every night."

I prop myself on my elbows so I'm closer to her.

She's so beautiful. But that isn't what draws my eye.

Or, at least, not all of it. I want to stare because...it's Alyssa. My Alyssa.

Those blue eyes, that soft skin, the light hair...that's all my Alyssa.

Even the wary look in her eyes is all my Alyssa too.

"I want all of it," I say. "I want to eat breakfast with you, and text you on my breaks, and eat dinner with you every night."

"Awfully fixated on meals there."

I frown, frustrated myself now.

"It's not about your... problem."

She gives me that look.

That *really?* look.

"You mean my eating disorder?" "Yes, your...eating disorder." I don't know why I avoid saying the words. Maybe it's because it sounds so...serious. So real. "It doesn't have anything to do with your recovery." I cover her hand with my own, trying to anchor us. I can feel her pulling away. Not what I want to happen here. "I see a future for us. I see us building our lives together. Buying a house. Picking out furniture. Arguing over how to decorate the bathroom."

Some of the stiffness, the tension, leaves her body.

"Hot pink of course."

"Hot pink is perfect." I run my fingertips over her arm. "I want to travel with you, to run around Europe watching you sip espresso in Italy, while I'm outraged over why I can't find a decent cup of tea in the entire country. I want to watch you agonize over what outfit to wear."

"I don't agonize."

I chuckle, pulling back.

"I'm trying to be romantic here."

"I know. But you shouldn't misrepresent me in your fantasies."

"I've seen you agonize," I insist. "On occasion."

She looks away. She's nervous. "What are you really saying?"

I know she doesn't mean her clothing selection process.

"I don't want you to hear this as an accusation."

"But?" she prods, looking back at me. "But...you act like we're still sneaking around. Like I'm a dirty secret you don't want anyone to know about."

I can see the surprise flash across her face.

"What? No I don't."

I start ticking off the points.

They've been eating away at me, picking at me like a thorn in my side that just won't go away.

"We hang out here or at Laurie's. You refuse to go out for dinner. And it's not about food. You refuse to go out for coffee with me, and I know you'll drink coffee anytime, anywhere. You'll take walks around the marina, but only around the marina."

"I like hanging out here," she interjects.

It's defensive.

"I know you're not ashamed to be with me..."

At least, I don't think she is...

"It's not you." She bites her fingernail. "It's Ryan... because I... well, you were there when I was cheating on him."

Ryan.

Is he ever not going to be a specter in our relationship?

I'm so fucking tired of hearing his name.

"Can't we get past that?" I run my fingers through my hair, trying not to tear it out. "Don't get me wrong. I love spending time with you here. But I need more than that. We both do. "Her eyes turn to the pool once more. "Like what?"

I wait until she meets my gaze. "You could move in here."

It's something that's been on my mind for a while now.

"Into your ex's house?"

Her voice is dry, but there's a vulnerability lurking behind it.

"We can get a new house. Hell, where doesn't really matter."

Her shoulders drop.

"Luke..."

I don't like the tone she's using.

I quickly interject before she can finish.

"Okay, I get it. It's only been a few months. I shouldn't move so fast. But I feel like we're on hold. Do you..." Fuck, what if she says no? She could break my heart. "Where do you see this relationship going?"

She looks away, at the dark blue sky outside the windows.

What is she thinking?

Do I want to hear it?

And how the hell did I end up being the one pushing for more again? "Somewhere great." My stomach relaxes. She looks back to me. "But not yet."

"Okay. When?"

I need an answer here, something to hold on to.

"Sometime in the future."

"When in the future?"

"A year, maybe."

That's an eternity.

She turns back to me, her eyes clear and bright. "I love you, Luke, and I want to be with you. But I didn't do this relationship thing well before. I made Ryan my whole world. I relied on him so much, I didn't think I could survive without him. I just... I can't do that again."

"I won't let you."

I would never take her strength from her.

It's one of the things I love the most about her.

She runs her hand through my hair, her look tender. "I'm still here. Just not all the time."

"But I want you all the time."

I grip her wrist, but she breaks the light hold gently.

And then her hands are on the back of my head.

She pulls me closer, until we're almost kissing.

"I'm not going anywhere."

I sigh.

"Not unless I fuck it up."

"Not unless you fuck it up," she agrees. She laughs, kissing me again. Her fingers dig into my hair.

I try to shut my doubts out, to feel nothing but her lips and her body under mine.

Alyssa is with me now. I have her now.

But I know it's not enough.

I need more of her. All of her. All the parts she wants to keep hidden.

Chapter Two

I know it's fast.

My feelings are undeniable, but it has only been a few months.

And I don't doubt her when she tells me it's not personal.

Ryan was an asshole—he's still an asshole.

And I have no doubt being with him fucked with her head.

It's not like I was in the world's greatest relationship before. I can empathize.

I know all of that.

But... how long will it be until she's ready? What if it's months or years?

I don't want to keep waking up without her.

Lately, it feels as though the emptiness of the bed is mocking me at night.

Being with Alyssa...it's highlighted a hole in my life I didn't even realize was there.

Before her, my life was lacking something. It had been lacking something for years.

And I can now even pinpoint when the void first appeared.

I was barely seventeen.

A stupid kid with no clue of how good I had it.

It was late one night or maybe early one morning—that in-between time where a hush seems to settle over the world.

Or it's supposed to.

That particular night, my mother and my father had been fighting for hours.

It consisted mostly of him treating her like shit, assuming her opinion had no value. He'd never admit it, but he assumed everyone else's opinion had no value.

I remember hearing my name thrown around, feeling that particular sinking in my stomach when I recognized it.

I closed my bedroom door to get away from it, so I could plausibly deny they were fighting over me. Again.

I'd done something stupid to piss off my father—I lived for doing stupid things to piss off my father—but Mom was sticking up for me.

She always did. Hidden in my bedroom, I could only hear them. But I knew exactly how the scene would look.

I knew the look on my mom's face—the sheer frustration, the contortion of her forehead as she choked back tears.

She never would have stayed with him if it weren't for me.

She would have left him years before. This never would have happened if it weren't for me...

He screamed.

She fought back the way she always did, trying so, so hard to stay calm and not show any of the emotion he'd mistake for weakness.

Finally, she had enough.

I heard the front door slam, her car turn on, the tires screeching as she rushed out of our godforsaken neighborhood.

It was foggy that morning. That night. Whatever it was.

But it was always foggy. She should have been used to it. She would have been okay if she hadn't been crying.

If she hadn't been upset.

All I felt at the time was relief at the interruption of the fight.

It didn't last long.

The police were at the door a few hours later.

The sun was just peeking through the horizon, illuminating the vibrant green lawns, the pure azure ocean. The whole damn sky was filled with color.

I was still a kid, but I knew what was coming as soon as I saw their faces.

Pity. They looked at me with pity.

And I felt my heart squeeze in my chest. "I'm sorry, son." The officer had kind eyes. Not that it mattered in that moment. "Your mother was in an accident. She... didn't make it."

Everything changed with those three words.

She didn't make it. The color drained from my world.

Everything was dull and dim. They kept speaking, but their words were a jumbled mess in my ears.

Everything was wrong.

I couldn't just stand there, but I couldn't leave with them on the porch. So I waited until they went inside to talk to my father. And then... I ran.

I didn't stop to put on shoes or change.

Who cared? Nothing mattered.

I ran barefoot, in my pajamas. Until the sun was high in the sky. Until my legs gave out. I finally collapsed under some overgrown tree as the pain seeped in passed the shock. I curled up into a ball and cried.

I learned that no matter what cruel blow life dealt you, it just...went on.

There was no pause button on life. I didn't spend the next ten years numb and empty.

But the colors were never as sharp.

Food never tasted as good.

From then on, there was always something missing, some awful gray dullness layered over the world.

I was with other women before Alyssa, and I was happy. But there was still something so drab about my life.

Until I met her.

She stared at me, sizing me up. So very bad at hiding how much she wanted me.

And, I can admit it—I wanted to mess with Ryan.

I wanted to flirt with her, to rub it in his face. A nice jab for existing as such an awful human being.

A nice revenge for rubbing his relationship with Alyssa in my face every chance he got.

It was always my gorgeous girlfriend this, my gorgeous girlfriend that.

It was like an irritating tick.

As if I cared that his girlfriend was gorgeous.

But the second she opened her admittedly gorgeous mouth... I was hooked.

She was so smart and articulate.

And not at all narcissistic or self-conscious of her fame.

And even though she'd just met me, even though she clearly wanted to fuck me, she called me on my bullshit. She saw right through me, called out my obvious ploy to fuck with Ryan. She called me on assuming she was vacuous.

She even corrected my grammar.

And when I touched her, the most delightful red flush spread across her face. It was so bright and vibrant.

I wondered how far down the flush went.

It sounds so corny, but it was like a trigger that pumped the saturation back up in my life. Everything is better when she's around—the air, the music, the food.

Even me. I'm so much smarter and kinder and more honest when I'm with her.

I know it's still early, but I see a future with her.

A vibrant and bright one.

I see her lying next to me at night, her soft body pressed against mine, her arms wrapped tightly around my chest. My T-shirt—the one she claimed as her own—drapes softly over her curves. In the morning, she stretches out on the couch with her Kindle and a cup of coffee. I can smell the coffee on her breath, taste the honey on her lips. I feel the nerves in my body turning on, everywhere all at once, just from her hands on my skin.

I know it won't be that perfect. I know we'll have fights, we'll have bad days, we'll have miserable shit just like everyone does.

But it can be that good. We can be that good.

I really meant what I said.

I'd marry her today if she'd have me.

———

Mrs. Pike is immaculately put together.

She's the kind of woman who spent her entire marriage immaculately put together. One of those wives who serves as a very special kind of trophy—beautiful, educated, conservative.

Usually, by the time these women make it to my office,

they've lost interest in being the symbol of their husbands' good taste and manners.

Or their husbands have gained interest in a younger woman.

But Mrs. Pike is still immaculate in her freshly pressed suit and her small silver earrings.

"I should have known better," she says. "I did. I knew this would happen, even when we got married. I thought I could look the other way." Her attention turns to the window, but not like she's focusing on anything actually in front of her. "I have a good life, Mr. Lawrence. I have a beautiful home. I have all the money I could spend."

Implicit in those words is that all of that just isn't enough.

And perhaps not as fulfilling as she was led to believe it would be.

A common realization among my clients.

"How old were you when you married him?" I ask gently.

Her attention returns to me, her eyes focusing once more.

"Twenty-two," she says.

"You had no idea what you were giving up." I lean back in my chair. "You can't blame yourself. No one has their life together at twenty-two. It's a terrible age."

Mrs. Pike smiles, but it's short lived. "I was in graduate school. And he asked about my thesis. He pretended like he wanted to hear about it."

She's miserable over this mistake. Too miserable.

If she believes it's her fault, she won't ask for the settlement she deserves.

She'll let herself be fucked over once again.

She'd be an easy client for any other lawyer—a few billable hours to agree to whatever her husband offers.

But I know what she deserves. She deserves half of everything they made together.

Right now she needs someone on her side. She needs someone who will listen to her.

"What did you study?"

"Literature."

This is exactly how Alyssa would have ended up if she'd stayed with Ryan. She'd have spent her life ignoring her wants and dreams, instead playing the role of the perfect trophy wife.

"Not enough people appreciate literature," I remark. "Where did you go to school?"

"Columbia."

I smirk.

"What a show off."

She finally smiles. "Mr. Lawrence—"

"You can call me Luke."

"Okay, Luke." She nods. "I want to take care of this quietly and quickly."

"California is a community property state. You're entitled to half of his assets."

"I don't care about the money."

"Mrs. Pike."

"You can call me Kate," she says.

She's hooked. She's going to sign a retainer at the end of this meeting.

I almost hate how easy it is to charm these women.

All I do is listen to them, remind them they're valuable human beings.

And they're hooked.

They'll sign anything I put in front of them. All it takes is fifteen minutes of care and attention and they trust me.

"Okay, Kate. I understand your position. Your husband provided for you. It was a sacrifice, but it's the smallest sacrifice he could offer. It's only money. You've given up years of your life. How long have you been married?"

"Twenty years."

I lean in towards her so she can feel the full weight of my words. "I'm sure men have been interested in you."

She hesitates, but then nods slowly.

"But you were faithful. Because of your vows."

"Yes," she murmurs.

"You could have lived somewhere less awful than Los Angeles."

She laughs, life sparking in her eyes. "I wanted to stay in New York."

"And you gave up your career to raise your daughter. Isn't that right?"

Finally, Kate gives me a real smile. "She's fifteen. She's such a sweet girl. I know she's old enough to decide if she'd rather live with me or her father, but I want full custody."

"We'll get it."

Her face brightens. I see this a lot—she's mostly concerned with her daughter.

It's sweet, yes, but she's leaving too much on the table.

We can get custody and half his assets.

It isn't one or the other.

"I don't want to push him, Mr. Lawrence... Luke. I just want to be done with it."

"Then let me take it from here. I'll make sure you and your daughter never have to worry about money again."

"But he won't... he has so many lawyers."

"Yes." I offer Kate my hand. "But your lawyer is better."

She smiles, taking my hand. "Is he?"

"Trust me. Your daughter is going to be so proud of you for standing up for yourself."

I show her our standard retainer.

She signs without hesitation.

———

R YAN CALLS ME INTO HIS OFFICE AS SOON AS I ARRIVE AT work. The Monday after Alyssa left Ryan for me, I asked him to dissolve the partnership.

But he refused.

The way he saw it, there were two options—we continue working together with no mention of our personal lives, or I sell him my half of the firm and resign immediately. I hand over all of my clients, even those in the middle of difficult cases.

I want him out of my life, but I can't abandon the clients who need me.

I clench and unclench my fists.

Ryan is always irritating, but I'm not going to let him get to me today.

I knock on the door briefly and step into his office.

Ryan doesn't look up from his computer.

Maybe he thinks it's a power move or some other bullshit.

"Several new clients requested you. I put the consults on your calendar."

"I have a full calendar." And taking on new clients will make it harder to get out of this firm.

Ryan moves his gaze from his laptop to me. "They specifically requested you. You do have a certain reputation."

I offer him my best *I don't give a damn what you think* smile. "I'd rather focus on making the clients I have happy."

"It's perfectly good business. You need a better reason than that to turn it away."

He holds my eyes.

It's a business stare, cold and emotionless. And so very Ryan.

He never gives anything away.

He never even raises his voice.

"If we dissolve the firm, you can take on all the clients you want," I point out.

"Out of the question," he responds immediately. "We have a reputation, and I do all the work to maintain it. Seventy percent of our billable hours if you want an exact figure."

Asshole.

But I swear, if I look closely, I can almost see a sign of weakness.

I can almost see some little hint of how much it hurt him to lose Alyssa.

So I offer him a smile, a real smile this time. "When we decided to start this business, we agreed we'd work reasonable hours."

He narrows his eyes, his brow furrowing.

I'm sure Ryan regrets asking me to start Lawrence and Knight. I know I regret getting into business with him.

But it made sense at the time. He was the only competent person I knew who wanted to specialize in divorces and he was willing to actually run the firm so I could devote my attention to actually practicing law.

He doesn't know what to say to my parry, so he deflects.

Typical.

"You need to start pulling your own weight." It's as calm as it could possibly be. He flips through a file on his desk. "Starting with your latest client, Mrs. Pike. She can't afford the kind of aggressive negotiation you outlined, and there's no way she's going to get full custody. Convince her to take a more reasonable offer."

I fold my arms. "No."

Ryan looks at me with pity, like I'm an idiot for being so idealistic. "I appreciate that you can sell the hot, hopeless-romantic divorce lawyer. It attracts clients. Hell, it's your best asset. But you need to be reasonable. She'll never get full custody. And her daughter is a teenager. Any sane judge will let the daughter decide. You're only wasting her money and getting her hopes up for nothing."

I grit my teeth.

I can't lose it.

Not when he's so damn controlled.

"I will continue to run my cases my way. If you'd like to run things a different way, we can dissolve the firm." "That's out of the question."

"Then so is me taking on these new clients."

I need to get out of here.

I turn to leave but Ryan clears his throat. When I bring my gaze back to him, he's sporting a small smile.

I don't trust it.

"How is Alyssa?" he asks.

Dick.

"She's great."

"I've been meaning to ask her to dinner." He folds his hands in his lap. "We were best friends for years. I'm sure she'd like to get back in touch."

I laugh, wiping the sly smirk right off his face.

Does he think I actually see him as a threat?

"Knock yourself out, man. I need to get back to work."

He can say whatever the hell he wants.

I'm still the one with Alyssa.

"Yes, you have two briefs to finish. You don't want to work too late." A heavy, deliberate pause. "She gets lonely."

There's an ugly glint in his eye.

He doesn't like that I laughed in his face.

Tough break.

"Don't worry—her days of being left unsatisfied are over."

His face turns red with anger, but I turn and leave before he can pull himself together enough to respond.

Chapter Three

I t's almost nine when I arrive at Alyssa's place.

She puts her finger to her mouth in a *shh* gesture. "Laurie is sleeping one off, so..." She creeps to her bedroom, opening the door slowly.

There's a sound from Laurie's room. She's up.

Alyssa bites her lip, shaking her head. She motions for me to follow her into the bedroom. Mouths *now*.

This has got to be good.

Laurie pulls her door open and bounces out of her bedroom. She looks at Alyssa, then at me. Her eyes narrow. "Are you coming to the premiere party?"

A guilty look creeps onto Alyssa's face. She knows she's been caught.

"What party?" I ask.

Laurie puts her hands on her hips in exasperation. "Alyssa Summers! You promised me you informed Luke about this party."

Alyssa groans.

"Laurie...

"You're not getting out of this," Laurie warns.

Alyssa looks at me like she's begging for a lifeline. "I'm sure Luke has other things to do."

Barking up the wrong tree this time, sweetie.

"Nope." There's no way I'm missing a party celebrating the premiere of Alyssa's show. I'd celebrate it every minute if I could.

Alyssa glares at me, but it's a mock glare, an *I hate but I really love you* glare. "I have other things to do."

Laurie shakes her head. It's Laurie's show too—she's the head writer. It's how she and Alyssa became friends. "What other things?"

"Anything except for watching the premiere."

Alright.

I offer Laurie a smile. "Don't worry—we'll be there."

"You better." She points a finger at Alyssa. "Or I'll throw your Kindle in the ocean."

I laugh. "That's not going to convince her." I squeeze Alyssa's hand. "But we will be there."

Laurie nods, finally satisfied.

"Okay, good. I'll let you guys...you know."

Alyssa rolls her eyes pulling me into Laurie's spare room.

I suppose, by now, it really is Alyssa's room. She's been here a few months even if it lacks any real personal touch.

She sits on the bed, pulling her feet towards her crotch. Her eyes are turned down, her lips pressed together. "Are you mad?"

I shake my head. She doesn't have to worry about disappointing me. But I know it's a hold over from Ryan. "Of course not. But I wish you'd told me."

She sighs. "I was going to ditch it at the last minute. When Laurie was too drunk to notice."

I raise a brow at that.

"And where was I in all this?"

"You were going to pick me up and take me far, far away. To somewhere with no TV."

I kneel next to the bed and take her hands. "Why? You worked so hard on that show. Aren't you proud of your accomplishment?"

Her eyes are on the bare, white wall. "It's too nerve-wracking. People are going to have opinions. I know it's cable, but I'm going to be recognizable soon." She shakes her head. "Let's talk about something else."

"Are you sure?"

Her brow furrows, her forehead scrunching. Somehow, she even makes stress look adorable.

"Positive." She squeezes my hands. "How was work?"

"You're telling me you want to talk about Ryan instead?" I ask incredulously.

She shrugs as if it's no big deal, though I know it's not true. It's far from ideal that I still work with her ex-fiancé. The subject change definitely has more to do with her aversion for talking about the premiere more than anything. "Sure."

I move closer, until her legs are at my hips and my head is at her chest. "Fine. Except for the part about Ryan being there."

She runs her hands through my hair. It's sweet and affectionate, the change of subject releasing a lot of her stress. "Why don't you sell?"

Tension knots my shoulders. "I have a dozen clients in some stage of a divorce. If I leave them, Ryan will botch their settlements."

She brings her hands to my shoulders, frowning. "Can't you sell then finish up with your clients?" "He won't accept anything other than my immediate resignation." I look at Alyssa, into her clear, blue eyes. Some of my tension eases. "This is how he gets his revenge. The fucker."

She arches a brow.

"You did steal his girl."

"Please. You wanted to be stolen."

And I don't regret taking her up on it.

"I wanted to be with you." She runs her hands over my suit jacket. "You were working late." She's concerned.

But Alyssa doesn't need to worry about me. I can handle it.

"How about we don't talk about work at all?" I suggest. Feels like we're just going from one hard topic to another in that lane.

She nods, dragging her fingertips across my cheek. They stop at my lips. "I have to ask you something."

"Shoot."

She bites her lip.

She's even more nervous about this than she was about the party.

"It's not a big deal."

"Nothing is a big deal to you. You have no awareness of what is or isn't a big deal," I tease.

Her smile is brief, but genuine.

"This isn't a big deal."

"Alright. What is it?"

She sighs. "I have this assignment... from my therapist. To do a food challenge."

"Oh yeah?"

This sounds like a big deal. Like a huge deal.

And she wants to include me.

"Have you heard of it?" Her voice is soft, unsure.

"No. But I want to help if I can."

"It's not a big deal." She shakes her head like even she doesn't believe that. "I eat a small portion of something that would normally be off limits. One cookie or one scoop of ice cream or something like that."

I rub my thumb against her fingers. "That sounds like a big step."

"It's easy in theory." She grimaces at her own words. "Well, not easy. But simple. I eat the food and I sit there. I don't binge or purge."

There is so much need in her eyes, a vulnerability that makes me want to just hold her tight.

"All you have to do is babysit." She pulls her hands to her lap, shifting like she's uncomfortable. "Sit there with me. Keep me distracted if I start freaking out. Can you do it?"

I brush my fingertips against her cheek. "Of course, Ally."

My body is lighter than air. She's asking for my help. Finally. She's always so tight-lipped about this, but she's letting me in now.

"It's not a big deal."

It's almost like she's trying to convince herself of that.

"Okay." I nod. "Thanks for telling me."

"Luke..." Her voice is shaky.

"Yes?"

"Don't make it a big deal, okay?" she whispers.

I nod. It's clearly a big deal, a huge deal, but she's scared. Arguing is only going to make that worse.

I understand battling demons that just won't fucking quit.

What we need here is a distraction.

Worrying about it before it happens is only going to set her up for more anxiety.

And I know just the thing. I grip her hips and pull her closer, until her chest is only six inches from my mouth, until her knees are pressed against my hips.

Damn, her tank top is so thin. It's straining against her chest and she's not wearing a bra. And those boxer shorts

—my boxer shorts—are riding up her legs, exposing every inch of her thighs.

Her eyes connect with mine as I slide my jacket off my shoulders and down my arms.

I let it fall on the floor behind me and I scoot closer to her, until there's only an inch between my mouth and her chest.

Her fingers brush my neck. "Luke."

"Mhmm?" I slide my hands over the soft skin of her shoulders.

I pull her straps off her shoulders. Down her arms. Her tank top pulls with it.

It slides over her chest, slowly revealing her breasts.

My cock constricts. Her tits are fucking perfect, begging for my hands.

I cup her breast and bring it to my mouth, brushing my lips against her nipple. Her skin tastes so good, like Alyssa. I trace it with my tongue, as slowly as I can.

She groans, tugging at my hair. It's a plea to move faster.

But I want to savor this. It feels too good, watching her face contort in pleasure, hearing her groan, feeling her body shake.

I slide her tank top to her waist. She shudders, her legs wrapped around my hips. I lick her again and she arches back, shifting her breasts into my mouth.

Her fingers slide over my neck. Then my collar.

Her eyes flutter open, looking down at me like she needs me more than she's ever needed anything.

She tugs at my tie, pulling me closer. I press my lips into hers. Her tongue plunges into my mouth.

She needs this now. No more teasing.

I dig my hands into the waistband of her boxers and

slide them to her feet. She's wearing pink panties, soft cotton things that look divine against her skin.

This is my Alyssa. In... well... out of her pajamas. No pretenses.

Nothing but desperate need.

She loosens my tie and tosses it aside.

Her eyes are on me. She looks me over slowly, taking her time.

I love how she looks at me.

Love the need that fills her eyes as she does.

"You're wearing so many clothes." Her voice is heavy, strained.

I slide her panties to her knees. She squirms as she kicks them off.

Her eyes find mine. She tugs at my collar, working her way to my buttons. She undoes the first.

Then looks at the rest of my shirt like it's an impossible challenge.

"How the hell do you wear this thing every day?" She shakes her head and undoes the next button. Then the next.

The next.

Her eyes go to half mast as she pushes the shirt off.

She drags her fingertips over my shoulders, my chest.

Another button.

Then the last.

Finally.

I shrug the shirt off, ready to feel more of her touch.

She slides her hands down my stomach, her teeth sinking into her lip.

Her eyes rise to meet my own as she unbuckles my belt.

The gentle clink followed by the buzz of the zipper heightens the anticipation.

Not that I need any more of it.

I take a deep breath as she pushes my slacks off my ass.

"Still too many clothes," she remarks, her voice husky.

I'm not going to argue with that.

She traces the waistband of my boxers, completely absorbed by the task.

But she stops at my front, her hand inches away from my cock.

So fucking close.

Her lips curl into a smile, as if she can hear me.

Her hands slip into my boxers. Her fingers slide over my tip.

My breath catches at the delicate touch.

Damn. Heat rushes through my body.

She grips me firmly and strokes me, her eyes on mine.

No more waiting. I need to be inside of her.

"Ally..."

My voice is rough with strain.

She moves her hands back to my waistband and slides my boxers off.

"Mmm. That's much better."

Shit.

I run my fingertips over her hips, down her thighs, to the backs of her knees.

I stand, lifting her legs, pushing her onto the bed so she's flat on her back.

She trembles slightly as I pull her legs apart.

"Luke..."

I shift closer, until my tip is straining against her.

She digs her hands into the sheets.

No more preliminaries.

I slide inside her.

Yes. Hell yes.

She's so warm and wet, and it feels so right. Like I'm home.

Her eyes go wide, then flutter closed at the sensation.

She arches into me, tugging harder at the sheets. Wrapping my hands around her ankles, I hold them to my chest.

She's all mine now. And entirely at my mercy.

I thrust into her, keeping her pinned.

Her body is shaking.

Her lips part and a tiny groan escapes.

I need more of that noise. I need her screaming.

I thrust into her with long, slow strokes. I can feel every inch of her around me. Pleasure pools inside me.

Nothing matters but this, but us.

Her breath is heavy. Another low groan escapes her lips. I dig my nails into her ankles and thrust.

Harder and deeper into that tight perfection of her pussy. Until her groan is louder, lower.

Until she's panting.

Pleasure suffuses her face. Her eyelids are heavy. Her lips press together.

Her hands twist in the sheets.

It's the best thing I've ever seen.

I can never get enough of it.

I thrust into her again and again. And again.

She arches into my movements, throwing her head back like it feels so good she can't take it for another second.

My pleasure grows.

My body tingles.

It's desperate to fill her, to mark her as mine.

But not yet. Not until she comes.

I slide my hands down her calves and thighs, all the way to her hips. I move her back and climb onto the bed.

She shudders as I lower my body onto hers.

Her legs are pressed against my chest, her ankles around my shoulders.

And she's closer now. Close enough I can look into her eyes. They're wide with desire.

"Luke..." she groans.

It's all the encouragement I need.

I plant my hands next to her and I thrust into her.

She feels so good around me.

She arches into me, hard. Throws her head back.

She reaches for me, scraping her nails against my back.

I move deeper, slower, feeling every inch of her around me.

It's maddening.

But I have to hold out.

Alyssa groans. She digs her nails into my back. Hard enough to draw blood.

I shudder.

Her nails are the sign she's close.

Everything else fades away.

It's only Alyssa. Only her lips, her teeth, her nails, her lush tits, her curvy legs.

And her groans.

Her groans build and build, louder and louder. The only thing I know is that I need more of them. I need her coming around me.

I thrust into her.

She groans.

I move faster. Harder. Deeper.

Her tits shake and bounce with the force I'm using.

I reach out to squeeze one soft mound.

Her eyes snap open.

She screams. "Don't stop."

No possibility of that happening. Her nails scrape against my back. She's panting, screaming, shaking.

Then her eyes flutter closed. Her moans reach a crescendo and she comes, convulsing around me.

Afterwards, her breath steadies once more.

Her eyes find mine.

"Don't stop."

She unhooks her ankles and wraps her legs around my waist. Her hands press into my back and she pulls me closer.

Her lips find mine. She kisses me hard, her tongue sliding over mine.

And she rocks her hips into me.

I thrust into her, desperate.

Her lips stay on mine, her tongue still probing my mouth, her nails still sharp on my back.

The ache inside me grows. I'm tingling everywhere and she feels so damn good.

A chill passes through me. The ache is too much.

I groan into Alyssa's mouth. She pulls me closer, rocks harder. Her nails sink into my back again. She moans.

The ache builds until it's too much to take.

That's it.

My orgasm rocks through me, a harsh wave of almost painful pleasure. I release everything I have in me inside of her, my cock convulsing in ecstasy.

Her lips stay on mine, but her kiss turns softer, sweeter.

My breath is loud in the silence.

It takes me a minute to recover.

But then we untangle our bodies and I collapse next to her. She smiles at me, her expression deliciously satisfied.

I bring my hands to her back and hold her as closely as I can.

It can't get any more perfect than this night.

———

AFTER, ALYSSA AND I LIE IN BED, NOT REALLY WATCHING sitcom reruns on TV.

I curl up behind her, tracing the soft curves of her body.

I can never get enough.

She shifts constantly in a hopeless attempt to pretend as if she's not tired.

I whisper in her ear. "Go to sleep."

But she shakes her head and presses her body against mine. "If I'm asleep, I won't feel you holding me."

"I'll hold you anytime you want." I consider pushing it —reminding her how much easier it would be to hold her if she moved in—but I don't.

I don't want to ruin the moment.

She turns back to me, pressing her smiling lips against mine.

"You can't see the TV like this," I murmur.

"I'll live."

The kiss is soft and sweet, and there's no sense in arguing.

This is exactly where we need to be.

We stay like that for a while, our bodies tangled up on the bed. Until her breath is heavy and slow.

"Okay," she sighs. "I'll sleep."

She shifts, stretching out.

I take one last look at her—damn she's gorgeous— before hunting for the toothbrush in my overnight bag. My phone rings.

I ignore it—who the hell could be calling this late?

But it keeps ringing.

Damn it.

I find the phone in the pocket of my slacks.

It's probably a client. Or a client's angry spouse.

Someone overeager, someone who'd think nothing of calling so late.

I don't recognize the number.

But I know the area code.

It's in San Diego.

Fuck. It can't be...

"Hello?"

"May I speak to Luke Lawrence?"

It's a male voice, a stupidly matter-of-fact tone.

I've heard that tone before.

That's the *I am going to relay this bad news to you like I'm ordering a sandwich* voice.

"This is Luke." My response is unthinking, my heart rate already speeding up.

"I'm calling from Santa Barbara Cottage Emergency Room."

No. This isn't happening. There's no way Samantha is...

The voice continues, so even and calm. "I'm sorry to call you, Mr. Lawrence, but you're Samantha Brooks's emergency contact."

My heart is racing. My mouth is sticky.

"What happened?"

"I'm sorry, I'm not at liberty to discuss the specifics of the incident."

"Is she okay?"

"She's in the ER, and she's expected to be checked in for the night. Visiting hours start at nine a.m."

I can't hear anything except for the static on the phone. He won't tell me if she tried to kill herself again. He isn't at liberty to discuss it.

"You can ask for her room number at the visitor's desk." He pauses, as if to let it sink in that he's not allowed to tell me what happened to her. "Do you have any questions?"

"No," I say.

He's still talking, but I drop the phone.

Alyssa looks at me. I can't place the expression on her face.

I can't place anything.

She did it again.

I know she did it again.

I've been responding to her texts and calls, but not in the same way I used to.

I've been keeping a deliberate distance, trying to establish healthier boundaries now that Alyssa is in my life.

Was it enough to push her over the edge again?

I haven't been ignoring her.

Nor have I been rubbing Alyssa in her face, though I don't avoid mentioning her.

That feels wrong.

She's a big part of my life and I don't want to hide her. But Samantha's stuck in her parents' summer home.

With no job, no relationship that I know of.

Just a lot of fucking time to spiral.

Was there any indication? A word or a tone in a phone call, something odd in her texts?

I don't know.

All I know is she did it again.

And I didn't even register any warning signs.

Chapter Four

I feel like I'm reliving one of my worst memories.

This can't be possible. I was in San Diego a month ago. Samantha was happy.

She seemed so okay.

Didn't she?

I think back to the visit, trying to remember every detail.

We were sitting on the hardwood floor of her parents' house, playing rummy. She was sipping a glass of wine. And she looked fucking happy.

It was such a nice moment.

Cool air. The clear blue of dusk. Just enough light that we could still see the cards.

"I met a guy."

That got my attention.

"Where did you meet a guy?"

"At the store," she responded nonchalantly.

Like it wasn't the first time she'd mentioned a guy in a long while.

"You went to the store?"

"I know I'm staying with my parents, but I'm perfectly capable of driving myself to the store," she scoffed, adjusting her cards.

I don't touch that comment.

"Which store?" I ask instead.

Safe enough question.

"Whole Foods."

Of course she went to Whole Foods and not to any of the co-ops closer.

And of course she met some guy at Whole Foods.

He's probably another rich yippie. Some business casual stockbroker who drinks green juice and drives a Tesla.

He'd be perfect for her. For a minute, I saw a future for her. It was like the future I used to see for us, but it fit better.

She and the stockbroker fell in love fast. He asked her fast. She said yes. The wedding was fast. And then, a year later, they had a kid, a dog, and a house on the beach.

They had everything she pretended she wanted with me. Everything she really wanted with Edward.

She had hope again.

She stayed near her family. In San Diego. Her parents were happy about the match—they loved his clean haircut and his polite demeanor. They told her how proud they were—that she finally found a stable man, instead of some starter boyfriend.

She found a job at a law firm downtown. It was still corporate law, still boring, but it paid well and she felt important. She spent too much on designer suits.

She was happy. They were happy.

She didn't need me anymore.

It was a fantasy I sincerely hoped became a reality.

"What about this guy?" I asked. *"What's he like?"*

"He's a guy," she smiled. *"It's nothing, but we're going on a date next week."* Another expression flickered over her face, her smile fading. *"You don't mind, do you?"*

"Why would I mind?"

She shrugged. "You get jealous."

"I used up all my Samantha jealousy during that whole Edward debacle," I responded dryly.

How could I be jealous of a random guy when she'd literally had an affair with my dad?

"Still... I'd understand if you weren't totally over it. Actually... I was surprised when I heard about Alyssa." She looked at me and smiled. "In a good way. You deserve to be happy, Luke."

Had there been a tinge of sadness to her expression there at the end?

I don't know anymore.

When I open my eyes, Alyssa is staring at me.

Her expression is soft, filled with sympathy.

Her fingers graze my cheek. "Are you okay?"

I don't move. I don't say anything. I can't even think.

"Luke..." I can hear the worry in her voice. She wants me to say something. She wants me to reassure her that I'm okay.

"Luke..." She says it again. It's gentle and sweet. She sits next to me and presses her palm into mine. "Samantha?"

I nod.

"Is she going to be okay?"

That's what he said. She's expected to make a full recovery.

But that's just the physical.

"Maybe," I say. My keys are on the dresser. It's past midnight. If I leave now, there shouldn't be any traffic.

"Luke, talk to me." I know she doesn't really want me to talk about Samantha. At best, she tolerates our friendship.

But she cares about me and wants to help.

Even though it isn't her battle.

"Are you okay?" She wraps her arms around me. Her cheek presses against mine.

It's warm.

But all I keep focusing on is that Samantha did it again. "I'm fine."

"And I thought it would be easy being the one on offense for once." She smiles slightly, her eyes serious.

I hug her back.

She's right.

I can't push her and not myself.

"I... I just keep wondering if I missed warning signs, you know?" I admit. "She seemed completely fine when I saw her, but...she tried to kill herself again."

She wasn't okay.

"She probably tried to hide it from you," Alyssa points out carefully.

I nod.

"Maybe." I feel... lost. "I should go. I have to help her."

"Luke... it's midnight."

"So?"

She looks away, out the window, as the blackness engulfs the front yard.

It's so silent, I can hear every inhale and exhale. I can hear my heart beat. I can hear the wind rustling the rosebushes.

Alyssa bites her lip.

"Do you have to go tonight?" she asks. "Maybe you can go in the morning? The hospital won't let you in this late."

She hugs herself.

Alyssa needs me too, though she won't say it.

I know how nervous she is with her show premiering.

My chest is heavy and my throat is tight.

"What if she's alone when she wakes up?"

Alyssa shakes her head.

"She's in the safest place she could be—the hospital. But if you feel like you need to be there... you need to be there." She sighs, rubbing her face. "But don't pretend this is just about what she needs."

"What?" I draw back. "What is that supposed to mean?"

She meets my eyes head on.

"If you want to go to her, fine. She's your friend and you guys have been through a lot together. I can't say I fully understand your relationship, but I trust you. However, don't pretend that this is only about what Samantha needs."

"What else could it be about?" I demand, frowning.

What is she implying?

She doesn't back down. "It's also about what *you* need." She taps my chest to emphasize the point. "You need her to need you."

Is that what she thinks?

"No," I say, shaking my head. "It's not like that at all."

She raises her brows at me.

"Not at all?"

"She needs me. It's not about how I feel. Fuck—do you really think I'm that messed up?" "Maybe you don't realize it," she says, searching my face. "But you like that she needs you."

How can Alyssa say that? I thought she understood.

Samantha is my friend.

Yeah, it feels good to be there for her. It feels good to bring a smile to her face.

But that's normal. That's friendship.

Friends help each other.

"Forget it," she adds on the heels of that bomb. "This isn't the time to talk about that."

"It's never the time to talk about anything with you."

It pops out before I even think about it.

She grips my arms.

"Then start." She shakes me a little. "Tell me what you're thinking. Tell me why you need to rush to see your ex—the ex who cheated on you, who left you, who made it very clear she wanted nothing to do with you."

"She just tried to kill her fucking self!" I step back. "I really don't think this is the time to hold her indiscretions against her."

She winces in acknowledgment.

"Maybe. But do you even want to be there?" she pushes, not backing down.

"It doesn't matter what I want." Irritation pricks at me. "She's my friend. I have to—I want to—help her."

"Alright." She tilts her head, considering me. "And what if I *had* to flee to a suicidal Ryan's side?"

My jaw clenches.

"That's not a fair comparison."

"Why not?" she challenges.

"Samantha and I are friends. We have a history—a long one."

"Fuck your history," she mutters. She uncurls her body and pushes herself up. "I've known Ryan since I was four-teen. We have history. If I'm not allowed to be his friend—or even talk to him without you getting jealous—don't you think running off to your suicidal ex in the middle of the night is a little hypocritical?"

I shake my head, unsure how to deal with this.

How the hell did this turn into a conversation about that asshole once again?

"Do you even want to be friends with Ryan?"

That sets her back on her heels a little.

"Maybe... he was an important person to me."

"But he's such an asshole."

She sighs, picks her top off the floor, and pulls it over her head.

"I don't think Samantha is a shining example of a perfect person either."

I sigh.

She isn't wrong.

Shit.

"You can come with me," I offer.

She gives me a look.

"You're kidding, right?"

"No. If it would make you feel better, I want you to come. Hell, it would be great to have you with me."

Her expression softens.

"That's okay," she says, her voice gentler.

"I can't stay. Not for something like this."

Even if she wants me to.

"I know." She searches my face. "You wouldn't be the guy I fell for if you didn't want to help so badly. I just don't want to be imagining Samantha throwing herself at you."

"It's really not like that." My smile is a little grim. "She's made it really clear she doesn't want me like that."

"Maybe not," she concedes. "but I'm still going to imagine it." She picks her boxers off the floor and slides them over her legs. "You should go. You'll hate yourself if you don't."

She's right.

But it also feels like I can't win for losing here.

"Alyssa..."

I don't like this tension between us.

"No. You need to help her now." "I get it. She needs you a lot right now." She smiles a little, though it isn't a happy one. "I can relate. I just hope that she isn't going to need you quite so much soon."

I feel like I'm being ripped in two different directions here.

But I also know I have to go, even if Alyssa isn't fully okay with it.

Fuck.

Should this be this hard?

"I'll be back soon."

"How soon?" she asks.

"By the weekend." I reach for her hand, pulling her close. "I love you." "I love you too," she sighs.

I kiss her goodbye.

Knowing I'm going to be thinking about her the entire time I'm trying to help Samantha.

———

THE FREEWAY IS A BLUR AS THE SUN RISES OVER SOUTHERN California.

It's too damn early for traffic. It's too early to be on the road. I arrive hours before the hospital opens to visitors.

It's too early to find an open coffee shop in San Diego. I'm stuck with a twenty-four-hour diner and shitty Lipton tea.

There's also no way I'm making any of the meetings I scheduled for today. It kills me, but I need Ryan's help.

I pull out my laptop and attempt to be civil.

It isn't easy.

Ryan,

I have a personal emergency and there's no way I can make it into work today or tomorrow. I'll reschedule my 11:00, but I need you to take my 3:00. Your calendar says you're free. It should be an easy meeting—everyone is ready to sign on the dotted line.

Luke

HE RESPONDS THIRTY MINUTES LATER. OF COURSE, RYAN IS awake already. Hell, he's probably in the office, trying to figure out more ways to fuck me over.

I wish I could suggest that you're kidding, but I know better. I'll do what I can to take your meetings through Friday, but if you aren't here on Monday morning at 9 A.M., you can find another job. Agree to the terms, or you're on your own.

It was difficult enough last time you went MIA for two weeks, after Samantha's incident. We've barely recovered from the damage.

This early, this last-minute, it must be Samantha again. It's not like you have any family that could need you.

I'd think she'd finally be happy now that she's gotten rid of you.

Ryan

I CLENCH MY TEETH.

Motherfucker.

My fingers hit the keyboard harder than they need to.

Just a reminder—we are still business partners. You can't fire me. And if shit goes wrong with my clients, it affects you too. Though I would be happy to dissolve the firm. You keep your clients, I keep mine. Hell, you can keep the office, the name, and Janine. I'll reschedule everything with my clients. You won't have to touch a thing.

Luke

He replies quickly.

The only way this partnership is ending is with me owning 100 percent of the business. I'll happily buy your half for twenty percent over its value.

Agree to the terms or agree to leave. You may care more about chasing suicidal women than about your clients, but I'm still interested in running a business.

Ryan

Does he think he has actual leverage here?

If that's how he wants to play, fine.

I planned on being back Monday anyway, but I'm not telling him that.

I don't have to agree to anything. Take the meeting or don't. I have my laptop. I'll do everything except take those meetings. If you won't handle it for me, I'll reschedule.

Luke

Rescheduling isn't ideal, but I'll do it if I have to.

He's quick with his next reply.

I'll take the meeting.

How is Alyssa? She can't be happy about this.

I bet she needs some comforting.

And we both know that fidelity isn't her strong suit.

Of course, you're used to women cheating on you, aren't you? Maybe it won't be too bad.

Ryan

I resist the urge to throw the laptop across the room.

Instead, I close it gently.

I got what I wanted.

Chapter Five

The hospital waiting room is sterile and drab—designed to be as unpleasant as possible.

I stop at the plastic reception desk and ask if I can visit Samantha.

The frowning woman in her fifties looks at me like I'm an idiot.

I doubt she'd look at me like this if I was in my suit and tie instead of jeans and a T-shirt, my tattoos on display.

Like that, I'm the dignified professional. Like this, I'm the asshole boyfriend.

But who knows.

Maybe she treats everyone like this. Probably a byproduct of not getting laid for too many years.

"I'll see if Ms. Brooks is accepting visitors." She hands me a form and points to the spaces I need to fill out.

I scrawl my answers quickly, handing it back to her.

"Thanks," I say, my tone cool to match hers.

I sit on one of the ugly green chairs and flip through the faded paperback I keep in my pocket.

It's *Murder on the Orient Express*, an Agatha Christie novel

I bought at the used bookstore a million years ago. I've still never finished it.

Today isn't looking any better. I can barely read a sentence, much less a chapter.

I lean back in the chair, close my eyes, and accept that this is the best rest I'm going to get today.

It feels like forever before the receptionist finally calls me back to the desk. "Ms. Brooks doesn't want any guests right now." She frowns, surprisingly apologetic now.

Clearly, Samantha doesn't want to see me today. She definitely said something to this woman about how little she wants to see me.

I don't think there is anyone else who would visit her.

My guess would be her parents aren't in the loop at this point.

The receptionist looks at me with pity. I must be the asshole ex-boyfriend now.

"There's a cafeteria in the basement," she offers.

I nod a thank you and I leave the waiting room.

It's cool outside and the sky is a blinding shade of white. It's the kind of white that covers Southern California beaches in the morning, before the sun rises and turns everything a brilliant shade of blue.

My shirt is sweaty, sticking to my chest, and my hair is a mess.

This isn't going to work itself out in the next few hours. Samantha refused to see me. She wouldn't refuse to see me if she was in a car accident or if she fell and broke her leg.

My jaw locks up.

My head is aching and my back is sore.

I'm at a loss about what my game plan should be now.

Okay, first I should make sure Samantha won't see me today.

It's a fucking waste if I got in an argument with Alyssa and drove all this way for nothing.

I call her phone. It rings three times, all the way to voice mail. Not a good sign.

"Fuck, Sam. Come on," I mutter under my breath.

I call again. This time, it rings once, then voice mail. She rejected the call.

Fine, she doesn't want to see me today. She needs time to build her nerve.

I walk back to my car, thinking.

Sam might change her mind today. But I don't want to just wait around for the off chance that happens.

Alyssa's party is tonight. I know how much she's dreading it.

I get it.

She's been bitten by the fucking sharks in her industry too many times to not worry about it.

I check the time.

I could easily make it back in time.

Yes, work will suffer for it.

But Alyssa is so fucking worth it.

And I can always drive back here tomorrow. Maybe Samantha will even deign to see me then.

I feel a weight lift from my shoulders and know I'm doing the right thing.

Maybe it's wrong to feel this way, but I'm kind of glad Sam didn't want to see me if it means it frees me up to support Alyssa.

I'm actually excited on the drive back, a marked difference from the previous drive.

I feel a twinge of guilt, but shit, I'm only human.

I don't even get mad when I hit the cluster fuck of traffic.

———

It's well into late afternoon when I make it back.

I text Alyssa, wanting to be sure she's home.

She is.

Anticipation bubbles up in my stomach as I knock on the door.

"Coming!" I hear through the door.

It's Alyssa. I can tell even though her voice is muffled by the barrier.

The door opens quickly, the expression on her face distracted.

But her eyes quickly sharpen when they land on me, the mixture of surprise and joy on her face making the trip so worth it.

"Luke!" she cries, jumping right into my arms, peppering my face with kisses. "What are you doing here?"

I laugh, wrapping my arms around her.

"Turned out Samantha didn't want any visitors today. And I didn't see any reason to wait around when I could just drive back in the morning."

"Oh." She frowns. "I'm sure she's just embarrassed. It's not like she wants you to have to rescue her every six months."

I nod.

"I'm sure you're right."

"Are you okay though? I know, if I abandoned all my responsibilities to be at someone's side and she rejected me... I'd be pissed as hell."

"I'm okay." I really am. "It was a shitty round trip, but at least now I can be at the party with you." I tuck a lock of hair behind her ear, studying her face. "How are you dealing?"

"You know me. Nothing I love more than crowded parties where I'm the center of attention."

Her tone is snarky, but I can see the anxiety in her eyes.

I squeeze her closer.

"I'll be there with you."

She smiles, cupping my face in her warm palm. "That will make it easier, at least."

"Good. I'm glad. And if you want me to sue anyone afterwards, I'm always down."

She laughs, rolling her eyes.

"Come on," she says, pulling back. "You can take a nap while I get ready." She gives me a concerned look while she tugs me inside. "You look beat."

"It was a long drive," I acknowledge, following her into her room.

A nap sounds like nirvana.

So I do exactly what she suggests.

I strip down to my boxers and fall into the bed.

"I'll wake you up when you need to throw on some clothes."

"Hmmm."

I drift into sleep, barely feeling Alyssa kiss my forehead.

———

"It's going to be fine."

"God, I wish I was anywhere else," Alyssa mutters, surveying the crowd.

She looks fucking gorgeous, as usual.

What I really want to do is drag her back into her room and remind myself that she tastes just as good as she looks.

My cock is already more than a little interested.

Unfortunately, it's not in the cards right this second.

So I content myself with looking.

Her blond hair tumbles around her shoulders, her simple calf length sheath dress highlighting her body, but in an understated way.

Her makeup is equally simple and pretty.

But she really does look like she's about to bolt.

I squeeze her hand, drawing her attention to me.

"They're going to love the show, love you."

"You don't know that," she counters, but her eyes lose some of that edge.

"Sure I do. I'm a smart as fuck lawyer, remember?"

She rolls her eyes, a grin tugging at her lips.

"Don't you mean smart*ass* lawyer?"

I grin back, happy to see the smile.

"Who says the two are mutually exclusive?"

"Come on guys—it's about to start!" Laurie announces, shushing everyone.

We all turn towards the big screen television.

I feel Alyssa tense once more next to me.

I wrap an arm around her and squeeze, watching the opening credits along with everyone else.

The show starts.

Five minutes into the thing, I know I'm right.

This thing is going to be a hit.

And Alyssa is flat out amazing in it.

Amazing.

I knew she'd be amazing—she was amazing in all sorts of tiny films, and even in the terrible teen soap she was on for years—but she never got the chance to be so fucking hilarious. She's a force of nature. She's selfish, and rude, and completely awful, but lovable all the same. She's never been more on fire, more bright, more brilliant.

This brilliant, talented woman wants me.

And I know I'm the luckiest guy in the fucking world.

When the show fades to black, there's a moment of silence.

For a second, I have a taste of the doubt that must plague Alyssa.

It's not at all fun.

And then everyone starts to clap and whoop, offering their enthusiastic congratulations.

Thank God.

"You were amazing," I whisper to Alyssa as she fields compliments left and right.

"You were so good, Alyssa! I can't believe..."

"They couldn't have cast anyone more perfect for the part! I mean..."

She smiles at everyone, but I can see the anxiety still brewing in her eyes, in the tight grip she keeps on my hand.

But she gets through it.

Still, she stays out only long enough to be polite.

And keep Laurie away from what I assume is trouble.

"I'm going to have to make sure Laurie doesn't try to sleep with Danny... not that I can blame her. He's hot."

"Excuse me?"

I look over in the direction she's focused in, taking in the generically handsome guy flirting with Laurie.

She throws her head back and laughs at something he says.

"Doesn't seem like she wants to be saved," I observe wryly. "You think that guy's hot?"

She chuckles.

"Not as hot as you, but still... not bad."

I mime her favorite *Law and Order* quote. "I'll allow it, but you better watch yourself, Summers."

She laughs, a big belly laugh. "Make me."

I have a quick flash of some of the things I want to do to her.

None of which are fit for public consumption.

"Maybe once we're alone."

Her cheeks flush in reaction, her eyes darkening.

But then they dart away from me again, back towards Laurie.

"One second," she murmurs, hurrying away.

I turn to watch her expertly deflect Danny away from Laurie and towards another willing young woman.

Laurie looks put out, but only briefly.

It doesn't take her long to get involved in conversation with someone else.

Then Alyssa is right back with me, tugging me back to her bedroom.

"Impressive."

"I have some experience," she tosses over her shoulder.

I bet.

She's the bell of the ball, so she has to interact as we move, but she does with an expertise that doesn't leave anyone feeling slighted.

That's an art in itself.

I have the urge to shove a couple of people away myself.

Finally, we make it to the bedroom.

"You did it," I murmur, pulling her into my arms in the sanctuary of the closed room.

She leans against me, sighing out a breath, her shoulders finally dropping.

"Yeah. But..."

"But what?" I urge, rubbing her back.

She peeks up at me.

"Now I'm worried about what the reviews are going to say."

I shake my head.

Time to get her mind off of all this.

There's too much that could bring her down and she's already drained from the socializing at the party.

"Why don't you take a break from thinking about the show," I suggest, turning her towards the bed. "The show was good—everyone really enjoyed it. That's enough for tonight."

She raises her brows as I push her gently onto the mattress.

"I think you might have an ulterior motive," she accuses, smiling while she rubs her hands down my arms.

"Me?" I ask innocently, nudging her thighs apart with mine. "I don't know what could possibly give you that idea..."

I lean down to settle my mouth onto hers.

And pull the front zipper of her dress down to split the fabric, exposing her ridiculously perfect tits to my eager hands.

FUCK, YES.

It doesn't take too much convincing to get her mind off the show.

———

AN ODD BUZZING HAS ME OPENING MY EYES.

I'm wrapped around a naked Alyssa in bed.

This better be good.

Blearily, I reach out for my phone, blinking a few times before I can focus on the screen.

It's a text.

My heart skips a beat before I even read it.

It's from Sam.

Room 203.

It's still early. The sun is far from being up.

But I'm suddenly sharp and alert.

Samantha is ready to see me.

I look over at Alyssa's sleeping form.

I don't want to leave. I want to spend the weekend celebrating the premiere with Alyssa.

But I need to make sure Samantha's okay.

I don't know if she has anyone else to turn to.

"Alyssa."

I smooth a hand down her slender back.

The touch has her eyes fluttering open.

"Hmm?"

"Sam just texted me. She wants to see me."

The haze of sleep dissipates quickly at that news.

She sits up, shoving her hair back from her face.

"What?"

"I need to drive back to the hospital," I explain. "She finally reached out to me."

She takes a deep breath. Like she's working up her nerve?

"Do you have any idea how long you'll be visiting?"

"A couple days? I'm not sure. I don't know what state she's in."

"Oh." She nods. "Okay." "I'll call after I see her."

"Alright." She draws me in close, giving me a gentle kiss. "Drive safe."

I hesitate before I get off the bed, feeling like we should talk more about this.

Feeling shitty for just leaving.

But also not knowing what more to say.

Yes, Sam and I have a complicated relationship. But she was there for me when I needed her.

How can I not be there for her?
So I just get dressed and kiss her goodbye.
But that unsettled feeling doesn't leave me.
Something feels... off.
Unfortunately, I don't have time to dive deep.
Later. Later, we'll talk more.
About everything.

————

I SPEND THE DRIVE THINKING ABOUT WHAT TO GET ALYSSA.

Something to commemorate the premiere.

Something better than flowers, candy, or stuffed animals. She'd recede into herself and lock me out if I even dreamed of buying her candy. I would never be that insensitive about her recovery.

And she isn't really a stuffed animal type. Hell, the only two things she wants are coffee and books for her Kindle.

Huh.

Maybe I just need to stay in those two lanes then.

I tighten my grip on the steering wheel, switching lanes on the still sparsely populated highway.

I hope Samantha is getting the help she needs.

It sounds awful, but the sooner she's better, the sooner I can be back home with Alyssa.

Chapter Six

When I reach San Diego, I drive to the cheapest hotel in the area.

I have the money to stay someplace nice, but I'd rather this trip not feel nice in any way. I'd rather solve this problem and get back to my life with Alyssa.

The room is an ugly shade of beige, but it's not altogether unpleasant. It has everything I need—a bed, a TV, a shower, curtains to block out the obscenely bright sun.

The hot water of the shower feels perfect against my skin. It would be so much nicer to have Alyssa in here with me, to press her against the tile wall and slide my hand between her legs, feel how slick she is. To run my lips over the wet skin on her neck, to watch her bite her teeth and arch her back, to hear a perfect, soft moan escape her lips.

But I'm not here to have a good time.

Shit.

I force my mind away from Alyssa.

It takes some doing, but my cock finally figures out nothing is happening.

I rough dry myself and finally leave the shower for the room.

As soon as I'm ready, I head over to the hospital.

It's quiet here. The air is stale. There's something horribly uncomfortable about it, but I push it to the back of my mind.

Samantha's room is around a corner and down a hallway. I knock on the door briefly and enter.

She's sitting on the hospital bed, a cardigan over her paper gown.

Her features look hard and tired. Her brown eyes seem dull. Her long, brown hair is in a messy ponytail. Even her glasses seem old and faded.

It's difficult to see.

"Hey," I say in a low voice.

She looks at me like I'm an idiot. "I was expecting something more dramatic."

I know it's defensive.

"I'd say maybe next time, but I'm hoping there isn't a next time."

She shifts in her hospital bed. Looks at the curtain next to her, shaking her head. "This isn't a repeat, Luke." She looks back at me. "I wasn't trying to... I was prescribed a new anti-anxiety med."

"What happened?" I prod when nothing else is forthcoming.

Is she lying?

I want to believe her. "Do you know you're not supposed to mix that stuff with alcohol?" She sighs. "I took one before eating. After a few glasses of wine at dinner, I wasn't thinking all that clearly." She frowns, her fingers picking at the sterile white blanket. "I got into bed, but my mind was still racing. I couldn't turn it off, you know? So I took another. But I still couldn't stop thinking, couldn't get to sleep. So I took another...Too much wine and too many prescription pills." She gives me as sardonic smile. "A stupid mistake. I woke up in an ambulance. The housekeeper found me and called 9-1-1 when she couldn't wake me up."

I know the easy delivery is to distance herself from what happened.

Was it an accident, like she's trying to convince me it was?

"Samantha..."Her eyes pass over me like she's studying me. "Sit down. You're making me uncomfortable."

I sit in one of the ugly green chairs. "Does this really make you more comfortable?"

She sighs and folds her arms. Her voice is rough and irritated. "You must feel so embarrassed in a shit hospital gown, no makeup, no access to even a hairbrush. And then your ex hauls ass to come and rescue you. Very embarrassing for you." Why does she always try to chase me away before she begs me to stay?

"I'm here because I want to be here," I say. "And I don't give a fuck what you look like."

"I look like shit."

She isn't her usual polished self, but she looks fine. Samantha was never a knockout, but that never mattered. "You didn't deny it. It must be true."

"Don't be so vain."

She gives me a real look at that.

"Said the guy dating the hot actress."

"She has other traits."

"Like?"

I shake my head. "She's thoughtful. She's sweet. She's smart as all hell. Reads most English grad student stuff. And she's so passionate about what she does. You know how that gets me."

Samantha unfolds her arms, sighing. "I get it, Luke. She's hot and smart and puts up with shit like you being here. She's a catch no matter how you slice it"

"I don't care that she's hot."

"Uh-huh."

"Don't get me wrong. She's amazingly hot. But I'd be with her even if she was a hideous beast."

She smiles, humor glimmering in her eyes.

"That's what guys always say when they're dating hot women." The mood is finally starting to lighten a little, and the room feels a little brighter and more colorful.

She looks down at her blanket, entirely focused on pulling lint off it. "I thought you'd leave after yesterday."

"I did leave. Alyssa had a premiere party for her show. But I came back down when you texted because I care about you. You idiot."

She laughs at the soft jab. Then takes a moment to compose herself. This time when she looks at me, it's direct and no nonsense. "You shouldn't be here. I don't want to take you away from your life."

"I want to be here for you."

"Why?" Her voice is low.

I know she's thinking about what she did.

It's always in the back of my mind when I'm around her.

"You're my friend. This is what friends do." I scoot my chair closer to her. "Like you were there for me when I needed you."

She looks at me, her defenses stripped away for a moment. "Are you sure?"

"Positive."

She nods.

"Did you visit your mom?"

I think of the manicured cemetery, the crisply carved tombstone.

I push the image away.

I can't think of that right now.

Not while one of my oldest friends is lying in a hospital bed.

"No."

My answer is short.

Sam gets the point, her eyes softening in sympathy.

She changes the subject.

"My dad is going to flip if he sees you around."

This is as good an opening as I'm going to get.

"Why isn't he here now? Why isn't your mother here?"

She looks down at the blanket.

It's as good as an admission.

"They don't know."

"They don't need to know." She meets my eyes once more. "And you're not going to tell them."

"Sam—"

"No," she repeats firmly. "They can't go through that again. I want to at least let them enjoy their vacation without worrying about me."

"When will they be home?" I ask, my stomach sinking.

"After the weekend."

"Okay." I take a deep breath. "That's good."

At least she's seeing someone if she has a prescription for anxiety medication.

Her eyes stay on the window. "I wasn't trying to commit suicide, Luke. I already told you that." She turns back to me, a little irritated. "If you want to stay and keep me company, I'd be glad to beat you at rummy, but I'm not talking about it anymore. It's none of your business."

I tamp down on my frustration, though it wants to turn to anger.

That won't be helpful in this situation.

"I'd say it is my god damn business," I return firmly. Her expression changes to one of surprise. Maybe she was expecting me to just roll over. But fuck that shit. "I'm still your emergency contact. I'm the one who showed up when you needed me—hell, I'm the one who always shows up."

"Then don't! I didn't tell you to be here," she growls, her hands clenching in the sheets.

"Didn't you? Why else did you text me your room number?" I push. She doesn't have an answer to that. I soften my voice, reaching out to cover her hand with my own. I take it as a good sign when she doesn't immediately pull it away. "I care about you Samantha. I want you to get better. I worry. Okay?"

She looks at the window. It's flooded with light, but the curtains make the whole room dim and dull. "I...yeah." She sighs. "I get it. Sorry I'm so defensive."

"It's alright. I get it," I murmur.

She nods slightly, picking at her fingers now.

An anxious habit that only comes out when she's the most stressed.

This definitely warrants it.

"Was there anything I could have done?"

It just comes out without real thought.

She gives me an exasperated look. "Jesus, Luke. Not everything is about you. Sometimes people are just fucked up."

She shakes her head. She's right.

I know it's not about me, but still... I could have done more maybe. I could have helped more.

Maybe it's stupid, but it's how I feel.

She brings her gaze back to my eyes. Her face is completely unreadable, but I know she's hurting. I know there are things she can't bring herself to say.

She folds her arms. "Now go buy a pack of cards at the gift shop. We have enough time for a few games."

"Next time, I'll smuggle in a bottle of Cabernet."

She smiles. Finally, a full smile.

"I won't turn it away."

I smile back.

It's possible this will work out okay.

––––––––

I SPEND THE REST OF THE DAY GLUED TO MY LAPTOP. I'M buried in work, but my mind keeps drifting back to Alyssa.

I still need to find some way to make this up to her. A small gesture for the premiere at the very least. She deserves more. Hell, she deserves everything the world has to offer, but my options are limited.

It has to be something she'd really enjoy.

Something just for her.

So basically, tequila or coffee.

And I'm not sending her a drink typically reserved for drowning sorrows.

But the coffee... She's mentioned Laurie's shitty coffee maker before. There's this horribly futuristic contraption she wants. It's Japanese and it's supposed to make the world's most amazing coffee.

And she's always going on about what shitty coffee Laurie buys—awful generic stuff from the grocery store.

God, Alyssa is adorable during these rants. *Why would she do that to herself? It's like eating drugstore chocolate. I assume. Or like... like going out for fast food when she could eat at a five-star restaurant. That stuff is shit—the bottom of the barrel. Like the tea dust you're always going on about. You know, the shitty bags with no flavor. That's what this is. And she buys it ground. She doesn't even have a coffee grinder! I'm not saying she needs to spend twenty dollars a pound on beans, but for the love of God, she could do better. I mean, she only shops at Whole Foods—they have good shit there!*

She gets the most satisfied look on her face when she takes her first sip of good coffee.

There's only one other time where I've seen her that satisfied.

I pour over the options online.

Then I see it. The perfect coffee maker for her.

It's hot pink to boot.

But I can't give her this if she's only got crappy store brand coffee. And it's unlikely Alyssa will allow herself the pleasure of buying beans she actually enjoys. What was that brand she liked? Something from Portland or Seattle or some place that actually has trees.

Stumptown.

I buy her a bag of beans, the glorious hot pink pour-over contraption, and a grinder. I overnight all of it.

My fingers hover over the keyboard, thinking over the message.

It has to be real. She has to feel it.

I compose an email.

Ally, I'm so glad I was there for your premiere. You were so fucking great, I can't get over it.

I've felt lucky every day, ever since the moment when you told Ryan to go fuck himself. Ever since you chose me.

But I've never felt luckier than last night.

I still can't believe my luck that you want anything to do with me. I pinch myself when I wake up, because I think I'm dreaming.

I'm sorry I keep trying to rush you. I didn't do things well before either. But, God, I love you so fucking much. I feel it everywhere, all the time, wherever I go. I love you so much, and every single inch between us hurts. I want you to live with me. I want you to be my wife.

But I know I'm getting ahead of myself.

I just want you to know I'm in it for the long haul, Ally.

You're the best thing in my life. I don't even know what my life was before I met you, because I can't imagine it without you. I can't imagine not coming home to see you glued to your Kindle again, pretending not to gasp over the dramatic twist in whatever it is you're reading. I can't imagine not arguing over what to watch on TV. Or not mocking old movies with you. I can't even imagine waking up and drinking all my tea, instead of losing half of it to you. I'd so much rather you have that half of my tea.

I'm sorry I'm here. I promise it has nothing to do with us. I'm still all in.

And I promise that when I get back to Los Angeles, I'll make this up to you in a much more... exciting way.

I'm all yours.

Love,

Luke

Chapter Seven

Samantha almost shrieks when I pull out the Cabernet.

It's not a bottle. It's a juice box. Well, a wine box.

Her jaw drops. "I thought you were joking."

"I'm not that cruel." I place two water cups—flimsy plastic things—on the table attached to her bed. "When are you getting out of here?"

"Tomorrow."

I pour the wine into the tiny cups. It's such a violent, vibrant shade of crimson that the whole room fills with color.

She brings the cup to her lips and takes a tiny sip.

"Is it acceptable?" I ask.

She smirks. "I'm not in a position to be choosy."

The wine stains her lips the same vibrant shade. Her whole face floods with color.

She takes another sip. "Better than I expected from a juice box."

"It's easier to smuggle than a bottle."

"There's nothing in the hospital policy that specifically forbids wine."

I run my fingers over the edge of the cup. "You didn't just take your medication, right?"

She rolls her eyes. "I'm not a complete idiot. Even I can learn from my mistakes."

My shoulders relax a little.

Though maybe bringing wine might be enabling her... shit, I just don't really know what to do anymore.

I drag the ugly green chair, placing it next to her bed.

"I've been thinking... you know, you don't have to stay with your parents."

It clearly hasn't been a good thing.

"I thought it would help," she explains, sighing. "Get away for a while. There was so much gossip floating around the office, especially when people heard I landed in the hospital. You must remember."

"You were vague about what happened."

She looks at me like I'm an idiot, again. "What am I supposed to say—I was fucking the boss, who, as you guys probably know, is my fiancé's father? And I got so depressed after he died that I swallowed a bottle of sleeping pills?"

I wince.

"It's okay for a first draft."

She shakes her head. "It was better to say nothing."

I can't say she's wrong.

We're quiet for a while. We stare into our plastic cups of wine, sipping it so we won't have to talk.

Samantha stares at her fingers. She squeezes her cup so tightly I think it will break.

I bring my eyes to hers. "Why don't you come back to Los Angeles, Sam? Maybe it's better you get away from the house at least."

She nods.

"I might. I certainly can't stay with my parents. They treat me like I'm fourteen. I don't have anything to do except sit in the study and look at my law school textbooks longingly."

"Read them. I'm pretty sure they aren't meant to be art installations."

She laughs.

"I do. It's pathetic. It's like I'm taking Torts 101 for the first time." She finishes her glass and motions for me to refill it.

I give her a look—should you drink so much?

She strains not to roll her eyes. "You don't get to boss me around anymore, Lawrence. I'm not your girlfriend. I don't have to listen to you."

"When did you ever listen to me?" I oblige her with a careful refill.

Two glasses worth of wine and she's happy. Three, and she's mouthy. Four, and she throws a fit. A very tiny, contained fit that no one will ever see. She does care about appearances, even with me.

She smirks, her voice brimming with confidence. "When I was trying to get in your pants." I'm not touching that comment. Color floods her face as she drinks, like the red of the wine is bleeding into her cheeks. She looks down at her cup. "I feel like I finally remember why I ever cared about the law."

I study her as she studies the wine.

"He killed your passion, didn't he?"

We both know who I'm referring to.

Samantha gives me an imploring look.

"Luke, please don't—"

"Why the fuck not? I can handle it."

"Maybe I'd rather not talk about it with you," she

mutters. "Have you considered that?" It's painfully obvious that Samantha doesn't want to talk about her affair.

I don't know what in me keeps me picking at the subject.

She finishes her cup and sets it on the table. "I'm sorry, okay. I don't know if it's possible for me to apologize enough, but I am sorry. I should have told you from the beginning. I shouldn't have lied for so long."

I swallow, hard. "Don't you hate how 'I shouldn't have fucked him' isn't on that list?"

I thought I was over it.

But maybe it's something I'll never be completely over.

Sure, there was a lot to hate about my father.

But he was still my father. He still cared about me in his own way.

At least, I thought he did.

Maybe that's why I can't fully get over this.

She lowers her voice, her eyes on the floor. "I'm sorry. I really am. I should have ended things way before I did. You didn't deserve that."

"It's okay. I wouldn't have let you end things if you'd tried."

She adjusts her glasses and looks me square in the eye. "Please, Luke. Don't tell me it's okay again. I'd feel so much better if you called me a cunt and told me you never wanted to see me again."

Fuck.

God knows I called her that and every name in the book in my head.

But what did that get me?

"Would that do us any good?"

"Tell me the truth."

"We've been over this."

"But you always sugarcoat it." She holds my gaze,

staring at me like she really wants me to unleash a flurry of insults.

I did hate her, for a while. But she was such a big part of my life. We went through so much together.

Everything but how shit ended between us was great.

But, man. That bad part was a fucking nuclear explosion.

Still...it tainted everything else, yes—but it didn't erase it.

And then, when she tried to kill herself...It was hard to stay mad.

Even though I had more than enough reason.

I finish my cup of wine and place it on the tray. "You're not a cunt. It wasn't the best thing you've ever done. But you're not a cunt."

She makes a frustrated sound in the back of her throat.

"I'd feel so much better if you hated me as much as I hate myself for it."

I shrug.

"Too bad. I don't."

"You didn't hate me when I told you I was in love with Edward?"

"Fuck, sure. Maybe," I say honestly. "But really I hated him." He was my father. The betrayal cut deeper. If I was honest, Sam and I had been drifting apart before that.

"Luke..."

I give her a sharp look.

"Do you want the truth or not?"

Samantha lowers her voice to a whisper. "Are you ever going to get over it?"

"Why should I? He was a fucker. He basically killed my mom. He almost killed you—"

She interrupts me.

"No, I almost killed me."

"It was at least partially his fault." I frown, thinking back. "You were different before him. You were happy."

"Maybe we shouldn't talk about this." She pushes her blanket off her chest.

She looks so small and fragile like this, even with the sweater covering her tiny paper gown.

I scrub at my face, trying to pull back from that emotional edge.

"Okay." I drop my hands. "Okay."

She's right. There's no good way for this conversation to end. And I don't know if a hospital room is the place to delve deep into our screwed-up past.

"Maybe we should start that game of rummy before someone notices our raised voices and confiscates our wine."

She nods.

I pull the cards from my pocket and start to shuffle, my mind having trouble shifting gears.

When I look up, Samantha is holding my gaze.

"Thanks," she says.

"For what?" "For being here."

———

I PORE OVER WORK ALL EVENING.

As usual, that fucker Ryan is attempting to bury me in a pile of it. He's willing to do whatever it takes to convince me to sell.

But my irritation fades away when I see an email from Alyssa.

She never emails. She barely even uses the computer.

Luke,

Why didn't you warn me how fucking sweet you are when we met? Completely insane, but sweet :).

How the hell did you get a pour-over to Laurie's place so quickly? You know what—don't tell me. I don't want to know about the freaky drones that are going to take over the world.

Anyway, thank you. I really need the coffee today, and OH MY GOD it is so, so much better than the crap Laurie keeps in the freezer. Can you believe how low her coffee standards are? It's one thing to not like coffee. Fine. Plenty of people don't like coffee. But to keep it ground up in the freezer in that stupid plastic tin! It should be illegal to drink such awful coffee.

And before you even start, no, it should not be illegal to put honey in coffee. Honey and coffee are madly in love. Even more than we're in love.

And we are, Luke. I love you so much. But the scary thing is, I know what my life looks like without you—and it looks like total shit.

I'm so happy with you. I really am. I feel like I'm lighter than air when I'm around you. You're my trigger whenever I need to project love or joy or, obviously, lust.

And it's not that I'm not all in. I am. I just need more time. I need to feel like I know who I am. Because you're all consuming, and as much as I love that, I can't get consumed again.

I worry I'm going to be like the Alyssa of the past. But I don't want to be her anymore. I want to be strong. I want to be independent. I want to stand on my own.

Because that's how we'll know it's real—if we're together by choice, not out of a lack of better options.

I've already been there, done that.

God, I'm rambling. I'm sorry. I'm trying really hard to stay away from reviews, but they're so fucking tempting. And they're all at my fingertips.

Come back soon, okay?

Love,

Alyssa

P.S. If you, for some reason, come back in love with Samantha, I'll take Laurie up on her offer to have you killed. Don't make me complicit in murder. I'll crack on the cross, and I'll be an awful prisoner.

P.P.S. This isn't a threat... more of a hypothetical. For legal reasons, of course.

Chapter Eight

I wish Alyssa was here.

I need to hold her and whisper in her ear how much I love her. I need her to know that this trip has nothing to do with us—I still love her more than anything.

But the weight of this is so heavy. I can feel it pressing down on us, taking up space between us.

She knows I have to be here.

But she doesn't like it. If I leave now, Samantha might sink back into her depression.

I'm not entirely sure what happened was an accident.

Even though it does seem like Sam may have convinced herself it was.

I take a deep breath. I've only been here two days. Two days is nothing in the scheme of my life with Alyssa. And she's an actress. There are going to be so many times when she's out of town filming a project. There are going to be so many times when we're going to have to be apart.

I need to make peace with that.

I call Alyssa, but I only get an "I'll call you back" text.

I resort to killing time—leafing through a faded paperback I've already read half a dozen times, flipping through channels on the TV, staring out the hotel window at the awful view of the parking lot.

And then my phone rings.

I answer after the first ring. "Hey."

She laughs. "That's a lot more restrained than I expected."

"You're obviously trying to kill me."

"Obviously." She clears her throat, nervous. "Did you get my email?"

My lips curl into a smile. "I did."

"Did I sound like a rambling idiot?"

"No, it was really sweet. I loved it."

I can hear the embarrassment and the pleasure through the line.

She quickly changes the subject.

"I love this pour-over. And this coffee is amazing." She sighs like she's in heaven. "I didn't realize how desperate I was for an easy supply of good coffee."

"I'm glad," I say. I shift the phone to my other ear. "I watched *Model Citizen* again. You were really amazing."

"I was okay. I can't believe you watched it again."

"You were amazing. And I enjoyed it just as much the second time."

It's true.

"But that scene in the laundry room—ugh! I was acting so hard. I could see it on my face."

"You're the only one."

She groans. "You're biased."

"Admit you were amazing."

"I was okay."

"Admit it."

"Good even." She takes a long breath, like she's waiting for me to respond. "Maybe even really good."

I lower my voice. "You were amazing. Anyone who says otherwise is an idiot. If you tell me of anyone, I'll kill them."

"Kill him." It's a smug correction.

God, how I'd like to wipe that smug look off her face with my lips, to press her against the wall, fuck her until there's nothing on her face but ecstasy.

But this isn't the time. I shake my head, bringing my focus back to my brain.

"Also... I've had a few questions about my boyfriend... people trying to figure out if the gossip blogs are right—if I really left my fiancé for a mysterious hottie."

I chuckle.

"I saw that blog."

"Hmm. So who did you tip off?"

"Oh, you know, just Perez Hilton and Harvey Levin. No big deal."

"You wish." She giggles. "More like Joe of Joe's Blog."

"Hey! You can say what you want about me, but don't speak ill of Joe."

"Never."

She laughs. It's so pure and warm that it fills the room with color. "What about you? It can't be easy trying to comfort your suicidal ex."

"She says it was just an accident. New medication."

"Hmm." She doesn't argue, but I can hear the skepticism even in that sound. "What do you two do?"

"We talk and we play rummy."

"What do you talk about?" She asks like she's curious, like she really wants to know.

I smirk. "How much I love fucking you."

Alyssa laughs, but it's awkward. Tense.

She wants me to reassure her of something, but I'm not sure what.

"We don't talk about anything important," I say.

"No? The woman's back in the hospital and you don't talk about anything important?"

"Nothing worth rehashing."

She sighs and takes a long, slow breath. "I won't get upset. I understand that you loved her once."

There's a pounding in the back of my head. I shift the phone, lowering my voice to a whisper. "She was there for me when nobody else was."

"I'm glad she was there when you needed her," she murmurs, her tone softer.

I nod, even though she can't see me.

"Yeah. I want her to actually get better, not go from crisis to crisis. But I'm sick of talking about Samantha."

She murmurs some acknowledgment. Alyssa must understand. She's always trying to get out of conversations.

She clears her throat twice. Exhales a heavy breath into the phone. "Well, um, here's the thing..."

I like the sound of that. "Yes?"

"I was thinking... We could do things... on the phone." She's so breathless she can barely get through the words. She exhales, harder this time.

I really like the sound of that. But still, I need to torture her as much as I can.

I am as coy as possible. "What kinds of things? Chess?"

"I hate chess."

"Pawn to A4."

"Not chess!"

"That's a terrible opening!"

"How would I know? I hate chess. It's awful and boring." She groans. It's a low, throaty groan.

It's sexy as all hell.

But still, I need to torture her as much as I can.

I exhale into the phone. "And the whole point of the game is protecting the king."

"But isn't he useless? Isn't the queen some kind of Lady MacBeth with all sorts of mad skills?"

"And you acted like you knew nothing about chess."

She groans, louder this time. "Goddammit, Luke. Why do you make my life so difficult?"

"Because you like it better when I make you wait." And I like it better when I get to watch her contort in pleasure for as long as possible.

She sighs, giving up any pretenses. "You know what things I mean. Where are you staying?"

"Miss Summers, that doesn't sound like an appropriate question."

"Oh, God." She mumbles something.

I can practically see her cheeks turning red, her teeth sinking into her lip. She's flustered.

She's so fucking cute when she's flustered.

"A hotel," I say.

"A nice hotel?"

I look around the room. It's yellow from the fluorescent lights, but dim at the same time. I need something more vibrant. It would be more vibrant if she was here to brighten it with her smile.

God, if she was here, I could feel her body against mine. I could feel her breath on my neck. Her nails on my back. And she would whisper in my ear. Maybe we could...

She'd blush, a little shy about it. And the color would be so fucking gorgeous on her skin. So pink and bright, like her lips. And she'd press those lips into mine, and they would be soft and sweet. So fucking sweet. And I would run my fingertips over that amazing, soft skin, and she would groan and arch and shake, and I'd keep doing it until she was writhing in pleasure. Until I was so hard I couldn't take it anymore.

"Luke?"

"It would be nicer if you were here."

"And you're alone in your room?"

I grin.

"Miss Summers, what exactly are you getting at?"

Chapter Nine

"It's weird to talk about it. I've never done anything like this before." She lets out a nervous laugh, her voice lowering. "But I miss you. I want to feel like you're next to me. I want to hear you..."

She takes a deep breath. God, it's so fucking adorable that she's nervous.

She exhales slowly, adopting her most confident voice. "I want to hear you come."

Blood rushes to my cock at the explicit words.

It would feel damn good to groan into the phone, to listen to her panting and screaming. But not yet.

Not until she's desperate.

I play coy. "Oh yeah?"

She groans. "Jesus, Luke. You're torturing me. I'm never talking about this again without two shots of tequila first."

"Why do you want to hear?"

"Because you're incredibly sexy." She clears her throat. "And I like it when you come."

"Do you?"

"You're evil." Her voice is low, desperate.

I swallow and dig my hands into the sheets. "And how do you propose we accomplish this task?"

She laughs. "I'm getting a drink. And then, maybe, we can talk about this further."

I shut the blinds.

"I could start."

"Drink first," she says.

She puts down the phone, and the room is quiet for a minute. I haven't done this before either, but God, I would do so many damn things to Alyssa.

If she was here, I'd peel off her clothes and touch every part of her. I love the feel of her body, the way she responds to me. I love looking at her. I get hard just picturing her naked—the soft curves of her body, her firm breasts, those pert nipples, so perfect and pink.

Fuck.

I hear her breath first.

"I'm putting you on speaker." She sounds so nervous. "So, um..."

"Your hands can be occupied by other things?"

"I should have taken two shots." She pushes out a throaty exhale. "I, um, what are you wearing?"

I glance in the mirror on the wall. "Jeans and a cotton V-neck."

"Take them off." Her voice is so desperate, so needy. "Please."

Suddenly these clothes feel heavy. Like they're in the way. But I'm not going to let her know that. "What's in it for me?"

"My undying appreciation."

"I think you can do better than that."

"I'll tell you what I'm going to do to you when you get back here."

"And what is that?"

"Suck you off," she says.

Fuck.

Intelligible thought flees my brain. Instead, it floods with the memory of Alyssa's mouth on me—that soft, sweet mouth driving me out of my fucking mind.

I clear my throat. "And what are you wearing?"

"That blue dress you like," she says.

"That's far too much. Take it off."

I expect her to object.

But she doesn't.

I slide my T-shirt over my head. It's only fair.

My senses start turning on. The air conditioning is blowing hard, making the hairs on my neck rise.

If she were here, I could throw her on the bed and get this room so fucking hot.

She breathes hard into the phone. "It's off."

Heat spreads through my body, but I can't give in. Not yet. "What's left?"

"A pink bra and a thong."

Fuck, she must look amazing. The pink pressed against her soft skin. The fabric straining over the curves of her hips. Her lips curled into a shy smile. Her cheeks flushed the same pink as her bra.

Mhmm.

I want to be there, be able to peel her bra off her shoulders and bring my mouth to her nipples. To slide her panties down her hips and rub her until she's screaming my name. She's so fucking sexy, and she's so far away.

My cock pulses. God, if she was here...

"I bet you look fucking divine," I say, my voice gravel.

"If you ask nicely, I might send you a picture."

"Hell yes."

She moans into the phone. "That isn't that nice." She's enjoying her turn at torturing me.

"Pretty please." I need that picture.

Her moan is lower, louder. "That's pretty nice..."

"Please, Miss Summers, let me see how amazing you look, so I can go crazy wishing I was next to you."

My phone buzzes with the picture message. She's looking at the mirror with *fuck me* eyes—that look that says she'd kill to have me inside of her.

Her teeth are sinking into her lip. One hand is on her phone. The other is running over the cups of her bra. It's that pink lacy one, and its straps are falling off her shoulders. Her back is arched and her cheeks are flushed.

It's like she's begging me to touch her. Like she's begging me to run my hands along the edges of her bra. She'd be squirming and groaning, her eyes closed as she fills with pleasure. And she'd arch and groan and pant, begging me to go inside her bra.

"Fuck." My breath is heavy. "You're so fucking sexy." I put my phone on speaker and slide out of my jeans. "Fuck, Ally, I'm going to get you back for all this torture."

"What are you going to do?" she asks.

"I'm going to peel off that bra," I say. "Slowly. Very slowly. And I'm going to take in every inch of you with my eyes, because you are the most beautiful woman I've ever seen. I love your body. And fuck, your breasts are amazing. They're so round and firm, and honestly, it's a crime that you ever wear clothing."

Her breath gets heavier. "And?"

"And I'm going to touch you so lightly you can barely feel it. Just my fingertips on your back and your stomach and your shoulders. And, slowly, very slowly, I'll work my way to your breasts. And then I'll stop. I'll wait until you're writhing in agony, until you tug my hair and scream my name. Then, and only then, I'll rub my thumbs over your nipples."

She moans into the phone.

"God, I wish I could do it right now. It's so sexy when you do that. It drives me fucking crazy. I want to fuck you so badly, but I can't stop watching you fill with pleasure. It's the most beautiful thing I've ever seen."

I want her so much; my body is tingling with desire.

"Are you still dressed?" she asks.

"Just the boxers."

"Take them off," she says. "I want to hear you touch yourself."

I slide out of my boxers and shift onto the bed. If she were here... Jesus, if she were here.

I put the phone on speaker, and run my fingers along my cock. "I'm going to fuck you properly when I'm back home," I groan. "But not until you're begging me to do it."

My breath gets heavy. Flashes of Alyssa fill my head. The taste of her skin. The way she groans when I suck on her nipples. God, those nipples, so perky and firm and responsive. I stroke myself. Harder and harder and harder.

Pangs of pleasure shoot through my body.

"Jesus, Ally," I groan.

She moans into the phone. She moans like she's in heaven.

"Take off your bra," I say. "Now."

I hear her shifting.

Her breath gets heavier. "It's off."

"Now run your fingers over your breasts. Slowly, the way I do."

She groans. "Luke... I want to... I can't wait."

"You will," I say. I stroke myself, harder and harder, filling my body with the sweetest pressure. "Do you want to fuck me?"

"Yes," she moans.

"Do you want to touch yourself?"

"Yes."

"Not yet," I say. "Rub your nipples. Slowly."

Her voice is a low groan. She's not holding anything back. She's mine, even if she's far away.

She's mine.

I stroke myself. "You're so fucking sexy, Ally. The way you move when I touch you... it drives me out of my fucking mind."

"Luke," she groans, her voice needy and desperate

She's touching herself, moaning, probably writhing the way she does when I touch her. Fuck, I bet she's so wet. I bet she's desperate for me to touch her. She'd beg if I made her. She'd scream in pleasure if I slid my cock inside of her.

My grip around my cock gets tighter. The warmth spreads through my body, filling me with pleasure. I'm close.

"Are you wet?" I ask.

"Mhmm."

"Now," I say. "Touch yourself. I want you to come, Ally. I want you to scream my name when you do it."

She groans some agreement, and I stroke myself harder and harder, faster and faster.

Fuck. The room fills with her pants and moans. It's like she's here, like I'm the one filling her with pleasure, the one making her come. My mind is a jumble of Alyssa. The taste of her. The sound of her groan. Her hands tugging at my hair as she rocks into my mouth, practically screaming. Her moan filling my room. The warmth flooding my body. The pleasure and pressure and need building. Her back arching. Her nails on my skin.

I'm almost there. I stroke again. Again. Again. Everything in my body fills with pleasure.

"Fuck, Luke," she says.

Her voice is high and needy, and it pushes me over the edge. The pressure is too much. It feels so fucking good, and I can't hold off any longer. Another stroke, harder and faster. It's deep and intense, so intense it almost hurts.

I lose any conscious thought. Almost there. I groan. "Fuck, Ally," and I tighten my grip. One last stroke and the pressure builds to a climax. Pleasure rips through me as I come. I groan again, releasing everything, my body filling with a pleasant warmth.

It takes forever to catch my breath.

"Jesus, Luke," she says.

"Look at what you do to me." Every part of me is sensitive. I feel my inhale all the way to my toes.

"That was amazing."

Her voice is still high, still needy. She still needs to come. She needs to feel as good as I feel.

"You know," I say. "I only went first because you made such a nice request. I want to hear you too. I need to."

She doesn't say anything, but her breath gets heavier. Her moans get louder.

"Mhmmm."

Her voice is high, and she's so, so full of need. She's so fucking sexy. It builds slowly, getting louder and higher, until she's not just moaning. She's panting. She's screaming. She's desperately close.

It's the most beautiful thing I've ever heard.

"Luke," she moans.

Her voice fills the room, enveloping me in the ecstasy of her pleasure.

"Louder," I say.

And she groans louder. She's moving fast, I can tell. I know how she looks like this—her eyes closed, her back arching, her nails digging into the bed. It's the most gorgeous thing I've ever seen.

"Luke," she groans again, louder this time. "Fuck, Luke."

She's almost there.

She loses control of her breath, panting, practically screaming. "Fuck, Luke."

Her moans build as she gets closer and closer. "Jesus, I'm going to... Fuck..." And she gets louder and louder.

She's all animal—groaning and panting and breathing heavily. She's loud and deep, and she's so fucking sexy.

She builds to a crescendo. She groans, one more time, deeper and louder, more and more and more.

And she comes, panting and screaming and moaning through her orgasm.

Her breath is still heavy and strained. It gets louder. She must be moving the phone closer.

She attempts a slow inhale. A calm exhale. "That was amazing."

I murmur some kind of agreement.

We breathe into the phone for a minute. It's almost like she's here, almost like my arms are wrapped around her.

"I'll send you all the pictures you want if that's how you'll react," she says.

I laugh hoarsely.

"I can agree to those terms."

"But I want some pictures of my own."

"I think that can be arranged."

She murmurs in pleasure. "If I think about that, I'll want to go again."

"I'll fuck you senseless when I get home."

"Well, don't wait too long. I'm not sure I have the patience for it." She sighs wistfully, her breath slowing until it's steady and even.

She's tired. I wore her out.

I can't help but grin.

I press the phone into my ear. "Are you going to bed?"

"Mhmm."

"Stay on the line. I want to fall asleep with you, even if you're far away."

She takes a slow breath. "Give me five minutes to brush my teeth."

And we spend the next hour sharing, listening to each other breathe.

I keep her up too long, talking about nothing.

She almost falls asleep half a dozen times, but she catches herself and begs me to change the subject to something that will keep her awake.

But she can't last forever.

Sometime after midnight, she stops responding.

Her long, slow breaths fill the room, and I almost feel like she's sleeping next to me.

Almost.

Chapter Ten

"So... my parents are out of town this weekend," Samantha reminds me.

We're in her hospital room, playing another game of five hundred rummy.

She's winning, as usual. Though in all honesty, I'm not paying much attention.

It's much more fun to replay last night's phone call with Alyssa.

"I was thinking of leaving Friday."

"Oh." Dread spreads across her face. She sinks back into her chair and motions for me to play my card.

I do. She stares at it like it's everything she needs.

"Is that a problem?"

She shakes her head. "No, of course not," she says quickly. "I was just thinking..." She stares at her cards like they're the most interesting things she's ever seen.

I fight a sigh. This would be much easier if Samantha would admit how much she needs someone.

I lean a little closer. "What were you thinking?"

She slides her fingers over her cards. "It would be nice to have someone around."

An ache builds in my forehead. I want to get back to Alyssa, but I can't exactly leave Samantha if she's worried about being alone. Not after what just happened.

But I can't be here for two more days than I planned.

I have to get back to my own life.

"I can't stay through the whole weekend. But I could swing Saturday," I offer.

She looks up from her cards.

"You can't do Sunday too?"

"Sam... I can't."

She nods, looking away. "Yeah, I totally get it. But you're sure you can stay Saturday?"

I nod.

She sighs in relief.

"Thanks Luke."

She plays her hand—she's won this round—and she marks the points on a notepad.

She squeezes her pencil, once again not meeting my eyes. "Do you think you could stay in the house?"

The air in here is so stale. The windows don't open and the air conditioning is utter shit.

I clear my throat. "That's not the best idea."

"Oh." The relief fades a little. "Is it because of Alyssa?"

"She wouldn't like it." I want to help Samantha, I really do, but not at Alyssa's expense.

"You can stay in the spare room. It's not like I want to get you into bed." She shuffles the cards. Her voice rises until it's confident. "I could have done that a long time ago."

"Is that right?"

She nods. I try to read her expression, but I can't place it.

"You probably forgot how good I am."

She rolls her eyes, then stares at me like I'm an idiot. That's the Samantha I know.

"Luke, I remember perfectly." Her voice is matter-of-fact, like she couldn't be less impressed if she tried.

I may not have been the world's best boyfriend, but I sure as hell left her impressed.

"And?" I ask.

"Let it go." She looks down at the cards.

I tap her hand. "Sam."

She refuses to meet my gaze. "This isn't a fruitful area of conversation."

"You seemed satisfied."

She squeezes her cards. "I'm not discussing this."

"Because you don't want to tell me how much you preferred Edward?" The ache in my head is back.

I don't know why I'm pushing this.

"I'm not comparing your sexual abilities to your father's."

I sigh. "When you put it like that, it sounds insane."

"It is insane." She pushes my hand away from hers and deals the cards on the tiny table. "Besides, I'm the one in the hospital. I'm the one who gets to decide the conversation topics."

I nod.

"Fair enough."

"Besides... it wasn't about the sex." She tries to turn her attention back to the game, but it doesn't hold. She brings her eyes back to mine. Keeps her voice steady. "I feel bad enough about the whole thing, okay?"

I nod.

She taps her fingers, watching me.

"What if he was better? Would knowing that help you in any way?"

I stay silent. I don't even know how to answer that.

I really don't think that's the kind of fucking question a son should think about.

Literally.

"You're so full of it." She sighs, furrowing her brow and pressing her back against the bed.

"Sam..."

She throws me a curt look. "Maybe you should step outside and get some coffee. Call Alyssa."

I hold her gaze. "When you asked for honesty, I gave it to you."

She looks down at her cards and spends what seems like forever rearranging them. "By the time he and I first had sex, you and I weren't connecting. I swear, Luke." She meets my gaze earnestly, her expression pained. "I was looking for an out, and that was it. You have to admit, things were pretty strained."

She's not wrong about that. It isn't an excuse, but she's not wrong.

"Thanks for telling me the truth."

"Are you mad?" Her voice is hesitant, careful.

"No," I say. Though I don't know if that's entirely true.

Hell, there's so much shit swirling inside of me right then I don't know if I could even pick it apart.

"I'm really sorry, Luke. I don't know if I'll ever apologize enough for lying."

Her apologies feel like volleys I have to keep fielding.

"You don't have to keep apologizing. I forgave you a long time ago."

It's hard to stay mad at someone after she tries to kill herself with your bottle of sleeping pills.

I pull a card from the draw pile, but I don't look at it. My eyes are on Samantha. She's still looking at her cards, doing a poor job of hiding how much she hates this topic.

She usually looks so polished. She usually keeps up her brave face so well. I barely recognize her like this.

She needs me right now. She wouldn't let anyone else see her like this.

She trusts me.

Her eyes turn to the floor. "I get so guilty, I can't sleep." It's a low whisper. "We had our flaws. You have your flaws. But you treated me better than any guy ever has. And I wanted so badly to stay in love with you, but I couldn't. And, instead of telling you... I strung you along while I fell in love with someone else."

She runs her fingers over the edges of the cards. "I don't care what you think about it. I don't care if you're over it, or if you've forgiven me. I'm not over it. It was an awful thing to do, and only an awful person would do it."

"That's not true."

The words stick in my throat but I push them out.

She gives me side eye.

"Don't, Luke. I know you have different ideas about morality with your 'people can't be stolen' bullshit. But I don't care what you think or what your opinion is. I still feel awful."

I scoot closer to the bed, trying to understand. "Is that why..."

I don't even know how to complete that question.

She frowns, her eyebrows furrowing, her gaze on the ground. She looks... lost. "I fucked up my life so badly. None of my friends speak to me anymore. I couldn't face them if I wanted to."

I offer my hand, but she doesn't take it.

"They'll understand," I say.

"Don't, Luke." Her voice is heavy with emotion. "I don't want your empty encouragement. It only makes it harder when reality hits. I don't need you to lie to me and pretend like my friends don't hate me. Or like everyone at work doesn't think I'm a tramp."

Samantha blinks back a tear. She takes off her glasses and wipes her eyes with her free hand.

I can't just sit here. I need to do something.

But a hug would be too much.

This whole thing between us is so fucking complicated.

I hand her a tissue from the box on the counter. She nods a thank you, and pats her eye.

I keep my voice as steady and reassuring as I can. "I doubt anyone is thinking you're a tramp. Not unless you went back in time to the 1950s."

She cracks a smile. "You know what I mean."

I nod, and I wait for her to catch her breath. This room is so drab and ugly. Who could feel happy in here?

Samantha pats her eyes dry. She offers a tiny smile as if to say she's okay.

I know I should move past this subject, but I can't miss this opportunity.

I look her straight in the eye. "Why did you do it the first time?"

She bites her lip but she holds my gaze. "The weight of it was crushing me. It was the only thing I could feel. I wanted to stop feeling it, and... I didn't know any other way I could do it."

It was at least partially my fault.

I was distant. I was mean. Hell, I was an asshole.

But I had my reasons. It fucking hurt when she told me she was leaving me, and it hurt even more when she crawled back to me after Edward dumped her.

No, that isn't right. She didn't crawl back.

She picked up the pieces, and I begged her to let me help. I begged her to give me another chance.

I begged her to let me help and then I didn't.

Her eyes are on me. Samantha wipes another tear from her eye. She scrunches the tissue into a tiny ball. "It's still killing me. You come here every month and you're so nice to me. I'm so happy when you're here, but whenever you leave, I keep thinking that I took something I didn't deserve. That I'm dragging you down, ruining your life."

"You're not ruining anything." It's not ideal, but it also isn't that dramatic.

She shakes her head. "That's only part of it."

Part of it.

I have no idea what to do.

Did I not do enough the first time, triggering her attempt?

And now she's saying I do too much and that made things worse too?

That doesn't make any sense.

Lately, I sometimes feel like I can't win for losing.

She studies my expression. Her lips press together. Her hands press together. "It's not just you."

"But it's partly me?"

"No, I didn't mean... I'm sorry." She turns her gaze to the floor. "I have such long, empty days in that giant house. It's so lonely and the only respite is your visits. It hurts so much when you leave. It's like there's a weight in my chest and it's dragging me into the ground."

Does she want me to stay with her around the fucking clock? That isn't at all reasonable.

I bite my tongue.

"Luke, I... it's not your fault."

I nod. But it certainly sounds like she's also saying it's my fault.

"What about therapy and antidepressants?"

She shakes her head. "I don't have a real future. What's the best that could happen—I get another law job?"

"You loved being a lawyer."

"I loved studying the law. But writing contracts for sixty hours a week? I can do it. I can convince everyone there that nothing is wrong. And I even like going to the office, and making a cup of coffee with awful powdered French vanilla creamer. But God, when it's seven o'clock and I have another two hours of work so I can help some company squeeze a little bit more out of its employees?"

"You'd be a great teacher." I try.

"Yeah, right," she rolls her eyes. "It's more than the job, Luke. If it was just the job, I could take it. But the job is all I have now."

My head pounds.

This isn't how this is supposed to be going. I'm supposed to be convincing her everything is okay so I can go back to Alyssa.

I'm supposed to repay this debt, not make things worse.

She presses her hands together. "I think about my future, and it's empty. I'm never going to meet someone. I'm never going to have a family..."

"You'll meet someone else. You're a beautiful—"

"I'm not beautiful." She folds her arms. "And it doesn't do me any good to listen to your lies. Especially when you're dating the hot actress."

I rub my temples, but my head is still aching.

Fine. If she wants only the full truth, I can give that to her.

I meet her gaze. "Fine. You're not beautiful. But you are attractive. You're not at your best at the moment, but I've seen you in your suit and makeup. There's something very appealing about it. There must be. Edward would not have wasted his time with an unappealing woman."

She shakes her head, almost cracking a smile. "This is the strangest pep talk."

"Fuck the pep talk. You were right. It's pointless. It's bullshit. I don't want to lie to you. Your life sucks right now. But it will get better. You can find your passion again. You'll meet someone. Some shallow asshole who loves *Guns, Germs, and Steel.*"

"This sounds like a pep talk."

"Okay, it's a pep talk. And I swear, I'm not going to keep doing it. But I believe in you, Sam. You're going to be happy again one day. You just need a little help getting there."

"A little?"

"Everyone needs help sometimes." I reach out to set my hand on hers. "Just like I did after..."

That bitter, despairing edge to her expression fades, compassion returning to her eyes.

For a second, she looks like the girl who was my rock when I needed her.

I can almost forget all the shit that happened between then and now. "Yeah," she whispers, squeezing my hand. "Okay. Okay."

Chapter Eleven

I call Alyssa as soon as I get back to the hotel.

She's not going to be happy I'm staying with Samantha longer than expected.

She picks up after the first ring.

"Hey!"

She sounds happy and bright.

Makes me not want to say what I have to say even more.

"Hey yourself." I pull the curtains open to let some light into the dull room.

"Are you exhausted from saving the world?" she asks.

I smile slightly.

"I manage."

She chuckles.

"Did you sleep last night?"

"Mhmm. Someone wore me out."

She clears her throat. "Oh. Well, that's good. It's good to sleep." She's nervous, almost stuttering. She takes a deep breath. "What is it like spending the afternoon with your ex? That's a lot of baggage to deal with."

I lean my forehead against the wall.

"Me, baggage? That's ridiculous. I've never even held a grudge."

She laughs. "Uh-huh."

"Not even once."

"Then what do you call your deep and abiding hatred of Ryan?" She says it so cockily, like she knows she's right, knows she's got me.

I'll be able to kiss the smug look off her face soon enough.

"That's nothing. A little hostility towards a coworker."

Understatement of the century.

"And him being my ex-boyfriend has nothing to do with it?"

"Not a thing." I press the phone into my ear. "Him hurting you... that might have something to do with it."

"But it's not a grudge," she reiterates.

"Exactly."

She laughs like she thinks I'm ridiculous. "How is Samantha?"

It's still bright outside. It's barely late afternoon. The windows are flooding the room with light, bringing a bit of life to the drab, beige room. "Not as well as I would hope."

"Oh." The joy in Alyssa's voice is gone. She's trying to hide her disappointment, but it's clear as day.

"She's depressed. And lonely."

Alyssa voice lowers. "I don't like the sound of that."

I turn away from the windows. "For a friend. Only a friend."

"Yeah, sure..." She sighs. "No. I trust you. I don't trust her, but I trust you."

I sink into the bed. It's too soft. A crappy piece of a crappy hotel. "How have you been managing with Laurie? She's been a little crazy on Twitter." She posts about the show every hour on the hour. Not that I'm really interested in how Laurie is.

But Alyssa isn't going to respond to an obvious offensive move.

"She's been reading a lot of reviews."

Oh no.

"Have you?"

"Yeah."

I wait for her to say more, but she's quiet. The air is stale, immobile. It must be this quiet in her room. This motionless.

"How is that going?" I ask carefully.

"Not great." She sighs. "It was an awful, stupid idea. It's not like this is the first time I've been down this road. People always have their opinions. And even the people who like the show get things wrong, or have inane interpretations. I thought I learned my lesson on *Together*. Or *Mahogany*. Jesus. That one was brutal."

"It has almost ninety percent on Rotten Tomatoes."

"Yeah, ninety percent liked the movie. They didn't necessarily like my acting."

She takes a deep breath, no doubt waiting for my objection. I can't argue here. She needs to talk.

Maybe she's ready to open up more.

"Tell me about it," I urge.

"I can feel my stomach do somersaults because I'm so nervous to keep reading the review. Cause I know it's due to mention my performance any second. And then I spend an hour poring over the two lines devoted to me. I analyze every single word. And then I can't stop thinking about it for the rest of the night."

I shake my head, feeling second hand anxiety from how she describes the experience.

"Jesus. That sucks."

"I knew better, but Laurie was obsessing so much. I was too curious not to look. I should have more self-control." She sighs.

I hear her shifting. Getting on her bed, probably.

It's almost like we're together. Both of us in bed, in our empty rooms, our attention only on the phone.

"If I was there, I could distract you."

"Luke..."

I slide back on the bed. "What's wrong?"

I can hear it in the tone of her voice.

"Nothing... just... I wish you had been here."

I close my eyes, feeling that bite of guilt.

"I'll be back soon."

"I know. I just miss you. I feel like I'm... I don't know. It sounds pathetic, but I feel like I'm unraveling. I forgot how hard all this is. The production is one thing. It's stressful, but I love it. I love being there in the scene, even if the director is a tyrant or one of the other actors is an asshole. But the rejections, and the reviews, and the meetings... Jesus, the meetings are miserable."

Miserable?

"Have you had any problems?"

"No one has been direct, but I get this sense from so many of these people. I can see the rejection in their eyes the second they introduce themselves. I see them looking at me thinking no, she's not the right kind of woman. And then... I read the comments on this review. And a lot of them were about me. About my body." I should have been there to distract her.

"Don't listen to those idiots. Your body is to die for."

She sighs. "I should have known better." There's not much I can do from here.

Fuck. What are the right words here?

I press the phone into my ear. "It's understandable."

She sighs, lowering her voice to a whisper. "After I read the first one, I couldn't stop. It was just like the reviews. Then, before I knew it, I was sitting in front of the computer and crying like an idiot."

I feel my heart ache for her.

"When was this?"

"Earlier today."

I rub my temples. "Ally, why didn't you call me? You know you can call anytime. I want you to."

"I know."

She takes a deep breath. Like she's calming her nerves. "I don't need you rescuing me every time I'm upset."

"You'd rather cry by yourself?"

"You can't shield me from the world. People are going to start threads about how I'm too fat to play a sexy character no matter how close you are to me."

What she's saying is practical and logical. But...

"You're supposed to call me when you feel overwhelmed. That's our deal."

It's in place for a reason.

I worry that it can trigger her eating disorder, and that's a shitty, dangerous spiral I don't want her being sucked into again.

She's quiet for a moment, only breathing. "Okay. Fine. I'll call next time I'm overwhelmed."

"Promise me."

"I promise." Her breath is strained. She shifts again. "Never mind. I want to talk, okay? Can I just talk?"

"Sure."

"It's not like I believe these people. They're just idiots on the Internet. I mean, I wish I had the self-control to ignore them. I swore off the Internet for my first three months out of treatment. It was boring, but it was also kind of peaceful." She takes a deep breath. "This would be easier if you were here."

"You'd just jump me."

She laughs. "True. But after the first three or four times, I'd need a break."

She sounds so warm. So sweet. So okay.

I should be there.

I could leave now, but I'd be stuck in traffic for hours. I'd arrive at ten p.m. and need to leave by four a.m. if I wanted to get back to Samantha's place before she started freaking out.

"When are you going to be back?" she asks.

I take a deep breath. There's no way to soften this blow. "Sunday."

"Sunday?" Her voice falls.

"I'd rather leave tomorrow, but her parents are going out of town and she's afraid to be alone. She wanted me to stay through the weekend, but I offered a compromise."

"Oh."

Silence.

This really doesn't feel great.

"Well. I hope you come home with your hands clean of this." There's apprehension in her voice. "Wait. Her parents are out of town?"

"Yeah."

"And where will you be?"

"She asked me to stay at the house, but I already nixed that idea." "She asked you, huh?"

I can hear the implication.

"It's not like that. She just wants company."

"Yeah, if you were visiting me, I'd want company too." She exhales. "You can afford to drop four hundred dollars on a hotel for the weekend. Hell, I've seen your bank statements. You can afford a lot more than that."

"Snoop."

"You leave them on the kitchen table on purpose." "I'll break out all the stops to impress you," I tease. "And it doesn't mean anything, but I already refused the offer. She just needs someone nearby. We don't feel like that anymore."

"You don't." She agrees pointedly. "But I can't shake the feeling that she might not. What if she begs you to comfort her physically?"

I'm ready to start banging my head against the wall.

"She won't." "How do you know?" Because Samantha rejected my advances several dozen times. Because she'd rather sleep with my fucking dad.

I keep my voice calm. "I know. She's made that very clear. But even if anything like that happens, you have to know I would never cross that line."

Alyssa sighs.

"Are you okay?" I ask.

"Yeah. It's fine. But I should probably go."

"It's only this weekend," I say.

Alyssa sighs again.

I know what she's thinking.

Chances of that are slim with Sam.

And I can't even be mad at her for thinking that.

"How about you come over Sunday morning? I'm going to leave early. You can stay at my place so we don't wake up Laurie."

"Maybe."

"Ally..."

She takes a deep breath. "Do you have to stay?"

I rack my brain for reasons to leave. I'd so much rather be with Alyssa, but I need to stay.

I need to make sure Samantha is okay.

I run my fingers over the edge of the phone. "It will be

over before you know it. We'll be back together. And we can do your food challenge next week."

"No, I think I'll do it on my own."

A new anxiety runs through me.

No way. Fuck that.

"Ally... I really want to be with you when you do it."

She swallows. "I don't want to wait anymore."

I bite my lip. I can't let her do it all alone. "Just a couple more days. We can do it as soon as I get back. Okay?"

A small pause.

This is too important, too dangerous for her to move forward alone.

I start to sweat when she doesn't answer right away.

But she finally agrees. "Okay."

"Perfect."

Relief flows through me, but the anxiety doesn't fully go away.

It's not perfect.

But I really hope it's enough.

Chapter Twelve

I need to help Samantha.

I don't want to lose another person who was such an integral part of my past.

Mom's gone. Even my father, such as he was.

If Sam's gone...

I don't want to think about it.

And not because I'm still in love with her.

Honestly, at this point... I'm not sure I ever really was.

It was puppy love, friendship, admiration maybe. Something much less deep and true than what I have with Alyssa.

But back then it felt real. And I held on to it tightly, even after we graduated law school, even after she started to pull away.

I knew something was fucking going on. I didn't know what it was, but I knew something was different. She stayed at work late. She spent weekends with girlfriends she hadn't seen in years. She made excuses about why she didn't want to have sex.

She was having an affair with my father.

Edward fucking Lawrence.

He was her boss. Senior partner at the firm.

Hell of it was, I basically got her the job, more or less.

I put her right in his path.

She spent the better part of a year having this affair, lying to me, getting more and more obvious.

I just didn't want to see it.

That should have been a sign I was already checked out. I can't imagine looking the other way with Alyssa. Ever.

But then, one day, Sam broke down in tears. She told me what was going on. Not to beg for forgiveness, but to explain why she was breaking up with me.

She was in love with him.

Not that it ended up mattering. Asshole that he was, Edward rejected her when she tried to start a real relationship with him.

Because it wouldn't look right, would it?

She wasn't even mad at him for it. She understood completely. I guess they always had that in common, that obsession with how things look.

Fuck how things look. I should have walked away. I should have wiped my hands clean of both of them and moved on with my life.

But I didn't.

Instead, I begged Samantha to take me back. To give me another chance. I promised I'd treat her better, love her more, give her everything he did.

But I didn't.

I was too hurt, too angry. And not in love with her. Not even in infatuation. I ignored her. We went on like that for a few months. It wouldn't have lasted.

But then things went from bad to really fucked. Edward had a heart attack.

It was over in the blink of an eye. No one got a chance to say goodbye.

I had my issues with him, but he was still my father, even after everything he'd done.

It was a devastating blow on top of a horrifying revelation.

I never got any real closure. I was to angry to even talk to him.

And Samantha... she was heartbroken.

I should have done something to help her. Gotten her into therapy at least.

But I did nothing. I ignored her.

I was too angry at him, at them, at the whole fucking world.

She sank into depression.

I registered that she was unhappy, but it was a distant realization.

I was dealing with my own emotional turmoil.

Then she swallowed my bottle of sleeping pills.

My prescription was on the bedside table for weeks. A crutch that I needed more than ever.

I never thought...

I didn't know she'd prefer death to living with the shame of her dirty secret becoming public, the pain of losing the lover who didn't even want her.

A few weeks after Edward's death, she was in the ER having her stomach pumped, a suicide note tucked under the bottle.

I'd promised to help her.

But I wasn't strong enough. I tried so hard to forgive her, to be there for her, to hold her when she cried... but I couldn't.

I knew she was crying over Edward.

She was crying because he didn't love her.

She was crying because he was gone.

I couldn't comfort her.

Hell, I couldn't even comfort myself.

He was my father. An asshole, but still my father, and I was supposed to be comforting her about it?

But...

If I had been there for her the way she needed me...

Maybe she wouldn't have done it.

I failed her then. I can't fail her again.

———

SAMANTHA'S PARENTS LIVE IN THE RICHEST CITY IN THE SAN Diego area.

Their house is huge, one of those suburban mansions on a hill. It has everything—four bedrooms, a study, a formal dining room, a view of the California coastline.

I still know the way there from memory. I've been visiting her a while now.

It's sunset when I arrive, and there's a soft orange glow over the quiet streets. They're too quiet, like there's no life in these houses.

My shoulders tense. I'll always be Samantha's friend, but this is the last weekend of this. It has to be.

I want to help her, but I feel like I'm almost pulling myself apart in the process.

I park on the street and walk up the long stone path to the door.

Samantha answers quickly.

She's dressed like an actress in a movie. Not in pajamas, but in designer loungewear.

"I got takeout," she greets me.

I nod.

We move into the dining room. It's a huge, empty room with a sturdy oak table. Once upon a time, I made a joke about fucking on this table.

She didn't find it funny.

I set the wine on the table, a bottle this time, and Samantha squeals in delight.

She throws her arms around my neck and presses her lips into my cheek. "Oh my God, I love you."

I swallow hard. It's a friendly I love you. That's it.

She brings her eyes to mine. "My parents are trying to convince me to stay here again."

"Will you?"

She shakes her head. "If I do... it's not good for me."

I nod.

I agree with that. She goes to the kitchen and comes back with a wine cork. "Sit down."

I settle in, staring at the wine as she pours it.

Hoping I'm doing the right thing.

———

I text Alyssa Saturday morning to check in, but she doesn't reply. I try not to make much of it. It's early, and she likes to sleep in.

Samantha and I play cards at the dining room table for hours. She frowns every time I check my phone, but she doesn't point it out. She just taps her hands and waits for me to finish my turn.

The morning turns to afternoon. We order take-out. We trade gossip about our old law school classmates.

But Alyssa still doesn't respond.

It's three now. I text her again. *How is everything.*

I turn my phone over and play another round of rummy with Samantha. The damn phone doesn't buzz.

No new calls. No messages.

Samantha looks at me with concern. "Is everything okay?"

"Yeah." The screen is still empty. "It should be."

I stare at the phone. Alyssa isn't a huge fan of technology. It's possible she has her phone off, that she broke it and can't be bothered to fix it, that she's out and she just forgot it.

But I sent that first text hours ago.

My shoulders tense.

A hint of irritation enters Samantha's voice. "It doesn't seem okay."

I shake my head. I need to give Alyssa a little more time. "It should be."

She nods, but she keeps one eye on me as she takes her turn. "Alyssa?"

I nod.

"What is happening with Alyssa?"

I pick up my card and stare at it. "Don't worry about it." This card is not what I want. I don't know what to do with it.

Samantha frowns, but she says nothing until I finish my turn. Then she picks up a card and declares her victory.

She wins again. Truth be told, I let her win.

I ignore my phone for the next two rounds. Until it's nearly five. Until this damn phone is burning a hole in my brain.

This isn't like Alyssa.

But I pick up my card. I stare at it the way I always do, with my best poker face.

But then I throw it down.

Fuck me, I have to call.

I stand.

"I'm going to call Alyssa."

Samantha stares at me like I'm an idiot. "Finally! I'd like to get your attention back." I press the phone between my palms and make my way to the empty study.

It's a dark room in warm shades of auburn and brown. The kind of room that radiates wealth and prestige.

I dial Alyssa. The phone rings. It rings again. It rings straight to voice mail.

My shoulders tense. This is not good. But I won't jump to conclusions. I try again.

But again, the phone rings straight to voice mail.

I send a text.

Give me a call when you get this. I want to hear your voice.

It's probably okay. It's probably nothing.

But, just in case it's not, I call Laurie.

The phone rings straight to voice mail. "You've reached Laurie House. Please leave a message."

Deep breath. "Hey, it's Luke. I can't reach Alyssa. Let me know if you hear from her." I hang up.

It's probably nothing.

———

I'M DISTRACTED ALL EVENING, BUT I TRY TO GIVE Samantha as much of my attention as I can. She talks about little things—staying with her parents, her wish to return to her job, how sick she is of the only restaurant that delivers to her house.

We order dinner. We drink half a bottle of wine. We watch some show about Lincoln on the history channel. Samantha loves the history channel.

Finally, my phone buzzes. Samantha turns to me, her eyes laser focused on my expression.

I turn over the phone.

It's a text from Alyssa. *Sorry, I was at a movie. Is everything okay?*

I reply. *Just checking on you.*

Her response is quick. *I'm fine.*

I reply. *Did you do the food challenge?*

I told her to wait for me, but she isn't acting like herself.

It's the first thing that springs to mind.

And when she dodges the question, I know I'm right.

I'm tired. We can talk when you're home on Sunday.

I clench my jaw. She did promise she'd call if she was overwhelmed. I reply.

Right. But do me a favor?

No favors.

I reply. *Just promise you're okay.*

I'm fine. I'll see you Sunday.

There's a finality to it. She's done with this conversation.

I can't push her on this until I'm there in person. My back is aching and I'm thoroughly distracted now, but I do my best to push it aside.

I turn my attention back to Samantha. She's staring at me.

She nods to the TV. "They're about to get to the good part."

"He's finally executed and the show ends?"

She shakes her head and she holds up her wine glass as if to ask for a refill. "Please."

I nod. Okay. I grab her glass and mine, and push off the floor. It's a short walk to the kitchen. A short walk through this huge, dark, empty house.

There isn't a single speck of dust in the kitchen. There's nothing except a tiny crimson spot next to the bottle of wine. It's going to stain. Her parents are going to yell at the maid.

I wrap my fingers around the glass bottle. Twenty-four more hours and I'll be with Alyssa.

I return to the living room and offer Samantha her wine. She smiles, licking her lips like she can't wait to be just a little bit more tipsy.

She's sitting on the rug. It's the same crimson rug we always sit on. Once upon a time, I made a joke about fucking on the rug.

She didn't laugh at that one either.

I take a seat on the couch. Samantha frowns. Pats the spot next to her.

But I shake my head.

She pushes herself off the floor and plops next to me. She's close, closer than she should be. She rests her head on my shoulder. Wraps her hand around my arm.

"Sam, don't..."

"Please." It's a high-pitched plea. She takes a long sip of her wine, her cheeks flushing with color. "Just hold me for a while."

Fuck me. Was Alyssa right?

I push her off as gently as I can. "You know I can't."

She sighs, wrapping her fingers around the stem of her glass. "Right. I'm sorry... I shouldn't ask...."

"Sam..."

She hugs her chest with her arms, her eyes turned to the floor. "Wouldn't a minute be okay?" It's so desperate, like she'll fall apart if I don't immediately wrap my arms around her.

But it's not happening. "No." My voice is harsh. A warning not to ask again.

She shakes her head. "Of course. I'm so sorry. I didn't mean..." She brings her eyes to mine for a moment.

"You're the best thing in my life. Please don't think I have the wrong idea."

I nod. It's possible Samantha did forget. It's possible she really means nothing by her request. That it's just the wine.

But it's also possible she knows exactly what she's doing.

Chapter Thirteen

I wake up early Sunday morning to drive back to Santa Monica.

The sun rises on the way.

I want to spend the day with Alyssa.

I miss her. I didn't like being away, even for such a short period of time.

It's still early when I park in the driveway. The house is dim, but there's a low roar from the TV. Alyssa is curled into a ball on the couch. She's hugging a pillow and her eyes are closed. I almost don't want to wake her.

But the sound of me coming in is enough to do it.

She stirs. She's wearing my clothes—a T-shirt and boxers.

She looks so fucking hot in them.

I know part of it is I just like seeing her in something that's mine.

When she opens her eyes, she looks at me with the tiniest smile. She's still tired. It's completely adorable.

"What time is it?" she asks, that early morning rasp that always gets me going in her voice.

"Early." I drop my bags on the floor and move towards the couch.

She keeps her eyes on me, even as she struggles to keep them open.

She shifts to a seated position. "I have an audition tomorrow and I haven't rehearsed at all."

"I can help you later."

"I might take you up on that offer." She runs her fingertips along my arms, tracing from the veins on my wrist. "I missed you, you know?"

"I missed you more."

She brings her eyes to mine. There's such a need in her expression, but she blinks and it's gone. Replaced by something more demanding.

"Do you want to talk about it?" I sit next to her.

She shakes her head. "You always want to talk." She digs her hands into my hair, and she looks at me with those *fuck me* eyes. "Do you think, this time, we can talk tomorrow?"

I'm immediately hard.

"Ally..."

Her eyes connect with mine. There's so much need in her expression. Then her eyes are closed and her lips are on mine.

She tastes like mint, like her toothpaste.

She pulls back, her eyes connecting with mine. "Please."

She kisses me again. Her lips part and I slide my tongue into her mouth.

My body floods with heat. There is no sense in talking now. Not when we could do something so much better.

Her hands find my back. They dig into me, pressing my shirt against my skin. She's desperate. She needs this much more than she needs a conversation.

She pulls back. Her clear blue eyes connect with mine. "It's okay if you don't want to. If you want to talk."

But she still shifts her body into mine. She wraps her legs around my hips, her hands still digging into my back.

I smile. "You aren't even trying to be convincing."

"Uh-huh." She nods, sinking her body into mine. "If I wanted to convince you, I'd step up my wardrobe."

I slide my hand under her T-shirt, my T-shirt actually. It's clinging to her, highlighting every inch of her tits.

Her nipples are hard little points, showing through the slightly sheer white fabric.

"I like this wardrobe." I drag my fingertips over her soft skin. She feels so good.

She arches her back, fighting a deep desire to close her eyes. "But you'd prefer I get rid of it?"

I nod and slide my fingertips over her nipples. She groans, squeezing her thighs around me. I cup her breasts, rubbing my thumbs over her nipples slowly. She's putty in my hands, moaning and squirming and digging her hands into my back.

She kisses me again. It's hard and desperate, a demand. I squeeze her tighter, rub her harder. She moans into my mouth.

My blood rushes to my cock. All of her is soft and sweet, and I need to drink in that need. I need to feel her shaking and screaming around me.

She pulls her lips away from mine and brings them to my ear. "Fuck me, Luke. I need you inside me."

Jesus. That never gets old.

I pull her shirt, my shirt, over her head. She shudders, arching into me. Her eyes are on fire. She wants me. She wants me badly.

Is anything hotter than being so wanted?

I throw away any intentions of teasing her until she

begs me. She's already begging me. She's already desperate. And I need to be inside her, to make her feel so good she could die.

She kisses me, hard. Her tongue is in my mouth, her hands are on my shoulders. I slide my hands over the curve of her waist, soaking in the feeling of her soft skin.

My hands find her hips, and I pull her boxers to her knees. She shifts to help me, then kicks them off her feet.

I take a long look at her. Her delicate neck. Her lush tits. The dramatic curve of her hips. She's perfect and she's mine. She's in my lap, her thighs pressed into my hips, her eyes on me like she can't wait to fuck me.

I drag my hands back to her hips, and I pull her closer.

She groans, shifting into me, squeezing me tighter. "You're wearing too many clothes."

I nod and I press my lips against her neck. She sighs. Digs her nails into my shoulders again. It's sharp, a tiny hint of what I'll feel when I make her come.

I drag my fingertips over her thighs. She groans, holding on to me like she'll fall over if she loosens her grip. I stroke her inner thighs as softly as I can. Until she's shaking.

"Luke..."

I slide my fingers over her clit. She gasps and digs her nails harder into my shoulders. Her body shifts into mine. Her lips find mine. She kisses me, hard, plunging her tongue into my mouth as I stroke her.

She releases my kiss, shifting so her tits are pressed against my cheeks. It's practically a plea. I draw circles around her nipple with my tongue.

Her nails sink into my skin. Her eyes press together as she groans. I stroke her again, draw another circle. Again. Again. Again.

She moans, pressing her body into mine, her breasts

into my mouth. I suck on her nipple, harder and harder and harder. I bring my free hand to her chest, cupping her breast and rubbing my fingers over her nipple.

And I stroke her. Again and again and again.

Her legs shake. Her nails dig into my skin. She's panting, groaning, practically clawing at my shoulders. It's such a fucking beautiful sight, and I need more of it. I need her screaming in my ear, her nails so deep in my shoulders they draw blood.

I need to feel her come.

I stroke her. I sink my teeth into her nipple. Soft, then harder, harder, harder. She groans, her nails sharp against my shoulders, her head thrown back like she can't take it anymore.

"Luke," she groans.

And I stroke her. A little harder. A little faster.

She pants. "Fuck. I'm almost... Luke..."

Her breath strains. She groans. She screams. Her moans get higher, louder.

I stroke her, bite her, rub her.

And she groans into my ear. Her nails sink into my skin one last time, and she releases everything in a dramatic sigh. Her body relaxes into mine, her head resting against my shoulder.

She grabs my hand and presses it against the couch. Her lips hover over my ear. "One day, I'm going to make you go first."

"We'll see." I press my lips into hers.

She moves quickly, pulling my shirt over my head and gaping at me for a moment. Her hands are on my chest, digging into my skin like she could never possibly get enough of my body.

She slides her hands down my stomach. Over my jeans.

Heat spreads through my body. I need her hands on me. I need to be inside her.

She unzips my jeans and rubs me over my boxers. Fuck. My ache grows. I need her now.

I push my pants to my knees. Shift out of my boxers. I grab her hips and bring her closer, so my tip is straining against her.

Her eyes find mine. They're on fire. She wraps her fingers around my cock and slides me inside of her.

Fuck. Her eyes go wide. Her teeth sink into her lip. She feels so good. So warm, and tight, and wet. I squeeze her hips, rocking her over me.

She kisses me, grabbing my hands and planting them at my sides. Her hands find my shoulders and she presses me against the couch. She shifts, rocking into me again and again and again.

Her breathing strains. She groans. Close again.

I grab her ass and pull her body into mine. She squeezes my shoulders, riding me like I'm her plaything. Like she feels so damn good she can't help it.

I bring my tongue to her nipple. I need to feel her come again, to feel her cunt pulsing around me.

She groans, digging her nails into my shoulders. I suck on her nipple as she rocks into me. As her groans build again. They're higher this time. Louder.

Pleasure courses through me. I need those groans. Those screams.

I dig my nails into her ass. I sink my teeth into her nipple.

She rocks into me. "Luke," she groans. Her voice is low, heavy, like she can barely get it out.

I bite her harder.

"Luke." She sinks her nails into my skin.

Her moans build, higher and louder and higher and louder. She screams.

I can feel her coming, her squeezing my cock harder and harder, until everything releases and she's pulsing around me.

She collapses on me again, holding me tightly. Her eyes find mine. "Fuck me," she groans.

"Turn around."

She nods, shifting off me. I take one long look at her—she's fucking perfect—and move off the couch. She presses her lips into mine. Her hands wrap around my cock and she strokes me.

I grab her hips and turn her around, so my chest is pressed into her back.

"Bend over."

She leans over, pressing her hands into the couch. I have a perfect view of her ass, her hips. I dig my hands into her thighs, and I slide inside her.

She's still so wet, so warm, so tight. I squeeze her hips, pulling her body towards mine as I thrust into her.

She groans, a low deep groan that can only mean more.

I thrust into her. Again and again and again.

"Fuck me." She arches her back, her nails digging into the couch.

My body fills with pleasure. I move harder. Deeper. I thrust into her again and again and again.

I groan. She feels so damn good.

Her breath is low and heavy. "Fuck me, Luke. Come inside me."

I squeeze her hips. I thrust into her. Harder. Deeper. Again. Again. Again.

The ache builds. She's so tight around me, so warm, so wet, so perfect.

I thrust into her again.

She groans. "Come inside me." It's a demand.

I lose control of any conscious thought. It's only Alyssa. Her hips, her thighs, her cunt, her groans. I thrust into her, harder, and deeper, until the ache inside me is too much.

And I come, my cock pulsing inside her.

She sighs in pleasure, collapsing on the couch. I lie next to her, our bodies pressed together in the tiny space.

There's no sense in trying to talk after this.

Maybe after we eat.

Or maybe tomorrow.

Chapter Fourteen

The curtains are wide open, and the sunlight is falling over Alyssa's face. She looks so peaceful bathed in its glow. She sleeps on her side with her arms and legs crossed.

I still can't believe my luck that I get to wake up next to her.

She stirs and blinks her eyes open. Her lips curl into a smile as she looks me over. "What time is it?"

"Seven."

She groans and rolls towards the window. "What time do you need to be at the office?"

I brush a hair from her eyes. "Ryan demanded I show up at nine a.m., so..."

"You'll show up at four thirty to teach him a lesson?"

"Beautiful and smart."

She shakes her head. "Smart and beautiful."

True.

Alyssa pushes herself upright. The sheets fall to the bed, revealing inch after inch of skin. She never did get dressed last night.

She raises an eyebrow. ""I know how we could spend the extra time."

My cock is doing a victory dance.

But I haven't been sixteen in a while. My little head doesn't run the show anymore.

"How about we go out for breakfast?"

"I'd rather have you than breakfast."

I want to give in. But we really do need to talk.

I slide out of bed. "How about coffee?"

Her eyes pass over my body. I didn't get dressed last night either.

"How about after?" She runs her tongue over her lips.

"How about *after* after breakfast?" I stretch my arms over my head so she can take her time gaping at me.

I have to admit, I love the way she stares at me.

"You're so cruel." She crosses her arms in faux irritation, but she's smiling ear to ear.

"I'd be happy to finally christen my desk."

She rolls her eyes. "Yeah, and I bet it has nothing to do with the person sharing the office next to yours."

"Janine?"

"Yeah, Janine. Your assistant." She shifts off the bed. "Not my ex-boyfriend you want to hear us fucking."

"It was a joke."

"It's not funny." She moves to the dresser, opens a drawer, her drawer, and arranges her outfit for the day.

I move closer to her. "It's a little funny."

She folds her arms again, but she's smiling. "Only because of how ridiculous Ryan's expression would be." She mimics Ryan, furrowing her brow and turning up her nose like she smells something disgusting.

I laugh and wrap my arms around her waist. "It's not usually this difficult to buy you coffee."

"I know."

"Is everything okay?"

She lets out a tiny hint of a sigh. "I'm only going out on the condition that you don't ask that question again."

"This morning or ever?"

She moves away from me. Steps into her underwear. "Ever would be too much to ask."

She pulls her dress over her head. No bra.

She's doing it just to torture me.

"Okay," I say. "We don't have to talk about anything but our coffee."

"Deal."

———

WE DRESS AND DRIVE TO ALYSSA'S FAVORITE COFFEE SPOT in Santa Monica. It's a few blocks from the tourist mecca of Third Street Promenade, but this early it's nearly empty.

Alyssa is quiet, but she keeps her hand pressed against mine.

She doesn't want to talk about how she feels today. I could wait until she's ready, but I can't. There's a sense of dread in my gut. Something is wrong.

We order our drinks—they make one cup at a time at this place—and wait at a tiny table. The store is flooded with sunlight and it's falling over Alyssa like it was in bed.

She looks like an angel.

"Do you want to talk about anything?" I ask.

She shakes her head. "Maybe later." She turns to me and offers a half-smile. "I'm okay. Really."

"Then why can't I shake the sense that something is horribly wrong?"

"It's your natural state of being." She laughs like it's a joke, but there's no joy on her face.

"Ally..."

The barista calls out our drinks and Alyssa rushes to the counter. I'm not going to get anything out of her like this.

I need another strategy.

Alyssa squeezes the drinks, thanks the barista, and returns to me. She hands me a cup and I take a sip. It's her coffee, a dark roast with plenty of honey and plenty of almond milk.

"You like it?" she asks.

"It tastes like you."

She bites her lip. There's something to her expression, but I can't place it.

She switches cups. "How about we take a walk?"

"Perfect."

It's warm outside, but there's a pleasant breeze. The air smells faintly of salt and the sun is bouncing off the concrete. Alyssa digs her sunglasses out of her purse and slides them on. She's practically hiding behind them.

But still, she presses her hand against mine. She squeezes tight.

There has to be some way I can get her to open up here.

"You were at the movies when I called Saturday," I say.

She nods. "Yeah."

"What did you see?"

She swallows, squeezing my hand a little tighter. "Some thriller. It wasn't all that memorable."

"Where did you see it?"

She pulls her hand away. "What are you getting at?"

We walk past Third Street, past the long string of chain stores and restaurants.

I try to take her hand, but she keeps it pressed against her hip.

"Will you please tell me what it is that's upsetting you?" I ask.

She presses her thumb and forefinger together. "I recall you promising you wouldn't ask me anymore questions about if I'm okay or not."

"Fine. I won't ask any questions. But are you going to stay a million miles away or are you going to be here with me?"

Her voice lowers. "Hey, I'm trying. Also, I'm not the one who ran off to go save my ex-girlfriend."

Okay, I'm getting closer here.

"Is that really what's bothering you?"

She stops at the light. Second Street. Two blocks from Ocean Avenue, from the winding path overlooking the beach.

Alyssa takes a slow breath. "Part of it."

"Care to fill me in on the rest of it?"

She shakes her head, but she squeezes my hand again. The light changes and we walk across the street.

Her breath is slow and steady, but there's still dread in her expression. She squeezes my hand a little tighter, her head turned towards the ground.

We stop at the red light on Ocean Avenue. Alyssa opens her mouth like she's going to say something, but she takes a long sip instead.

The light turns, and we walk across the long street, to the path better known as Palisades Park. It's a mile or so of sidewalk sandwiched by greenbelt and a steep cliff that drops onto Pacific Coast Highway.

Alyssa walks to the edge of the path. She presses her hands against the railing. The ocean is maybe a quarter mile away and the skyline is an expanse of blue.

She takes another long sip of her drink. She turns to

the street, pressing her back against the railing. She points to a restaurant on Santa Monica Boulevard. "That's where Ryan asked me to marry him."

"Yeah?"

She nods. "That was barely six months ago."

What is she trying to get at?

"A lot can change in six months."

"Yeah." She squeezes her cup. "It looks so different than it did that day."

She brings her eyes to mine. "Where did you ask Samantha?"

"You don't want to talk about that."

"I'll decide what I want to talk about."

I bite my tongue. Fine. I can tell this story. "At USC. We were visiting an old professor and I asked her to stop by the building where we reconnected. She was barely listening until she saw the ring. And whatever was on her face then, it wasn't anything close to joy."

Alyssa presses her fingers into her cup. "I know the feeling."

I set my cup on the railing, turn to Alyssa, and lift her sunglasses off her eyes. There's so much pain in her expression. There's something she desperately wants to say.

"You want to tell me what you're thinking?"

"What if we had it right the first time? What if you were supposed to be with her, and I was supposed to be with Ryan?"

"Do you really believe that?"

She presses her eyes closed. "No." She shifts, her gaze turning back to the restaurant. "But I was a little scared you'd come back with...feelings, maybe."

I run my fingertips over her cheek. "I love you. Only you."

I've never meant anything more.

She moves closer. Wraps me in a hug and squeezes for dear life. "But she talks to you. What if you get tired of me keeping everything to myself?"

"That will have nothing to do with Samantha."

She squeezes tighter. And tighter.

I stroke her hair. "Something happened over the weekend, didn't it?"

She nods.

"You weren't at the movies, were you?"

"No."

I close my eyes, bracing myself.

"Where were you?"

"At Laurie's."

"Alone?" I ask.

She nods.

"Well, then it can't be that bad. It's not like you were out fucking Ryan."

She stifles a laugh. Her eyes turn to mine. "You're obsessed."

I nod and brush a hair from her eyes.

"You're going to be upset." Her voice is low, desperate.

"We already established that you weren't fucking Ryan, so it can't be all that bad."

A warm breeze blows over us. We're in such a perfect, beautiful place, but the only thing I can feel is Alyssa's pain.

I point to a bench. She shakes her head and presses her palms against the railing again.

Her eyes are on the ocean. "I did the food challenge."

Fuck.

"I told you to wait for me, Ally. I wanted to be there to help."

She shakes her head.

"I wanted to prove that I could do it myself." She half laughs, though there's no joy in it. "But…"

"What happened?"

"I didn't… I fucked it up." She looks at the ground. Her hands squeeze each other so tightly her knuckles turn white.

She doesn't need me to be mad right now about her not waiting.

Fuck, why didn't she wait?

"You know you can tell me anything."

She nods and takes another sip of her coffee. Her gaze moves back to the beach, to the expanse of sand and ocean.

"I thought it would be okay. I was stressed, but I thought I could handle it."

She takes a long sip from her coffee, her gaze flitting from me to her cup. "I didn't think it would be a big deal. It was just a chocolate bar. It should have been easy. All I had to do was eat a few squares of chocolate and not binge and not purge. Normal people do it every day."

She presses her fingers into her coffee cup.

I offer my hand. She takes it, but she still won't look at me.

"I couldn't stop at two squares. I ate the entire bar. And then I started to panic. I was alone, at Laurie's, and I was only a few blocks from Whole Foods. I didn't really think about it. I only knew that I'd fucked up and I'd have to fix it. And, as long as I had fucked up, I might as well go all the way with it."

She stops, still not looking at me.

"What…?" I don't know how to finish that sentence. I feel a guilt and anger and frustration swirling in my gut.

Why didn't she wait?

"I was walking to the store when I called Angela." Her sponsor. Was she able to help? I feel my hopes rise. "It...helped. I stopped in the parking lot for a while and we just talked. After an hour or so, I was able to turn around and head back home."

"Ally, that's great. You found a way to cope." She finally meets my gaze. "Barely."

"You did," I point out.

She frowns, looking away again. "Maybe."

"You're being too hard on yourself," I admonish. "I'm proud of you."

I don't know if she can really take in those words in her current mental state.

The silence falls around us. There's a soft breeze blowing through the trees. There are footsteps around us, other people walking their dogs or rushing to work. There are cars zipping down the street, honking, rolling their windows down to take in the Pacific Ocean.

"Why didn't you call me?" I ask.

Her eyes turn to the ground. "You were with her."

I need to stay calm, to prove to her that she can always trust me. But she should have called.

She promised.

"You're mad," she says.

"No, I'm just..."

"Disappointed?" She says it like it's the worst thing she's ever heard.

I sidestep the word.

"You promised."

She bites her lip.

"I'm glad you're okay. That's what matters."

"I'm sorry."

I shake my head. "I want to help you."

She takes a step back. "It's better this way. I should do this on my own."

"You're going to take on your entire eating disorder recovery all by yourself?"

She presses her hands against the railing. "I have my sponsor and my therapist."

That fucking hurts.

"You have me too."

"I have you if I'm doing well. But if I keep fucking up, you'll keep looking at me like I'm some priceless work of art in desperate need of restoration."

"That's not true."

I reach for her hand, but she takes another step away.

"Alyssa."

"I get it. I'm a disappointment. You thought you were different than Ryan, that you would be the one to fix me, but now that it's difficult..." She takes another step away.

I grab her wrists. "I'm here for the long haul. No matter how hard it is."

She shakes her head. "We should go. I don't want you to be late."

"I don't give a fuck about being late."

"I'd like to go."

I take a deep breath, letting it out in a low hiss. "Fine. But only if you promise to come over tonight."

"Not to talk," she says immediately.

"Yes to talk." I lighten my grip and take another step towards her. "I'm not going to let you lock me out."

Her voice is barely a whisper. "I don't owe you anything."

"So do it because you love me. Or because you know how much it would mean to me." I wrap my arms around her waist. "Or because you want to fuck me."

She lets out a tiny, surprised laugh. "I'll consider it."

"I'll do anything I can to help you."

"I know." She nods. "But, right now, I don't need to talk." She looks up at me with that hungry expression.

I need that too.

I need every inch of her.

Chapter Fifteen

Alyssa is sitting on the edge of the pool.

Her dress is hiked up to her thighs and her legs are dangling in the water. She doesn't look up when I step into the backyard. She keeps her attention on the clear blue water.

The sky is streaked with the red glow of sunset. It's dim, dim enough that the pool lights are illuminating the water with a pleasant glow. The light dances on her face, but I can't find the beauty in it. All I see is how much she hurts.

"Hey," I say.

She runs her fingers over the hem of her dress. "Hey yourself."

"I have a terrible problem."

"Oh yeah?"

"Mhmm." I step into the backyard. "I'd like to sit next to you, but I'm still in my suit."

She smirks. "That's quite the dilemma."

Her eyes stay on the pool. Her hands stay on her dress.

I strip to my boxers and leave my clothes in a pile on

the floor. The evening air is cool, but it feels good against my skin, like it's waking me up.

I move to the pool and sit next to her. She turns her gaze to me, looking me up and down like she wouldn't dare miss a chance to see me half-naked.

She starts at my eyes and works her way to my toes.

She laughs. "Nice socks."

"This is my seduction outfit."

She smiles. Her eyes are bright. "It's working."

I slip my feet, socks and all, into the water. She laughs again, and it's like some of the fog surrounding her has lifted.

"I'm sorry about this morning. I did want to talk to you about it. I do." She pulls at her dress.

"We're both here."

She nods and scoots a little closer to me. Her eyes stay on the water, but she rests her head on my shoulder. "I had a feeling I'd fuck up the food challenge on my own, but I couldn't bring myself to call you. I kept picturing Samantha sitting there next to you. I didn't particularly want her in on that conversation."

"I would have been happy to step away for an hour or two."

"It might have gone the same way if we were on the phone. I could have started freaking out and hung up on you."

"Maybe. Maybe not."

She presses her fingers into her dress. "It's not the same when you aren't here."

"I wanted you to wait for me to come back."

"I wanted to rely on myself. What if you leave to see Samantha again next weekend? I need to depend on me." She presses a hand to her chest to emphasize the point."

"It's not like that. I don't plan on being there every damn weekend."

Alyssa presses her palms against the concrete. "Maybe you don't plan on it. But what if she tries again?"

I run my hand through her hair. "You're much more important to me."

"Yeah, but I don't need you as much as she does. I mean, suicide attempts." She throws her hands up in the air. "How the hell am I supposed to compete with that?"

I scoot closer to her. "It's not a competition."

She brings her eyes to mine. "Isn't it?"

"No." I roll my shoulders back in a hopeless attempt to ease the tension in my neck. "If you tell me you need me, I'll be there."

There's something in her eyes, but I can't place it. She looks back to the pool and kicks her feet in the water.

Her voice is a whisper. "I needed you."

I shake my head, frustrated.

"You should have waited for me. But I'm here now. Tell me how I can help."

"I don't know."

I rub her shoulders. "We could do the food challenge again. I'll be your babysitter or your distracting human fuck toy."

She smirks. "Maybe." She makes circles with her legs. Tiny little circles. Then big ones. Then she kicks, sending water everywhere. "I'm sorry. I'm not good at this."

"At what?"

"Being in a relationship."

I run my fingers over her wrist. "Yeah?"

She nods. "No one has ever really loved me. Ryan was the only person, and he... it wasn't the same. He did care about me, and he wanted to help me, but only if I could fit into my role."

"That must have been lonely."

"Yeah."

I slide my fingers over her thumb. "What about your mom?"

"She doesn't love anything except the bottle." Her voice is matter-of-fact.

"Do you want to talk about?" I ask.

She kicks the water. "I've had my guard up for so long. It's hard to let it down."

"I get that."

"But I want to." She brings her head back to my shoulder.

I slide my arm around her waist and hold her as closely as I can. "I can be patient."

She nods, kicking the water again.

She wants to talk. She just needs a little encouragement.

I take a deep breath. "How did your eating disorder start?"

She chuckles. "You barely cringed at the words 'eating disorder.'"

"I don't like thinking of you in pain."

She turns her gaze back to the pool. "Are you sure you want to hear about this?"

I nod. "I want to know everything about you, no matter how ugly you say it is."

She takes a deep breath, like she's considering it. Then she nods. "I had a lot of time alone in high school. I was lonely. Empty. I had a friend who bragged about her bulimia. She thought it made her cool and edgy. So I knew it was possible." She presses her hands against the edge of the pool. "I tried it once in high school. I made my mom a cake for her birthday, but she never come home. She was probably out drinking. I don't know. But it was just me and the cake. And I knew eating it would make me feel better. But I also knew I couldn't eat all that cake. I knew I needed to look a certain way if I wanted to be an actress."

Her eyes turn to me. She's studying me for a reaction, to make sure I can handle this.

I nod. I can.

I will.

"So I got the idea to try purging. I ate a few slices of cake. I felt sick, but I kept going. I knew I had to get it right, to really stuff myself. And then I locked myself in the bathroom and I tried. It must have taken half an hour before I coughed anything up. It was so awful, and I felt like hell the next day. I was out of it; my stomach was a war zone. My throat was aching. I swore I'd never do it again. I swore I'd avoid temptation so I never even thought about doing it again."

"What happened?"

She takes a slow breath. "It was when I was on *Together*. It was a lot of pressure, and the producers made it clear I needed to stay at exactly my size, so I looked something like a teenager. A buxom teenager, but still a teenager."

Messed up doesn't cover it.

"If you tell me their names, I'll sue them."

I'm only half-joking.

Even if it doesn't go anywhere, I'm not above some paperwork harassment.

It's the least they deserve.

She laughs. "That would do a lot for my reputation. The poor, pathetic actress who can't handle criticism."

"If you want it to be anonymous, I bet Laurie knows someone who will take 'em out."

"Take them out?"

I nod. "I'll foot the bill too."

She smiles, and there's finally some life in her expression. "I'd rather stay a non-felon. But thanks for the offer." She draws another circle with her foot. "I had a lot of time to think about how badly I might fuck up. I had so much to prove. I had to show my mom, Ryan, the high school drama teacher who told me I was good, but not good enough to get my GED and move to L.A. I was terrified I would fail, and I didn't know how to deal with it. There was no one to talk to. Ryan was my friend, but he was against me acting. I wasn't going to drink myself stupid and turn into my mother. I couldn't just eat. The producers would have freaked out if I gained weight. But I remember that I'd tried and thought I could try again."

"And you did?"

"Yeah." She presses her fingertips into the concrete. "It was still hard, but it was easier. I swore I'd never do it, just stick to my 'healthy eating plan,' but I needed that release. I needed something." She brings her gaze back to mine. "You probably think it's pathetic."

I run my hand through her hair.

She leans into me, closing her eyes. She wants more, a quick end to this conversation followed by a thorough distraction. But I can't give that to her.

I'm not going to help her run away from her feelings.

"You've been alone your whole life," I say. "You found a way to get through a hard time. There's nothing pathetic about it."

She nods like she almost sort of believes me.

We sit there until the sky is dark and the stars are bright.

———

I MAKE DINNER. A BLAND DINNER, AT ALYSSA'S REQUEST.

She's certain the meal will be awkward, that I'm going to stare at her like a guard watching a prisoner.

It's not entirely comfortable. I watch her more closely than I mean to, but she doesn't call me on it. Hell, maybe she appreciates the concern.

After dinner we watch a movie on the couch. *The Apartment*, one of her favorites, though she's partial to anything directed by Billy Wilder. Sometimes I wonder where she found the time to see so many movies and read so many books. She's almost as well versed in film as my mother was.

But then I remember that she spent so much of her life alone. Even when she thought she had someone, she was alone.

Her mood lightens. She wraps her arms around me, laughing and gasping at all the appropriate parts of the movie.

And then my phone rings.

Alyssa brings her eyes to me. "At this time, it must be her."

"I'll turn it off."

She pushes herself up and moves to the opposite side of the couch. "What if she just attempted suicide again?"

"That's ridiculous."

She folds her arms. "Not that ridiculous."

"I'll text her that I'll call back later. I want to spend my night with you." She doesn't say anything. My phone is on the kitchen table. Missed call from Samantha Brooks. I send her a text.

I'm working late. I'll call you back tomorrow. Is everything okay?

She replies almost instantly. *I guess so, but I'd like to talk to you. It's important.*

I look over to the couch. Alyssa has her hand pressed

against her chin. She's trying to keep her attention on the TV, but she has one eye on me.

Whatever Samantha wants, it will have to wait. I set my phone on the table and move back to the couch.

Alyssa reaches for me. She presses her hand against mine. "I was snooping before you got here."

"Is that a habit?"

She nods. "You have so much of Samantha's stuff in that office."

I do. Not because it means anything. Just because I haven't had a use for the space and cleaning it out sounds like a lot of work.

"Do you want the office?"

As soon as I say it, I know it's the best way to use that room full of the past.

Fill it with my hopes for the future.

She swallows. "It seems like a waste of a room."

"What if it was your room?"

"My room for what?"

I take her hand. "Whatever you want. It could be your library or your rehearsal room or your masturbation room."

She laughs. "Just what I wanted."

I move closer to her. "I mean it. I want you to have your own space here."

She shifts back just a little bit. Her eyes turn to the floor. "You sure?"

"I'll clean it out this weekend."

She bites her lip, thinking it over. She looks over to the room then back to me. "I'll believe it when I see it."

Chapter Sixteen

Ryan is sitting in my chair, his feet on my desk. He's wearing a smug grin.

I motion for him to move but he stays put.

Just what I fucking need.

"I have work to do," I say.

His smug grin spreads to his ears. "Mrs. Pike's husband rejected your offer."

"Then we'll see her husband in court."

"You know as well as I do that she won't get full custody in court. Revise the offer and beg his lawyer to see you again."

My fingers curl into fists. "I appreciate your help during my absence, but I can manage my own clients."

He sighs. That you're-such-an-idiot sigh.

I unclench my fists. "I'd be happy to dissolve the firm. You can manage your clients and I'll manage mine."

Ryan's eyes narrow. His brow furrows. "It's my firm. You're not taking it away from me."

There's a tiny hint of something in his eyes. A weakness.

This isn't about the firm. It's about Alyssa.

"You can keep the name. I only want my clients."

He slides his feet off the desk. "No."

I take a step towards the desk. "I understand you'd rather not work with me after what happened with Alyssa."

"This isn't personal. It's a business decision."

Sure it is.

I take a deep breath.

"I'm serious about Alyssa. I'd rather not rub it in your face, but I don't think it's appropriate for us to continue to work together."

Ryan grits his teeth. "Is that right?"

"It must upset you working with the guy who stole your fiancée."

His voice is even and cool. "It doesn't bother me." He presses his eyes closed like he's willing any personal feelings away. "But if you're upset, I'll stand by my offer to buy you out."

"There's nothing in this for you."

He shakes his head. "I have my reasons."

"And they're professional?"

He clears his throat and moves away from the desk. "We're going to change our fee structure. Flat rates instead of billable hours."

I don't miss the fact that he doesn't answer the question.

"No."

"Janine is already reworking all the necessary paperwork."

"As per our contract, you can't make business decisions without my approval. We're partners."

Ryan shrugs like this means nothing to him. He steps past me and opens the office door. "It would be foolish of you to make a decision based on your 'commitment' to Alyssa. It's not like she's going to stick around."

"Whatever you say."

He looks at me with pity. "It's sweet that you believe she'd ever want something real from you."

"What can I say? I'm a romantic."

He shakes his head. " She's going to run as soon as she gets bored of fucking you."

He steps into the hallway like he's delivered a killing blow.

"Then I guess I'll have to keep things interesting for her."

That wipes the grin off his face.

He shakes his head. "I appreciate your Prince Charming thing. You have a nice face and you look good in a suit, and women eat it up. But you're going to have to step out of fantasy land. You're not taking any clients away from this firm, and you're not getting anyone to agree to your ludicrous offers."

"Thanks for the concern."

"You don't know her as well as you think you do."

"Well, that makes two of us. Doesn't it?" I shut the door in his face.

———

By lunch I'm calm.

Ryan is only trying to fuck with me. But I'm not going to allow him to rattle me. I'll find a way to leave this firm without abandoning my clients to Ryan and his obsession with the bottom line.

There's a text message from Samantha on my phone. *Can we talk soon?*

There's no urgency to it, but she's not in the best place mentally.

I call her. Whatever it is she wants, it can't be any worse than Ryan's attitude.

The phone rings to voice mail. I hate to admit it, but I'm relieved.

There's so much of her in my life already. Alyssa was right. Samantha's stuff is all over the house. She's taking up the entire spare room.

It could be Alyssa's. I can see her in that room, making it her own, decorating it with those silly wall decals in the shape of birds, hanging old movie posters. She could paint it hot pink. She could do whatever she wants with it.

It would be perfect.

———

I LEAVE WORK EARLY, AND SPEND NEARLY TWO HOURS packing Samantha's things into boxes.

There's still so much of her here. I need to get rid of it or this place will never be mine.

It will never be mine and Alyssa's.

I shake my head. I can't get ahead of myself. I'm only offering her space. She isn't moving in. She was very clear about that.

But the first step to convincing her is having her over more.

Most of this stuff is crap—tacky silk flowers, uncomfortable office chairs, matching desks from some furniture chain.

There's a picture on Samantha's old desk, a photo of the two of us at the beach. It was a week after we got engaged. We don't look happy, not really. I still remember the day we took this. She went out for "drinks with the girls" that night.

That was her code for going to fuck my father.

I toss it.

It takes a few hours, but I strip the room down to its bare essentials. There's a desk and a task chair, a couch, a bookshelf that will soon be teeming with Alyssa's messy stacks of plays.

The orange light of sunset streams through the windows, painting the walls in a soft glow.

There's something so perfect about the room like this. It's light. Hell, I feel light. The memories that were dragging me down are gone.

The ghost of Samantha is out of this room. This is only the first step.

This can be my home, mine and Alyssa's. The only memories that will matter will be the ones we make.

The front door opens. Alyssa. I hear her heels clicking on the hardwood floor.

"Lucy, I'm home," Alyssa squeals in her best Desi Arnaz voice.

I step out. She's in a gorgeous dress, made up like she's coming from an important meeting.

She slides out of her heels. "God, these things are so uncomfortable. Why don't I wear Keds all the time?"

"Because they're a very important part of your seduction outfit."

She smiles. "You look like you're up to something."

"I have a surprise."

"A sexy surprise?"

I shake my head.

She fakes a pout. "Such a tease." She shakes her head, a wide smile on her lips. "Is it a startling surprise? Because I think I'll need a cup of coffee first. I'm exhausted."

"Did you stay up late watching movies with some asshole who refused to turn off the TV?"

"Yes," she says. "But I only did it because I wanted to get in his pants."

"How did that work out?"

She moves towards me, wrapping her arms around me. Her eyes are on mine. Her hands are on my back. "I'll get him today."

I bring my lips to hers. It's so soft and sweet, and I can feel the need pouring between us.

I open my eyes and stare at her.

"Are you ready to see and believe?"

She laughs. "See and believe what?"

I take her hand and lead her to the former office. "I want you to feel like this place is home, even if you technically live someplace else. I want you to feel like you can take up as much space as you want."

"Luke, what are you—"

I push the door open. It isn't much right now, but it is hers for the taking. "It's yours now."

Her eyes go wide. "But yesterday... how the hell did you clean it out so fast?"

I grin.

"Magic."

She turns to me. "I can't take a room in your house."

"It's going to stay empty if you don't."

"But we're not... I'm not ready to move in yet."

"That's okay." I squeeze her hand. "This is your space, just for you. And you can do whatever you want with it. You can make it a library or you can fill it with makeup or you can store your extra coffee here. I don't care. But it's yours."

"I don't know."

"Ally, nothing would make me happier than knowing you can feel at home here."

She looks around the room, her eyes wide. She wants to jump in headfirst. She just needs a little encouragement.

"You gave up so much control of your life before," I say. "You deserve to take a little bit back. I know it's not much. It's just a small room in a small house. But it can be yours."

She steps into the room and presses her hand against the wall. Her lips curl into a smile. Her whole face lights up with excitement. "I'm going to make this the girliest fucking room."

"Hot pink?"

She nods. "And sparkles."

"I love hot pink and sparkles."

"And pictures of hot dudes on the walls."

"So you kept those pictures I sent you?"

"No, I..." She blushes and folds her arms. "Fine. No hot guys on the walls."

She presses her lips into mine. It's soft and sweet, but there's something under the tenderness.

She needs me as much as I need her. As badly. As urgently.

This is hard for her too.

Her eyes connect with mine. "Thanks, Luke."

"For what?"

"For being patient with me."

I can do patient.

While I nudge her in the direction I want to go. I can see our wedding, our honeymoon, the first home we have together. I can see us growing old together.

It might just take a little time to convince her of the same.

Chapter Seventeen

The rest of the day is bliss.

We swim around the pool, naked, splashing fights ending only in long kisses. We shower together, and I press her against the hard tile wall, rubbing her until she comes. We curl up on the couch, and I relinquish control of the remote to Alyssa. She squeals over *Downton Abbey*, reveling over the subtext in every scene.

I try desperately to teach her how to cook stir fry, but she's helpless anywhere near the kitchen. She holds the knife hesitantly, but gains some confidence as we go.

She takes a seat on the couch after dinner.

I move towards the couch, eyeing her.

I don't try to hide my intentions.

Sitting down next to her, I pull her onto my lap.

She straddles me, her thighs pressed around me tightly.

I brush a hair from her eyes, soaking in the sight of her. We'll be done with sweetness soon. I have to savor the moment.

"What?" she asks. A shy smile curls onto her face

"Just imagining what you'll look like when I make you come."

"Well, just this once, I might allow you to make that a reality," she says.

I raise a brow, squeezing her ass.

"Just this once? I seem to recall it happening many, many times in the past."

"That's... possible."

"Just for that, I'm going to make you come twice."

She laughs, a twinkle in her eye. "I should misbehave more often."

She arches into me and brings her mouth to mine, sucking on my lips.

I run my fingertips up her arms, my touch light as a feather. Then it's her shoulders and her back, and under the straps of her tank top. She groans, squirming, sucking harder on my lips.

She's already so full of want.

It's going to be difficult to torture her for long.

But I need to revel in it for as long as I can.

I pull the straps of her tank top off her shoulders, exposing the light pink fabric of her bra. She gasps, arching further into me, so desperate for me to touch her. I cup her breasts over her bra. The fabric is soft and smooth. I'm itching to get under it, to feel her skin, to rub her nipples until she's screaming.

But the wait makes it so much better.

She shifts into me, pressing her breast into my hand, her teeth sinking into her lips as she suppresses a moan. She's so fucking sexy. I wish I could spend my entire life torturing her like this, watching the beautiful agony spread across her face as she gets more and more desperate.

I slip one finger inside her bra, sliding it gently over her skin. Mhmm. She's so soft and firm at the same time. And she's rubbing her crotch against mine.

She moans, desperate for what's about to come. I unhook her bra and slide it off her shoulders. She closes her eyes, arching into me. Her nipples are so firm, and she shudders every time I touch her. I want to be inside her, filling her, making her scream in ecstasy.

But not yet.

I run my hands along her sides and bring my mouth to her nipple. She plants her hands on my shoulders, squeezing tightly. Hell, she's shaking with anticipation. Her skin tastes so good, like salt and chlorine and Alyssa. I suck, my tongue swirling around her nipples.

"Luke," she groans.

I suck harder, my hands making their way to her hips.

I unzip her shorts. She arches her back, shifting out of them, and I bring my hands to her inner thighs. I slide them up, and up, and up, closer and closer.

Her skin gives way to the soft fabric of her panties. I press my hand against them. They're already wet. She already wants me so badly.

She shudders again, her eyes squeezed shut, her head tilting back. I run my tongue around her nipples, and she shakes with every flick. I suck harder, and harder, until I feel her nails on my skin.

She looks down at me, her hair falling over her face, her eyes locked on mine. "You're wearing too many clothes." She pulls my T-shirt over my head and scans my body. "Still too many."

She reaches for my zipper, but I stop her.

"I'm not done with you." I slide my arms around her and run my hands from her back to her ass.

She shudders. "But... I want to... to you..."

"I want to eat you out, Ally. And I'm not going to stop until I make you come."

She groans and softens her body, relaxing so I can position her. I take her into my arms and lay her on the couch. She closes her eyes, lost in her desire. She's all mine. I dig my fingers into the sides of her panties and pull them off her hips as slowly as possible. She shakes as they pass her hips, squirms as they reach her knees, arches her back as they fall off her feet.

I bring my hand to her thighs, pressing her legs apart.

I take a second to just enjoy the view.

She's so fucking wet, so pink and ready. I press my lips into her thigh. My first kiss is soft. The next is harder. Closer to her.

"Oh," she groans. She reaches for my shoulders, squeezing tight. But I continue my pace, dragging my lips up her thigh, kissing and nibbling her soft, tender skin.

Then I reach her folds.

I soak her in as I slide my tongue over her. She tastes so good, sweet, and her groans are music in my ears.

I work my way towards her clit, sucking on her lips, sliding my tongue against her folds. She's so soft and wet against my mouth, and I lick her from top to bottom then back again.

Then, when she's panting loudly, when her nails sink into my back, I press my tongue flat against her clit. She nearly screams. I do it again, a soft, slow stroke. She groans, a little louder, her thighs falling flat onto the couch. I lick her again, and again, and again, soft slow strokes all the way.

"Luke." It rolls off her tongue like it's her favorite thing in the world.

She's lost in desire. She's so fucking sexy and she's close. I have to taste her as she comes.

I spread her lips apart with my fingers and lick her from top to bottom. She pants, her back arching, her legs squeezing my ears. I slide my tongue over her cunt.

Mhmm. She's getting sweeter, saltier, closer.

I press her thighs against the couch, hard, and I go deeper, my tongue plunging inside her. She groans. "Fuck. Luke. Fuck."

"Oh, fuck," she groans again. She shakes. Moaning. Rocking her pelvis into my mouth.

I lick her again. She gasps. Her nails are so hard on my shoulders. Her voice is so high. This is the spot. I lick her again, harder and faster. She wraps her legs around me. She pants. She moans. She screams. But I don't stop. I lick her again and again, all her want and need pouring into me.

"Oh, fuck, I'm... Oh, fuck Luke..." She rocks into me one last time, her voice cracking, her nails hard against me as she comes.

She tugs at my hair, pulls me back to her, a goofy smile on her face. "Jesus fucking Christ." She collapses next to me.

But she's not done. She presses her hands into my ass and wraps her legs around me. Her lips graze mine. A soft kiss. Then harder. Her tongue probes my mouth, swirling around mine.

Her hands are on my hips. She pulls my boxers to my knees and brushes her hand against my cock. Heat spreads through me again. I need to have her like this. I need to come inside her.

"Get on your back," she says

And I'm not about to deny her when she's looking at me like she's going to consume me. She presses her lips into my neck as she strokes my cock. I bring my hands to her chest and rub her nipples.

"Mhmm," she groans

Her grip tightens and she strokes me harder. Fuck. Warmth spreads through my pelvis, moving towards my legs. God, I want to be inside her, our bodies together as one.

I grab her hips and bring her towards me, the tip of my cock slipping inside her. A wave of pleasure rocks through me. But I can't stop to savor it. I need to feel her around me.

I go deeper. Fuck. She feels so good, soft and wet. I pull her closer, thrusting into her, filling her.

She groans. Her eyes squeeze closed again. She rocks against me, again and again. A warmth spreads through my body. Pleasure, everywhere. Her hands dig into my skin. "Luke. Fuck, Luke," she groans.

We lock eyes. She's so sexy like this, lost in her lust, her teeth sinking into her lips. "Fuck," she groans. I pull her closer, holding her body steady as I thrust into her. God, yes. Fuck, yes. She's so fucking. She's so...

I kiss her, hard, sucking on her lips. My hands are on her chest, circling her nipples, and she moans into my mouth. She's so close already, and she feels so fucking good.

"Harder," she groans.

And I thrust harder and deeper and stronger.

"Harder," she groans again.

I shift our bodies until I'm on top of her. She moans, pulling me close, wrapping her legs around me. "I want to feel you come again," I say.

She kisses me as she shifts her legs around my shoulders. She's completely pinned, completely at my mercy. I thrust into her, deeper and deeper. She's so soft and warm and tight. Jesus. I'm almost...

"Luke," she groans, her hands on my ass.

"Louder."

"Luke," she nearly screams it.

Fuck. Her eyes close. And then it's her nails again—a sharp pain against my back that only heightens my pleasure.

She groans. "Fuck, Luke, Fuck. Fuck. Fuck. I'm... fuck..." She squeezes me.

I thrust again. A little harder. A littler deeper.

I groan. I'm all instinct, thrusting into her, filling her, kissing her. Fuck, fuck, fuck. Her nails, her lips, her skin. Fuck, fuck, fuck. I sink my teeth into my lips as it overtakes me. Fuck, fuck, fuck.

I come, my cock throbbing as I fill her.

She pulls me close, her arms and legs wrapped around me.

Chapter Eighteen

T he shriek of my ringtone pierces the otherwise calm silence.

It's Samantha.

I peek into the bedroom.

Alyssa is in her own little world, her hands curled around her Kindle, her eyes glued to its screen.

She turns towards the sound, her eyes connecting with mine. "Samantha?"

"Yeah." She motions for me to close the door. That must be a sign of trust.

I answer. "Hey."

"Hey," Samantha replies. It's almost a whisper.

Her parents must be home.

"Is everything okay?"

"I can survive a few days without you," she says. "But this isn't really a social call. And I have to make it quick."

"Date with Mr. Whole Foods?"

"No, that's not happening. Not after my fun hospital stay."

Fucking hilarious.

"I have a few interviews in L.A.," she continues.

"That's great."

"I want to move back as soon as I can. My parents are driving me crazy."

Tension knots in my shoulders. "My friend Mike could help you find a place."

"Yeah, Mike is great." She takes a slow breath. "But I already know where I want to live."

I clear my throat. "Where is that?"

Samantha sighs. She wants me to say all this for her. She wants me to offer the house back, so she doesn't have to ask.

"Luke... you know where."

"Where?"

"I want the house."

She says it so bluntly, as if I have no say in the matter, as if it doesn't matter that I've been living here for six months. Or that she dumped my sorry ass and promised to move out. Or that she didn't even want the house when she tried and failed to leave me. She didn't even want me to buy her out of her half of the mortgage, not with Edward fronting the money for the down payment.

She wanted her conscience clean, so she could live happily ever after with him.

"Luke? Are you there?"

"Yeah."

"I know I don't have any legal standing, but I want it. It was a long time ago, but it felt like home."

"When did it feel like home? When you were fucking my father or when you attempted suicide in our bed?"

What can I say? I snapped.

Just a smidge.

She sighs. "It's not just where I tried. It's where I survived. And before that, we were happy. I was happy."

174

"When were we happy? Because most of what I remember is a crock of shit. Since you were fucking my father for, what, two years? Three?"

"Luke..."

I feel dizzy, like the air rushed out of my lungs all at once. Samantha wants this house. I knew she'd want it eventually. I promised it to her. I expected to give it away.

But that was before Alyssa. Before we kissed here, before we spent long, tired mornings here, before we started to make a life here.

"It's my house," I say.

"Can we not fight over it?"

"You didn't want it when you dumped me."

"Please." She's pleading. "I have enough to buy out your half and throw in a little extra for the interest. I don't want to go back to some sterile apartment complex."

"You can find another house. This is my home now. Mine and Alyssa's."

"Luke..."

"You don't even know if you'll work on the Westside. What if you get a job in Pasadena?" I lean against the wall to stay upright.

"It's always been mine," she says. "Edward wanted me to have it."

Really?

"Fuck you."

She immediately backtracks.

"Luke, I didn't mean it like that—"

"He was my father."

"I know."

"He was my father a long time before he was your boyfriend."

"I know."

"Do you fucking know? Because every time you bring

him up you act like you're the only person who ever cared about him."

"Luke..."

I dig my fingers into the phone. "I dealt with him my whole fucking life. I don't care if you loved him. I don't care if he hurt you when he rejected you. He was my father."

"I didn't mean that."

She sounds genuinely contrite but I'm so over this.

"You think it's your house just because your boyfriend fronted the down payment?"

"He told me—"

"You know what he told me?" Anger seethes through me. I usually fight it back, but not this time. "He told me that he was happy for me. Happy I finally got my life together. I had everything. A business, an ambitious fiancée, and now I'd finally have a home. It was the first time he'd said something nice to me since Mom died."

"I'm sorry." It's not earnest. It's not "I'm sorry for your pain." It's "I'm sorry you're such a fuck-up."

"He wasn't just the asshole you were fucking behind my back. He was my father."

"I know. I'm sorry."

"Did you ever love me or did you just want to get closer to him?" The room is spinning way, way too fast. I shouldn't push Samantha like this, not two weeks after a probable suicide attempt, but she's trying to take away my home.

"Of course," she says.

"When?"

She sighs.

"I always loved you. I just wasn't in love with you."

What the hell does that even mean?

"Don't bullshit me with clichés."

"Fine. The first year," she admits. "You were so sweet to me. You treated me so well. But after a while... you were different. Farther away."

"So it's my fault?"

"No," she says. "But he was so smart and successful, and he made me feel safe. It only got serious once I started working with him. All those late nights and work dinners." Her voice gets lower. "At first, we only talked about you."

"I asked you to marry me well after you started working with him."

"I know."

"Then why did you say yes?"

It makes no goddamn sense.

"Because I wanted to love you. I wanted things to be easy. I couldn't bear the thought of breaking your heart."

She takes a sharp breath, but right now I don't care how she feels. Her words are a knife in my chest.

"Luke, I'm sorry," she says. "I wish I could apologize enough."

"You could stop trying to take my house."

"I earned it." She sighs. "He was ashamed to be with me. He was the one who always talked me out of breaking up with you. I wanted to end it. I wanted to stop stringing you along, but he was worried about you. And about his reputation. About how it would look. Even when I offered to keep our relationship a secret for a while, to leave the firm, he wouldn't do it. He didn't want to look like some asshole who stole his son's girlfriend."

"But he was fine with fucking you as long as nobody knew about it," I remark harshly. I'll never understand putting perception above reality like that. "You could have told me," I add. "I could have used the mercy."

"I'm a coward." Her voice breaks. "I tried to tell you at the hospital. I'm a pathetic coward. I was ruining your life

177

then, and I'm ruining it now. You should stop talking to me. Keep the house. I don't need it."

"Sam, don't—"

"I don't deserve your friendship," she says.

"That's not what I meant."

I try to modulate my tone, frustration rising.

"I'm sorry." She chokes back a sob. "I'm a bitch," she says. "I was such a bitch. You should just move on with your life."

"No, Sam..."

"I'm sorry. No, you should have it. It's yours. He was your dad. You're entitled to it. Besides, you deserve the hush money more than I do."

Fuck.

"I need to speak with Alyssa before I can make a decision."

I hate this. It's either I say yes, or I worry that this is the thing that will push her. That she'll try to kill herself again because there's this hole in her heart that's shaped like our house.

She puts me in this position too much.

How long have her requests been veiled threats? *Do this for me or else I'll be so miserable. Come see me or I'll be so lonely. And I don't feel safe lonely. Please, Luke. Please, don't leave.*

Another wave of dizziness hits me. I know she's manipulating me. She may know it too.

Hell of it is, I still care.

I can hate it as much as I want. I'm not going to abandon her now.

I take a deep breath. This house means a lot to me, but only because it means a lot to Alyssa.

"Alyssa doesn't own the house, Luke."

"This affects her too. I won't give you an answer until I've had a chance to talk to her about it."

That much is non-negotiable.

Samantha's breath slows, until she's calm. "I'm going to figure out exactly how much I owe you."

"I don't care about the money."

"I do. I already can't pay you back for how much you've helped me. I'm not going to be in debt for half a mortgage either."

"We can split it exactly."

"No. He put in for the down payment."

"Why don't you draft a contract? I can look it over while we consider it."

"Alright. Thanks Luke."

I feel utterly drained by the time I hang up.

Chapter Nineteen

lyssa and I enjoy almost a week of normalcy.

She spends every night at my place. We do nothing of consequence. We read by the pool or watch TV on the couch or play cards in the kitchen.

It's a perfect picture of what our life together could be.

We touch and kiss and hug and fuck everywhere in the house. Now that I know I might be losing it, I want to mark every inch of it as ours.

I make her come in every spot where such an act is conceivable—the breakfast table, the kitchen counters, the desk, the pool. Every floor and wall in that house must be ours.

Everything is easy until Friday night. She sits on the couch, her arms curled around a pillow, her attention on the floor.

She shakes her head. "I don't know if I can do the food challenge tomorrow."

"You can do it."

She looks at me for a while. "Are you sure you can handle it?"

"Yes."

"And you won't get upset if I start freaking out?"

"I promise."

"Or if I want to use you as a distraction?"

"You'll be thoroughly distracted."

She bites her lip, digging her nails into the pillow. "Things are good right now. I don't want to ruin that."

"Things will stay good."

"What if you freak out?"

I sit next to her. "I won't."

Her eyes are glued to mine. Like she's studying me. "But what if it's too much and you lose all the respect you have for me?"

"Impossible."

She looks back at the floor. "Okay. We'll do it tomorrow. After dinner."

There's still so much dread in her voice.

"You okay?"

She nods but her eyes stay on the floor. "I'm going to hang out in the spare room for a while."

She offers me a quick smile and retreats into the spare room, her room.

Her room for another few weeks at least.

———

THE MORNING IS EASY. WE DRINK CUP AFTER CUP OF TEA and coffee. We spend hours watching TV on the couch. We eat lunch in the backyard.

But something changes in the afternoon.

Alyssa is a nervous wreck. She paces around the pool, her eyes on the concrete.

"How about a walk?" I offer.

She nods, but her attention stays on the ground. I'd

love to grab her and pin her to the couch to thoroughly distract her, but that is only going to make things harder.

She collects her shoes and purse and we make our way to the marina.

It's a nice day. Warm and sunny.

But Alyssa is obviously uncomfortable. She walks fast, clutching her purse like it's a lifesaver.

I give her space. I'm going to do everything I can to make it easier.

She stops at a curve and presses her hands against the metal railings. Her gaze is on the water, but she's a million miles away.

"We can talk about it," I offer.

She shakes her head and digs her hands into the railing. "No, we should probably pick up something to use." She motions to the shopping center a few blocks away.

"I can do it for you."

"No, I have to do it. Buy a box of cookies and only eat one." She turns her gaze to me, studying me.

She's watching for a sign I can't handle this.

"Let's do it."

I offer my hand. She nods, wiping her palms on her dress and wrapping her fingers around mine. She squeezes tight.

"You can do this," I say.

She nods. "Let's not talk about it too much."

I let her take the lead.

We change direction and move towards the store. It's a natural foods store, the kind of yuppie place Samantha and her future Tesla-owning husband would love.

The automatic doors slide open and we step inside.

Everything in the store is white and bright and the aisles are cramped. Alyssa wanders around the aisles, squeezing my hand tighter and tighter.

She stares at a shelf of chips like she doesn't understand it.

"Ally..."

"I'm fine." She turns quickly, moving to the next aisle. There's still a look of dread on her face. Like she's about to jump off a bridge.

"You sure?"

"The constant questions don't help."

She panicked last time. It was her thoughts tricking her and telling her she's a failure. I can't shrink myself and jump into her brain, but I can keep her attention here.

"You never told me which of your high school parts was your favorite."

She smiles slightly.

"You're so obvious."

"Still, not many high school students get to play two Shakespearean heroines."

She scans the next aisle, stopping at a row of cookies. "Abridged *Hamlet* cuts out all of Ophelia's best lines."

"Oh yeah?"

She turns her eyes towards me, shaking her head like I'm ridiculous. But she's smiling. "There's this great exchange between her and Hamlet where he asks if he can lay in her lap and she says no. But he corrects himself—he means his head upon her lap."

"Yeah?"

"Without the oral sex jokes she's just Hamlet's crazy girlfriend. Kills herself for no reason." Her attention turns back to the shelf. She picks up a box of sugar cookies and hugs it to her chest. "Of course, Juliet isn't really any better. She also kills herself over her boyfriend."

"So it's *The Crucible* then?"

She nods. "Abigail is a badass bitch. She starts all kinds of shit." She laughs and her eyes find mine. "Thanks."

"No, thank you for the free British literature lesson."

"*The Crucible* is American."

"Two lessons in one. How could I get so lucky?"

She presses her hand against my chest, pushing gently. "You better watch what you say."

"You're right. I wouldn't want to insult a depressing play."

"Ha ha." She grins.

A bit of tension releases. Then her eyes turn to the box of cookies in her hand and all the joy drops off her face.

"You want to get home?" I ask.

She nods.

She's white as a ghost at the checkout. And she stays quiet the entire walk back to my place. It's not until we're inside that she finally looks at me.

Her eyes are wide. Anxious. "This isn't going to be easy."

I nod.

"I might get upset. I might yell at you or try and run off. But it's not personal."

Her eyes connect with mine. She's still so scared, but I'm going to do whatever I can to help her.

"Do you want to talk about it at all?" I ask.

She shakes her head. "Let's just do it."

"How does it work?"

"I eat the cookie. It sounds so simple, but it's not."

She's already starting to freak out. I can see it on her face.

I reach for her, but she's receding further and further into herself.

"Ally, you need to try and stay here with me, okay?"

She nods. "I'll try."

She sits at the kitchen table, a serious look on her face. Those thoughts of hers are lying to her again, telling her she's a failure, telling her she's not good enough.

"I love you," I tell her. "No matter what."

I place the box on the table and sit across from her. She stares at it like it's something horrible.

"I can't do it." She presses her fingernails into her palm.

"Why not?"

"I'll be a pathetic failure if I eat one of those stupid fucking cookies. I can't do it." Her eyes are glued to the box. "But I have to. It's too exhausting to stay like this."

She looks to me for confirmation. I nod. We can get through this together.

She opens the box and pulls out the plastic tray. There are a dozen tiny cookies in it. She stares at them, studying them carefully.

"How many do you want?" I ask.

"Two." She swallows hard.

I take two cookies from the plastic and place them on the table.

Her eyes stay on the tray. "Can you put those somewhere else? Somewhere really tall that I can't reach."

"Of course." I repack the box and stuff it in on top of one of the cabinets.

She fidgets. She picks up one cookie and inhales its scent. There's something on her face, a look of wonder, like she can't believe she's actually smelling a cookie.

It's probably been years since she's had one.

She looks to me. It's a *should I?* kind of look. I nod and she turns her attention back to the pastry.

She takes the first bite. It's a tiny one, and she spends forever chewing. She keeps her eyes on the plate. She pulls her hand back, breaks the cookie in half.

She takes another bite.

"You okay?" I ask.

"Yeah." She stares at the treat like it mystifies her, like it's a paradox, something that shouldn't exist.

She takes another bite. I offer my hand again, but she ignores it. Something is different about her. She's pulling away, drifting to some other place. It's in her eyes—she's not there. She moves faster, almost frenzied.

I try to keep my mouth shut. This could be part of the process.

But it doesn't seem normal.

She eats the last bite and looks at her empty hands. She's mystified by them, like she doesn't know where the cookie went.

"Are you okay?" I ask.

She snaps out of whatever it is. "Yeah."

"You seem lost."

"I'm fine." She won't hold my gaze. She's somewhere else, closing off.

I lean closer. "Talk to me."

"I don't want to."

"You can't keep this bottled inside you."

"The whole point of the exercise is to keep everything inside me. That's why you're here."

"Don't be glib."

"I'll be however the fuck I want," she retorts, agitated.

"Okay." I can't let my feelings get in the way. "Be however you want."

That gives her pause.

"I shouldn't have done this, Luke. I need to fix it."

"How?"

"I have to get rid of it."

"Why?"

She stares out the window, at the bright light falling over the backyard. "Because..."

"Because why?"

She presses her fingers together with a sigh. "Because I do. I can't explain it, but it's so obvious. I'm not allowed to eat cookies. I shouldn't have eaten it. And I can't sit here with this horrible feeling of fucking up again. I have to do something to fix it."

"You can."

She pushes off the table. "I'm sorry, Luke, but I can't talk right now. I have to... I can't think."

I grab her arm. "I only have one duty and it's babysitting. You can yell at me if you want. You can hit me. You can spend three hours describing Ryan's sexual prowess. But you are not going anywhere."

She shakes her head. "I can't stay here."

"So we'll go somewhere together."

She shakes her head. She's fighting it. She's drifting back to that other world, but she's fighting it. "Okay." She bites her lip. "Anywhere. Take me anywhere else."

I walk her to my car and I take Lincoln until it turns into Pacific Coast Highway, until we're far into the curves of Malibu. Alyssa is quiet the entire drive. She leans against the window hugging her seat belt. She takes my hand, but her grip is weak.

She's still trapped in her head.

I hate seeing her like this. I hate her being far away from me. I hate her hurting.

But I have to focus on what she needs.

I park on the edge of the highway and walk her down to the beach. We sit on the sand, her attention still slipping away. She's a little calmer, but she's still not here.

I wrap my arms around her and hold her tightly. "I love you, Ally. No matter what."

She doesn't say anything, but she nods, and squeezes me tighter. We stay like that for a long time, our breath and heartbeats blending into the soft roar of waves crashing on the beach.

She calms slowly, clarity returning to her face bit by bit. She's fighting her urge to pull away, fighting hard.

She shakes her head, bringing her gaze to the sand. "I'm sorry."

"Don't be."

"You'd probably be better off with someone normal."

"I don't care. I want you."

The sun sets over the horizon, a violent burst of red bleeding into the blue sky.

Alyssa shakes her head. "I took your entire afternoon."

"I'll tell you a million times if I have to. I'd rather be with you than be anywhere else."

"Okay." She looks to the ocean. Watches the waves pound the sand.

"Do you want to talk about it?"

She shakes her head. "Not right now. I'm still..."

"Processing?"

She nods.

"I'll be here as long as you need me. I promise."

"Even if I relapse and need to go back to treatment?"

I nod. "No matter what."

She turns her gaze back to me. There's so much need in her eyes. So much desperation. She's never had anyone to count on. Not like this.

I swallow the hurt that bubbles up in my chest. She won't have to feel like that anymore. She won't have to be alone anymore.

Her gaze shifts away again. She moves closer, enveloping me in the softest, sweetest hug. "Thank you."

"It's nothing."

She shakes her head. "It's everything."

Chapter Twenty

It's late when we get home.

Alyssa rejects my offer to make her dinner, instead insisting on attempting sleep. I cook something anyway and leave her portion in the fridge.

I don't bother trying to sleep. It would be impossible. Instead, I flip through channels. Nothing on TV can pull me from my thoughts.

I have an email from Samantha. She's asking if I've spoken with Alyssa yet. There's no request for a rush but there's another attempt to guilt trip me. *I need to get out of my parents' house and back to my life as soon as possible if I ever want to get better.*

I close the email without responding.

It's almost eight when Alyssa wakes. The sun is already in the sky and it's casting a soft glow over the house.

She plops next to me, wrapping her arms around me.

I inhale the sensation of her—the warmth of her body, the smell of her hair.

She leans closer, her mouth hovering over my ear. "I know I'm a fucked-up mess, but please don't leave."

"You're my mess."

She squeezes me tighter.

It would be nicer, holding her so much in one day, if the circumstances were different.

She shifts and brings her gaze to mine. "You're upset, aren't you?"

"Yes, but it has nothing to do with you."

"What is it then?"

"Let's talk about it later."

She stares at the sliding doors. "Is it important?"

"Yeah," I say. "But we're both tired, and it can wait until after you've had five lattes and I've had five cups of tea."

"What is it?" she asks. She looks at me sincerely. Like she's all the way back here.

"We can talk about it later."

Light streams through those sliding doors, bringing soft highlights to her face. "Why are you the only one who ever gets to have any secrets?"

"Ally, it's not like that."

"Okay. What is it like?"

She looks exhausted. She's got no reserves left. No fight left.

I can't unload this on her now.

"I'm too tired for this conversation," I try.

"That doesn't sound like you."

"I know, but it's something new I'm trying."

She looks me over. "You could tell me. Put me out of my misery."

"After coffee."

She shakes her head. "Don't make me torture you."

I smirk. "Torture me how?"

"I'll tie you to the dining room table."

"I'm liking it so far."

She folds her arms. "And drink all your tea while you watch, helpless."

I laugh and all the tension in my back eases. She's trying.

"You win. That's much too horrible a fate." I bring my gaze back to hers. "Samantha wants to buy out my half of the house."

"What did you tell her?"

"That I needed to talk to you about it first."

"Oh." Her gaze turns to the backyard.

"I'd rather not go to war over it. Before we started staying here, I didn't want anything to do with this place."

"Bad memories, right?"

"Yeah." I move closer to her. "If you want me to keep this place, I will. I'll call her right now and tell her she can't have it."

Alyssa shakes her head. "What do you want?"

"I promised it to her a long time ago," I say. "And she needs the stability."

"Do you do whatever she asks?"

"No. She didn't see the point in me talking to you about it first. But you're part of the future I want, Ally. And your opinion is important to me."

She hugs her knees to her chest. "This time, it's a house. Last time, it was running off to be by her side for a week. Next time, who knows?"

"Ally... she's not well."

She shakes her head. Bites her fingernail. "And she milked that for as much as she could, didn't she?"

"It's not like that."

She sinks into the couch. "What the hell is it like then?"

"We're friends."

Her voice is low. "No, you aren't. Friends don't ask you to rearrange your life for them. They don't guilt you when you leave after a week by their side. Friends give as much as they take."

She isn't wrong.

"She's going through a rough time. She can't help it."

Alyssa lets out a sigh. "And this rough time has lasted what—a year?"

I sigh.

"About that."

She pushes off the couch and moves towards the window.

"I trust you," she says. "But there's no way she only wants to be your friend. Not with this kind of attitude."

I push off the couch. "It's only a house."

Alyssa turns back to me for a minute. "Was it only a house when you offered me your spare room?"

"No."

"So it's only a house when you want to give it up to Samantha?"

I shake my head.

"No."

Alyssa takes a sharp breath. "Listen, Luke, I really, really don't want to devalue your feelings. You have every right to feel guilty, even though it wasn't your fault. But are you going to keep bending over backwards for her just because you feel like you still owe her? Even after what she did to you?"

"She was there for me when I needed her."

"Does that mean you're in debt to her forever?" she asks.

I frown, scrubbing my hands through my hair.

"No. We're friends. I want to help her."

"Yes, and having friends is great. And it's normal for friends to *sometimes* be weird or needy. And it's also normal for her to *sometimes* ask too much or demand too much attention. But it happens constantly."

"We're normal friends."

I don't even believe myself.

Alyssa shakes her head. "You're not normal. I'm not going to be able to be patient if you're going to bullshit me."

"I'd never bullshit you."

She looks away, her hands curling into tight balls. "Things are so hard right now. Meetings, and press, and the show premiering. I need to feel like you're on my team."

"I am."

"What if you had to choose between us?"

"Ally—"

"No, just hypothetically. Gun to your head—would you rather be her friend or my boyfriend?"

"That's ridiculous."

"Still. Which would you choose?"

"Ally—"

She shakes her head. "I should go."

"I would choose you. I would choose you no matter what."

Her eyes connect with mine. She's upset, but she blinks it away. "I want to be supportive, but I can't watch you bend over backwards for someone who doesn't care the same way for you."

I know Samantha and I aren't normal friends. I know she's more than willing to take advantage of my generosity. But I help her because I want to help her. And I'm considering letting her buy out my half of the house because it could be the best option for both of us.

"Why don't you meet her," I say.

"I'm going home."

I move towards her. "Stay. We can look for a new place online, see what's out there. If you think you could live somewhere else. Hell, we can visit real estate listings."

"So in six months I'll be the ex-girlfriend who won't let go of her half of your house?" That stings. Enough that I can't answer before she continues. "Look—maybe it is a good idea to sell the house to her. It's just one more thing tying you to her." She leans against the counter, hunching her shoulders. "I have a callback Monday. I need to prepare."

"I'm not letting you leave until you eat something."

She turns the coffee maker on. "Fine."

"You'll feel better if you meet Samantha."

Her eyes find mine. "I doubt that very much."

"So do it because you want to fuck me."

She stifles a laugh. "You play that card too often."

"I know." I lean against the counter next to her.

She looks up at me. Her eyes are full of need. "Fine. But I'd like the court record to reflect my official rejection."

"It's reflected."

Chapter Twenty-One

The air outside is warm and dry. It's typical Southern California summer air, but something about it feels different today. It's heavy somehow.

I wait outside a fancy Italian restaurant on the other side of the marina.

It was Samantha's suggestion. She always wants the finer things. That's what she said when I asked her where she wanted to meet. "Someplace nice."

She should get it tattooed on her forehead. Someplace nice.

I swear, every time I've ever asked her where she wanted to go, she's said "someplace nice."

I wish she could get over her obsession with appearances. If she wasn't so determined to convince everyone she was strong, she might have gotten help sooner.

She arrives early. In her BMW. She's the picture of the educated, put-together lawyer—sheath dress, designer purse, black pumps, delicate jewelry. I wish I could say this isn't the Samantha I fell in love with, that I loved some earlier, less appearances-obsessed version of her. But she was like this back in law school. Even on the weekends it was designer jeans and designer shoes and eating at the nicest restaurants.

She hugs me hello. I could swear she lingers for a moment too long.

"Alyssa here yet?" Samantha asks.

"She's coming straight from a meeting."

Samantha nods. She motions to the host stand inside. "Let's get a table. We can order a bottle of wine while we wait."

"Sure." There's no sense in trying to talk Samantha out of drinking wine. The hostess leads us to a table by the window. It's overlooking a busy street, but the linen curtains block most of the view.

There's something so fake about this place. It has brick walls and soft lights, but it's manufactured. It's owned by a huge chain and its pasta sauce comes out of Costco jars, not from secret family recipes.

We take our seats. Samantha is giddy. Her first time back at some place nice, no doubt. She folds her hands together, practically sighing over the fake candle on the dark red tablecloth.

A dark red, no doubt, to hide the marinara stains.

"Luke?" Her voice is soft, but it's a demand for attention.

"Yeah?"

I peel my eyes away from the tablecloth.

"Is everything okay?" It sounds sincere.

"Yeah. Fine."

She mumbles something. "I'm sure Alyssa is just running late. It's not like she'd ditch this dinner."

I take a deep breath and offer her my best hey-this-is-just-business smile. "Of course not."

Samantha sighs. "She sounds very nice."

"She is."

She folds her napkin in her lap. "I had another job interview today. They seemed receptive, but there are a few details to iron out."

"I thought you were going back to Edward's firm."

She shakes her head. "There's so much gossip. Everyone thinks..."

I shake my head. This isn't the time. Hell, it's never going to be the time.

I just decide to ignore the awkward pause there.

"Where is the firm?"

"Right by the house," she responds, clearly relieved at the smooth over. "It's only a mile or two away from Lawrence and Knight, actually."

"And here I thought maybe Ryan hired you to replace me."

She smiles. "You couldn't pay me enough to do divorces all day. I don't know how you do it."

"There's something so magical about fostering a breakup. It's a beautiful thing."

She shakes her head. "Do you have a speech prepared?"

"It's hell to be stuck in a relationship you have no way out of."

Her eyes turn to the floor. "Like what?"

"Ryan and I, for example."

"Oh." She sighs in relief. Like she thought I was talking about her. "You know you're never going to outlast him. He was always the most stubborn person in our study group."

"It was a pretty close competition."

"Why stick around? If you're really serious about Alyssa... if you really do love her." There's something oddly stilted about the words.

Her attention shifts to the entrance. Her lips purse. Her eyes turn down.

I turn to where she's looking. Alyssa is standing at the entrance, and she looks divine. She's wearing a tight, black cocktail dress. Her hair and makeup are perfect.

There's no way she wore this to her meeting.

I smile. I never pegged Alyssa as the petty type, but there's something sweet about her getting dressed up. Like she's marking her turf.

I don't mind being marked.

She waves and walks over to us. No, she saunters.

"You look gorgeous," I murmur.

She smiles. "I know."

Samantha's jaw is almost hanging open. "Yes, you're much prettier than your pictures."

Alyssa turns to me. "You showed her pictures?"

I nod. "Before. We used to make fun of Ryan for bragging about his lovely girlfriend."

"Oh." Alyssa's smile fades. She takes a seat at the table and looks Samantha over. "What else did you make fun of?"

"It was Ryan we were mocking, not you," I say.

"I'm sure."

Samantha offers a smile. "That was a long time ago. And I admit I Googled you. I didn't expect to see Luke dating someone so... pretty."

Alyssa rolls her eyes. "Yes, well, that's my number one trait. The pretty actress with the great tits."

"Yes, Luke mentioned the great tits," Samantha says.

Alyssa looks at me. An of-course-you-did look. She turns back to Samantha. "If you'd like to see for yourself. I've done a lot of nude scenes."

Damn. She's on fire today. I should probably be

concerned with her attitude, but I love that she's claiming me.

Samantha offers a forced smile. "I'll take his word for it." She opens her menu. "This place is really nice. The pasta is great."

Alyssa grimaces but shakes it off. She places her hands over her menu. "I'm not really a pasta person."

Samantha looks Alyssa over. It's some kind of judgment, something women do that I don't understand.

"The fish is also great," I say. Since we both know Alyssa is ordering grilled fish and steamed vegetables.

Alyssa taps her fingers against the menu. "I appreciate the suggestions, but I've got it covered. I've been to restaurants before."

A waiter takes our drink order and delivers garlic knots. Alyssa ignores them. It's not the same way she looked at the cookie. It's a casual thing, like she really doesn't care that they exist.

I'm not sure that I've seen her eat a piece of bread.

But I know better than to interfere with her recovery without a specific request otherwise. I push the basket of bread to Samantha's side of the table.

Samantha raises her eyebrows. She clears her throat. "Usually I'd ask how you two met, but I think I have a good idea of how that went. Luke doesn't give up when he wants something."

"I wanted it as much as he did."

Alyssa looks at me. Her eyes are on fire, but I don't know what to make of it.

"That isn't how I imagined it," Samantha says.

Alyssa pulls her gaze away from me. "Well, look at him. And the mouth on him. Jesus, he can talk some serious trash. Of course, he does back it up."

Samantha's jaw hits the floor. She struggles to compose

herself. "Yes, he does. And he's very... handsome. But you were engaged."

"You know what that's like, being with a man you don't love, trying to convince yourself you should love him, drifting through life like a zombie. Then you meet someone and you finally feel alive."

Samantha swallows hard. "But that was awfully cold on Luke's part. I mean, he knew you were engaged to his business partner and he still went after you."

Alyssa shrugs.

"I'm sure he didn't mean for it to go that far."

"I'd hope," Samantha says.

"It's not like he owed Ryan anything. It's not like they're family."

Jesus Christ. She's flat-out challenging Samantha. Maybe I should be annoyed—Alyssa isn't playing nice— but truth be told, I kind of like this side of her.

Samantha clears her throat. "Luke and Ryan never did get along. Back in law school, they argued all the time. And he was always complaining about that asshole who wouldn't stop sucking up to the teacher."

"It's a good business," I explain.

"You could have started it on your own," Samantha retorts.

"Yes, well, you both know Ryan," I say. "He made a very compelling argument for starting the firm together. And I would have been a fool to leave a business partner who was willing to put in eighty hours a week."

Alyssa runs her fingers over her menu. "Nothing Ryan loves more than work."

Samantha offers a fake smile. Anyone can see how fake it is.

She shakes her head and looks at Alyssa. "I already

know so much about this obnoxious man. I want to hear more about you. He's quite taken with you, you know."

Alyssa smiles. "Is he?"

"You should see the look he gets when you text him. And then he tries to hide it and apologize like I asked him not to have a life."

"Don't start," I say. It's true, technically, but it's only half the story. It's only the part where she pushes me away, not the part where she breaks down and asks me to stay, to spend the night holding her, apologizing again and again for how she ruined my life.

"I tried to tell him he should be spending his time with you. But you probably know how he is by now."

"I'm sure," Alyssa says.

"He's very stubborn."

She nods.

A silence falls over the table. These two might be dead set on derailing dinner, but I'm going to keep the conversation pleasant.

"Alyssa is an actress," I say.

Samantha struggles not to roll her eyes, but she manages. "I'm afraid I'm rather TV illiterate."

"She's also been in lots of films," I say.

"Not lots," Alyssa says.

"She's been nominated for an Independent Spirit Award."

"Luke, it's fine," Alyssa says. "I'm sure Samantha can brag plenty about her law career. We're both more than our jobs."

"No, I'm interested," Samantha says. "What are you doing now?"

"I'm the lead on this cable show. It's niche, but it's doing well."

"What show?"

"It's called *Model Citizen*," Alyssa says. "It's a silly premise. I'm an ex-model, and I have no self-control. Always going after something—trying to win a shopping spree, trying to scheme my ex-boyfriend out of his car, trying to sleep with the hot next-door neighbor."

"That sounds interesting," Samantha says.

She's usually better at pretending to be polite.

"It's work. I'm sure you do plenty of interesting work too."

"Not in particular."

"That's a shame," Alyssa says.

It's cold, even considering her distaste for Samantha. I can't blame her. Samantha isn't being quite as polite as she usually is.

I try to step in. "Alyssa is an avid reader. But she's mostly interested in fiction. None of that *Freakonomics* stuff you love so much."

Samantha looks at me. "Let me guess. You finally found someone else who adores John Grisham?"

"He's a best seller. Plenty of people adore him. I don't need my girlfriend to be one of them."

"But he's so overwrought. You're too smart for that bullshit," Samantha says. I know for a fact that she's a closet Dan Brown fan.

"Alyssa reads like an English major."

Alyssa shrugs, smiling.

"I enjoy it."

Samantha nods like she doesn't believe this. "Let me guess. You force her to watch those shitty TV shows you like. Like *Law and Order*."

"How dare you speak ill of Detective Lenny Briscoe."

"Which one is he?" Samantha asks.

Alyssa laughs. "He's the one with all the cheesy one-liners. And he's Luke's absolute favorite. So you better watch yourself McCoy."

"Huh?"

"Jack McCoy is the assistant district attorney. He's badass and he has fantastic eyebrows and gorgeous wrinkles. You know, the silver fox type." Alyssa folds her arms, smiling as she leans back in her chair.

Silver fox isn't the most subtle reminder that Samantha was fucking my father.

But it's effective. Samantha recoils. "Yes. I know the type. I'm just glad Luke found someone whose taste in TV is as bad as her taste in men."

It's too friendly. Too familiar. Alyssa keeps a smile on her face, but she's clearly uncomfortable. I catch her gaze. I mouth "are you okay?" She nods yes, and directs her attention back to Samantha.

There's something in Samantha's expression, something that shouldn't be there.

"Let's order," Alyssa says. "I'm starving."

Samantha nods, but there's a smugness to it, like she's won this round of conversation.

But she already has everything I can give her.

Chapter Twenty-Two

The rest of dinner goes similarly.

I hate to admit it, but I watch Alyssa carefully. She takes such timid bites, and she looks at her food with such trepidation.

It's the kind of thing she'd normally include on her dreadfully dull recovery diet—grilled salmon and vegetables.

She can't stand it. Every time she catches me looking at her, she sinks further into her head. I try to include her in my conversation with Samantha, but Samantha keeps dominating it with trips down memory lane.

We finish our meals, but Samantha insists on dessert.

"Come on, it's been forever since I've had dinner at a nice restaurant."

"You know I'm not a dessert person," I say.

"And you'll complain about the shitty tea they serve in about five minutes." She looks to Alyssa. "What about you, Alyssa? Do you like chocolate?"

Alyssa tries to smile but it's pained. "On occasion."

"Do you want to split a piece?"

"No thank you." Alyssa looks out the window. "I'm full."

I clear my throat and give Samantha a look that demands she drop it. She folds her arms like I'm the one being ridiculous.

The waiter returns and Samantha orders for herself. Chocolate cake with ice cream. Alyssa orders a coffee, frowning when the waiter explains the lack of almond milk.

Samantha turns up her nose like she finds Alyssa's milk preferences horrifying.

It's a little much. Samantha is from San Diego. There's no shortage of hippie food there. I'm sure she's used to people requesting almond milk. She orders a cappuccino. Whole milk. Like she's showing off somehow.

I bite my lip. I can take anything Samantha wants to throw at me. But if she even thinks about doing anything to push Alyssa...

It will be the last time she ever hears from me.

We make small talk while we wait for dessert. Samantha and Alyssa talk about nail polish and clothing, apparently the only things they have in common.

I watch their exchanges. They're both trying to be polite, but it feels forced.

The waiter returns.

Chocolate cake, ice cream, and three spoons. Of course.

Samantha digs in, moaning like she's in the middle of the world's most amazing sex. "You really should try it."

Alyssa shakes her head. She takes a quiet sip of her coffee. She's trying to act strong, but there's a nervousness in her eyes.

"Are you sure?" Samantha asks. "It's amazing."

"Sam, drop it," I say.

Samantha shrugs like it's nothing. Like she has no clue this is upsetting Alyssa.

I swear... if she's doing this on purpose...

It's not completely absurd. Rumors of Alyssa's eating disorder are only a Google search away.

But Samantha would never sink that low. And she has no motive.

Alyssa steals a sip of my tea. "Wow, that is awful."

"I told you."

"Why drink something you don't like? Why not hold out for what you really want?" Alyssa's eyes are on mine.

She's not asking the tea.

"I already have what I want," I say.

She blushes and turns her attention back to the window. So this dinner can't be all bad.

Samantha drops the subject of the cake. She eats the rest of it without offering more bites or complaining she has to eat it alone.

The rest of the dinner is polite. Talk about nothing. No argument when I insist on paying the bill. Samantha lingers a little long when she hugs me good-bye, but it's still well within the normal length of a hug from a friend.

It's nothing.

———

ALYSSA BEATS ME HOME. THE LIGHTS ARE OFF. SHE'S sitting on the couch cross-legged, her attention on the darkness engulfing the backyard.

"Ally..." I move towards her. Sit next to her on the couch. "What's wrong?"

She takes a deep breath and shakes her head. "I hate to sound like a cliché, but do you really have to ask?"

"Of course I—"

"I don't want to fight."

I try to take her hand but she pulls it away.

"What are you talking about?" I ask.

She moves off the couch. To the sliding door to the backyard—a big mass of glass blocking out the darkness.

"You can tell me anything," I say. "Even if it hurts."

But she shakes her head. She presses her palm against the glass of the door. "I'm not in the mood to have some stupid drawn-out conversation."

"Don't be so oblique."

Alyssa turns back to me. She looks beyond frustrated. "She's in love with you. Why can't you see it?"

"I..."

Have no idea what to say to that. Not that long ago, I would have said it was completely ridiculous.

Now...

Alyssa starts ticking off points when I don't have anything more to say.

"You visit her. You dote on her. You soak up all that need of hers. Why wouldn't she be in love with you?" She shakes her head. "You know what? I can't keep doing this."

I move towards her. She presses her back into the glass door. But when I wrap my arms around her, she melts. She squeezes me back.

I'm causing her this pain. I need to stop it.

I move my mouth over her ear. "I love you. Tell me what I can do to make this better and I'll do it."

"It's not about love."

She holds me closer. Tighter.

"Ally, let's talk about this."

"She's in love with you, Luke. You're playing her boyfriend and you're playing my therapist, and I can't do it anymore."

"I'm not."

She takes a deep breath, melting into me a little more. "You need to figure this out. Because I don't think I can be with you if you're always going to be running off to help her."

"She needs me."

"She manipulates you," she corrects. "She isn't your friend. Your friend would be polite to your girlfriend. Your friend wouldn't spend dinner trying to make your girlfriend jealous. And you think I didn't notice that bullshit with the chocolate cake?"

I sigh.

"Maybe."

"You might not realize this, since your private life isn't visible to anyone with an Internet connection—but she knew about my eating disorder. And she was obviously reveling in it."

Alyssa pushes me. It's soft. A *give me space* not a *get the fuck away*.

She shakes her head. "I'm sorry, Luke, but I need you too. At least, I want to. But every time I start to get that feeling in my chest, every time I start to let myself need you, I have to stop myself. I don't know if you'll be around or if you'll be off with her. I don't even know if you'll keep your promises or if you'll be too busy conceding to what she wants." I take a deep breath, but it only makes the ground feel further away. It only makes this feel more impossible.

Alyssa is pulling away. I have to do something.

But I can't abandon Samantha. Ending our friendship could push her over the edge again. I move towards Alyssa again, wrap my arms around her again.

But there's a coldness to it. She's already made up her mind.

She's already somewhere else.

"Alyssa, please. I want to be with you."

"Until when? What if she tries to kill herself again? Will you be by her side again?"

"She's my friend."

"Yeah," she says. "She's your friend. And, if she gets her way, she'll be your girlfriend, so she can keep leaning on you forever."

"Ally..."

"I want to be with you too, Luke, but not like this. Not if you're always going to rush off to save her." She steps away, her back pressed against the glass. "I need some space. To think about this... to figure out if I can really handle it."

"I thought we were done with space."

"Me too."

She moves away from me, towards the couch, towards the other side of the room. She picks up her purse and hugs it to her chest.

"I want to help you through everything you're dealing with," I say. "You shouldn't have to do it alone."

She shakes her head. "I'm sorry, but I can't. Not if you keep trying to save her."

"Let's talk about this."

Alyssa shakes her head, hugging her purse tighter and tighter. "Are you still her friend?"

"That doesn't matter."

"And are you still going to insist she needs your help?"

"She does."

"Then no," Alyssa says. "We can't talk about it. Because any conversation I'm going to have is going to include some kind of ultimatum." She moves away from the door.

Her voice is a whisper. "I sat back idly while you went to rescue her. And really, I was okay with it, because it's who you are. You care too much and you want to help people. But this has gone too far. I'm losing you."

"You'll never lose me."

She shakes her head. "For all intents and purposes, you're her boyfriend. And I'm not going to share you."

"Alyssa..."

"I want to be with you. But not like this." She repeats, taking another step towards the door. "Think about it, okay? Because I'm going to get some breathing room, and I'm going to figure out exactly what I want. And when I come back, I expect you to know what you want too."

"I know what I want. I want you."

She shakes her head. "But you want to help her too. Think about it, okay? When I do this, I want to do it all the way."

"Alyssa... stay."

"I'm sorry," she says. "I love you. I hope you can figure this out." She steps out the door.

And that's it.

The color drains from the room. It's cold and gray and there's no rhyme or reason to any of it anymore.

Chapter Twenty-Three

I t was hard before, when Alyssa didn't immediately choose me.

It was unfair of me to give her an ultimatum, but I couldn't help it. My stomach twisted in knots every time I thought of her with Ryan. I know it's a dick move to start an affair with an engaged woman then get mad at her for being engaged, but I really didn't mean to fall in love with her.

I never thought things would get that far.

That day, three or four months ago, I pressed her to finally leave Ryan. She recoiled. She wasn't ready.

Even though it killed me, I understood. I understand better now, actually. She really believed she'd fall apart if she left him. That she'd spiral back into her mostly recovered bulimia without him around to keep her in line.

It was a punch in the gut, but it was nothing like this. I drag myself out of bed every morning. I stare at the electric kettle in the kitchen, barely able to force myself to find the teaspoon, to scoop Early Grey into the damn plastic tea maker. I stand there as the microwave timer counts down from five minutes, and I stare at the water as it mixes with the tea, becoming a darker and darker shade of brown.

Alyssa is gone.

It takes all the willpower I have not to call her every morning. She wants space. I have to give her space. I still have a chance. It's a tiny piece of hope.

She wants to be with me. She said she wants to be with me. Just not like this.

I have to show her she always comes first.

I push back another thought—that sting that screams that I have to choose. I can either repay my debt to Samantha, help her out of the mess I put her in and lose Alyssa, or I can abandon her and choose Alyssa.

There has to be another way.

Work is agony.

I am lost in my meetings. Some other version of me takes over. He is the charming, flirty man all my clients love. He woos them, compliments them, promises them everything they deserve. And then I am back to my zombie self, moving through prenuptial agreements and settlements as if I am simply entering data.

And I am. It's all the same.

Even Ryan can't rattle me. He must not know Alyssa is taking space again, because he doesn't gloat or brag. He just offers once again to buy out my half of the business.

But he's living in a fantasy.

He's not getting anything from me. Not anything but a punch in the fucking face.

After work, I run. I run and I run and I run some more, until my heart is pounding and my legs are shaking. Until the sky is dark, and I have no idea where I am. Then I turn around, and I run back to that stupid condo, and I stand in the kitchen, not paying much attention as I somehow conjure up a dinner.

The nights are the worst.

I'm parked on the couch for hours. I try watching every TV show I've ever enjoyed, but none of them stir me.

I have a drink, or two, or three, but it only makes me sink deeper into this ugly, gray feeling.

I have to give her space, no matter how much it hurts.

So, instead of calling Alyssa and begging her to hear me out—that won't work, not like this—I call Laurie.

She answers with a triumphant, "Uh-huh."

I can see her smirking, her eyes glowing behind her bright red glasses.

"Well, if it isn't Mr. Hot Lawyer," she says.

I try to fight a sarcastic response. "Those are my only two distinguishing characteristics?"

"No, there's three. Hot. Lawyer. And asshole who upsets Alyssa..."

"How is she doing?" I ask.

"She was upset for a few days—you know, hiding out in her room and reading, drinking fifty iced lattes in a row."

"Did she talk to you about it?"

Laurie scoffs. "What do you think?"

I rub my face. "She wants space. I just want to know if she's okay."

Laurie sighs. "Listen, Luke, I'll be straight with you. I like you. You're... different. And you're very attractive, and I can tell Alyssa appreciates that. And I think it's good for her to have a boyfriend who isn't in TV. We're fucking crazy, and we need saner partners to help even us out."

"Laurie—"

"I'm still talking." She clears her throat. "I like you. A lot of things about you are good for Alyssa. You help pull her out of her head, you know? And she really needs that."

I like where this is going, but I can sense that "but" coming.

"Thanks," I mutter.

"And, when things are good with you two... I've never seen her that happy."

"That's all I want."

"Yeah, me too. Well, for Alyssa." She pauses. "But, when things aren't good with you two, she's utterly miserable. She's despondent. She mopes when you're gone for more than a day or two. She'd deny it, but she does."

"Really?"

"Yeah, she's gotten better. Going to her acting classes, entertaining my dumb ideas about how to get out of the house. She's even taking art classes. Painting or something."

"She didn't tell me."

"Well, you should have asked."

"How is she doing right now?"

"She's okay," Laurie says. "She's staying busy."

"Did she say anything about me?"

"Are you kidding? You're all we talk about." She laughs at her own joke.

It's business as usual.

"Laurie—"

"No, she hasn't said anything. I asked her what was wrong, but she shrugged and said she didn't want to talk about it. I asked how things were with you and she, can you guess—"

"Said she didn't want to talk about it?"

"Bingo!" Her voice drops to a more serious tone. "What happened, anyway?"

"Honestly? I'm not exactly sure."

"Don't be such a fucking guy," she says. "I'm sure you

know. You probably just don't want to admit you were wrong."

"It's complicated."

"I'm sure you did something. I can tell you are this nexus of drama. It swirls around you. I mean, you did intentionally start an affair. And you did break up with her when she was on set." Laurie clears her throat. "And if you do anything like that again, I really will kill you. No one fucks up my show."

"Can you tell me anything?" I ask.

"No way," Laurie says. "I'm not stepping into that drama hurricane. I'm sure she has her reasons, and I'm sure you have your reasons. There's no way I can help you with this."

"Fuck. I know." I let out a breath, resting my head against the wall. "I just hate being away from her."

"Yeah, we all know you're desperately in love." She says it with such annoyance. She's probably rolling her eyes as we speak.

"What the fuck is that?"

"Hey! I'm the closest thing you have to an ally. Don't be rude."

"Okay. Ms. House, can you explain your hostility?"

"That's better," she says. "You don't listen. I just told you that you're not the only person in the world who feels things. You're not the only person in the world who loves people or has needs. I know you care about Alyssa. I know you want her to be okay. And I definitely know you love her and want to be with her."

"But?"

"But you need to listen to her."

"She's told you something," I say.

"Maybe." Laurie's voice gets serious. "But I'm sworn to secrecy. And, like I said, I'm not interested in the drama hurricane. No offense, Loverboy, but I'm much more invested in Alyssa's well-being than I am in yours."

"I'm sure there's a way I can tempt you."

"Not unless you can get Fox to offer me seven figures for my latest pilot." She laughs at her own joke, but there is an edge to it. She really is worried about Alyssa.

Maybe Laurie and I can be on the same team. We do have a common goal.

"We both want Alyssa to be happy," I say.

I wait for Laurie's response.

She takes a slow breath. "I'm listening. My patience is running out, but I'm listening."

"And we can both agree that she's happy when she's with me."

"Usually."

"So, don't you think that helping me here would lead to Alyssa's happiness?"

"You can't logic me into helping you. But apparently," she sighs, "apparently, you can inspire enough pity to get me to help you."

"So?"

"So, you need to listen to your girlfriend. She wants this to work. And I know for a fact that she told you exactly what she needs to make this work."

"You mean..." Deep breath. If Laurie doesn't know about Samantha, she'll freak out at the news. And I might have lost my only ally. But it's a risk I have to take. "You mean Samantha?"

"Yes, I mean your manipulative ex."

I'm not detecting much in the way of sympathy here. "Okay."

"So listen to what Alyssa wants and do the intelligent thing. And then give her some time. She's dealing with a lot. No thanks to me. I've been a little crazy about the show, and she's going to do a movie next week."

"She is?"

"She didn't tell you?"

"No," I say.

"Hmm... she probably signed on after this space thing. But it's good. She's excited about it."

I press the phone into my ear. "Do you think you can talk to her?"

"And do what?"

"Make sure she's doing okay."

"No way," Laurie says. "I'm not getting in between you two."

"Don't," I say. "Just make sure she's okay."

"Don't be such a guy. Talk to her. I'm sure there's a little more to this than your ex."

What?

"Laurie—"

"Okay, maybe I invented a little backstory in my head. But it was exciting to imagine some kind of crazy fight." She takes a deep breath. "Alyssa is a really reasonable person. I don't think she would leave you hanging if she didn't believe she had to."

I thunk my head against the wall.

"Yeah."

"Maybe I'm wrong and it's just the ex. And all you need to do is cut ties and you'll be okay."

"You sure she didn't say anything?"

"Yeah." Her voice gets higher, reassuring. "But you're a smart guy. I'm sure you can figure it out. Think about what you did, admit you fucked things up, and then unfuck them. Or at least send her some sexy pics or something. You need to use your assets to your advantage."

"Sage words."

"I know," she says. "I should write an advice column."

"Thanks, Laurie."

"Don't fuck it up any worse," she says. And she hangs up the phone.

It's not the most comforting suggestion.

But it's fair enough advice.

Chapter Twenty-Four

The next week is less painful.

I call Alyssa, not to impose, but to let her know she can talk to me. If she needs to. That I'm here, always. She thanks me, and tells me about her two-week film shoot in Vancouver.

"It's enough time for both of us to think this through," she says. "I'm going to leave my phone at home. I need time to air out my thoughts."

"Oh." I try not to make much of it.

"But Laurie has the number of my hotel. You can call her if there's an emergency."

"Okay." I suck the air between my teeth. If I push her, I'll lose her. I have to wait this out.

"I love you," she says. "I hope we can work this out."

"I love you too."

The air hangs between us for a minute. It's almost like we're close, almost like things are okay. "I'll see you soon," she says. "Take care of yourself."

"I'll miss you," I say.

"I'll miss you too." And even though the call fades to an end, it feels so painful and abrupt.

It's a good thing that she's taking time to think.

It's time for me to figure out how to unfuck this.

———

I BURY MYSELF IN WORK AND SHUT OUT EVERYTHING ELSE IN the world.

There are two weeks until Alyssa is back in Los Angeles.

But Samantha calls me every night. I text her that I'm at work. She resorts to begging. To her familiar guilt trips. *I really want to see you. I don't know what I'll do if I have to spend the night alone.*

I lock my phone in my desk and resolve not to reply. I ignore my phone all weekend. I run. I watch TV. I pack up the house—another thing Samantha is getting.

But I can't sleep. I've never had an easy time sleeping, but this is worse.

I close my eyes and there it is—the first time I ran to her side, the first time she tried to kill herself. It was about a year ago now. We were practically but not technically broken up. I wasn't even staying at the house. I was staying with a friend.

And then I got a call from the hospital.

It was just like it was this time—a calm voice explaining that she was in the ER. That time, maybe this time too, she called 9-1-1.

I try to remember a time when I loved her as an adult. But every happy memory I have of us is tainted.

That dinner after graduation, where I thought we had everything we'd ever need. My father was there, and she was falling in love with him.

This has been bullshit for so long. It's one thing for me to take on this burden.

But I can't let this ruin things for Alyssa. For us.

It's late Sunday when I respond to Samantha's texts. She's still up and she responds with a dozen smiley faces.

We agree to meet for dinner. To discuss the details of the move. She wants to come here. To scope out the house.

She's rubbing it in my fucking face.

———

SAMANTHA INVITES HERSELF OVER.

I make excuses, but she resorts to begging. Finally, I can't take it anymore and agree.

Truth be told, I've been avoiding her.

She's jealous.

I've denied it for a long time. It's not like Samantha to be jealous, and she did everything she could to throw me away. She's broken down crying a hundred times, apologized for leading me on, for never really loving me.

Is the change simply because she thinks she can't have me now?

I tell her to come by on Friday evening. We can sort out all the details of the mortgage. She can start salivating looking at the house that's going to be hers.

She arrives late. It's already dark and the only lights on are the fluorescent ones in the kitchen.

The door is open and she enters without knocking.

She looks like she's ready for a date—heels, designer dress, enough makeup I notice it.

My stomach drops. If she thinks she's going to impress me, she has the wrong idea.

"The place looks great." She offers a bottle of Cabernet like it's an amazing gift.

We both know she'll drink the whole thing.

"Did you eat?" she asks.

"Yeah."

"Oh." She frowns. She probably wants to make this a long dinner. "I guess we'll just have drinks."

I find the corkscrew and open the bottle of wine. Its rich, fruity smell wafts through the apartment.

"Luke." Her voice is low, like she's worried. "Are you okay?"

I nod.

As far as Samantha knows, everything is perfect between me and Alyssa. But if she really is jealous, if she really is in love with me... she'll be happy that Alyssa asked for space. She'll be happy that I'm losing the most important thing in my life.

I pour two glasses of wine and take a seat at the kitchen table. Samantha slips out of her heels and sits across from me.

Her eyes are fixed on me. "I have exciting news."

Please let it be that she has a boyfriend, something that will assuage the uneasiness filling my gut.

"What's that?" I ask.

"I got the job." Her face lights up with a smile. "Are you happy for me?"

"Of course."

She brings her glass to mine. It's time to toast. I am happy for her, but I'm happier for me.

A job is the first step to Samantha moving on with her life, to her needing me less.

"That's great." I take a long sip of the wine.

"I'm starting Monday. I couldn't have done it without you." She sets her glass on the table. "I wouldn't even be here without you."

"Yeah."

Samantha brings her gaze to me. She's happy. But something... isn't right.

Her gaze softens. "What's wrong?"

I shake my head. "Nothing."

"Please, I'd love to hear about anything except for the pathetic failure that is my life."

"You're not a pathetic failure," I say, but there's no meaning behind it. It's rote.

"Thanks. I was just... there's something bothering you." Samantha clears her throat. The joy on her face turns to something ugly. Just for a split second. But I catch it. "Is it about your girlfriend?"

She looks so earnest, but I know it's all bullshit. "You weren't very polite at dinner."

"I was trying to make conversation."

"And the cake?"

She shrinks back. "I ate some cake. Is that a crime?"

"Look me in the eyes and swear you didn't know about Alyssa's history with an eating disorder."

Her eyes turn to the floor. "I didn't know it was still a problem."

Her voice doesn't waver. But I don't buy it.

She polishes off her glass and refills it. "Why would I try to hurt her? What problem could I possibly have with your girlfriend?" It's a stupid question, and it doesn't merit an answer.

"Please don't make me choose between you," I say instead. "I'm not going to choose you."

"Choose what?" she asks, deliberately playing dumb. "Luke, you're my best friend. I'm happy you're happy."

"Then why all the trips down memory lane? Were you trying to make her jealous?"

"No!" she pushes back. "I only wanted to revisit a few

nice memories. I want to be friends with her. I want you to be with her. I want you to be happy."

They're the right words. But they don't sound smooth and easy.

She swallows hard. She's not selling it well.

"Alyssa asked for space."

It's a test.

My eyes are glued to Samantha. If she has any feelings about this, I'm going to catch them. She's not going to bull-shit me again.

"Oh, I'm sorry to hear that." She takes a careful sip from her glass, her eyes on the floor. "What happened?"

"It's kind of complicated," I say. "But mostly, I think... she's not really comfortable with our friendship."

"What's there to be uncomfortable about?"

I take a deep breath. I don't want to push Samantha this hard, but I have to know where things stand. "She thinks you have feelings for me."

"Oh." She presses her fingers into the glass. "I told you to go back to Los Angeles to be with her."

We make eye contact for a moment. There's some-thing she wants to say, but she's keeping it locked inside.

"You needed help," I say. "I couldn't have left you in that hospital alone."

She turns her attention to her wine glass. "Well, I'm sure it hurts. But... maybe it's for the best."

I grit my teeth. I'm tempted to kick her out of the house.

"For the best how?" I ask.

"Well, she was with Ryan. Aren't you the rebound guy?" She looks away. "I mean, she seems nice and smart and she's very pretty. But maybe you two aren't meant for forever. Maybe you're meant as a fling."

I try to swallow all the anger that bubbles up from my gut.

Samantha looks away. "Forget I said anything. It doesn't matter what I think. It only matters how you feel." She brings her gaze to mine. I search for intention in her eyes, but I still come up empty. "Do you really see a future with her? It's not like you can't find another pretty girl."

"Fuck you."

The words spill out without conscious thought.

But I mean them.

"Sorry." She clears her throat. "I didn't mean it like that. But you have to admit how it looks."

It's always about how it looks with her, isn't it? It must be why she can't bring herself to hate Edward the way I do. Because even though she loved him, she understood that he couldn't be with her.

Because it just wouldn't fucking look right.

"I love her," I say when I've found some control. "And I want to be with her forever if she'll allow it."

"That's great," she mutters. She tries to maintain her poker face, but it's fading fast. She looks at her cell phone.

"Does that bother you?"

"Of course not. I've told you a million times. I want you to be happy. I want you to move on." She shakes her head, presses her lips together. "Excuse me for a minute."

She moves into the bathroom. Her gait is calm. It's almost like she's normal. Like she only needs to fetch something in the other room.

I could leave her in there. Let her figure this out on her own for once, damn the consequences. She's an adult. She should be able to manage one of her contained fits.

But there are prescriptions in the medicine cabinet, and I can't trust her not to take them.

I knock on the bathroom door. "Go away."

"Talk to me."

"No. I'm only making your life harder."

"At least tell me what's wrong."

"It's nothing," she says. "I'm just a little stressed out. It's nothing."

I open the door. She's sitting on the tub, wiping a tear from her eyes. "But I'm getting in the way of your happiness. You love her and you want to be with her, and I'm a problem."

I want to tell her she's right. I want to tell her she brought this on herself. I begged her to stay, but she was done with me. She was so done with me, she'd sooner pine after a dead asshole than spend a single moment in my presence.

She was done with me, and I moved on. And I finally found someone who made me happy.

And now she's jealous.

I want to tell her to go fuck herself, to get over it, to stop being such a selfish bitch.

But I can't.

She clings to me, crying into my suit jacket. She doesn't explain what's wrong. She doesn't have to.

Alyssa was right.

Samantha is in love with me.

When she finally calms down, she wipes her makeup from her eyes. She looks so desperate.

I know I shouldn't try and make her say it, but I need to hear the words. I need her to admit it, so I can know for sure.

"Tell me what's wrong," I say. "Tell me why this upsets you."

Her voice is a low whimper. "Don't make me."

"Please. I need to know the truth."

"What difference does it make?" she asks. "You're in love, and I want you to be happy."

"You don't."

She doesn't deny it.

"I want to. I've done enough to ruin your life. I've done so much to hurt you, Luke. I can't burden you with this too."

"I can take it."

She shakes her head. "I had the right idea before. I'm causing you pain. You're the only person who cares about me, and I'm causing you pain."

"Sam..."

"You shouldn't have come to San Diego. You should have left me alone in that hospital with my thoughts. You should leave me alone now."

"I wanted to be there for you."

"Just go away! This is what I deserve!"

I bite my tongue. She's too old to have these kinds of tantrums.

The platitudes stick in my throat this time.

I can't get the empty words out.

All I can give is my physical presence.

She clings to me, crying until she's utterly spent.

Chapter Twenty-Five

Alyssa is back in L.A.

She texts me. It's not much, little how are you's and I miss yous, but it morphs into full conversations.

They're about nothing important.

She tells me about her film role.

It's a romantic comedy, she texts. *I'm the best friend. I've never been the best friend before, only the girlfriend. It was nice not having to do any heavy lifting. Just nodding and bouncing off the friend who is the star. I even get my own little subplot. My own love interest—the guy's best friend. God, I can't believe I took something so cliché. It's well done, I swear.*

And I tease her about unplugging from technology. *What were you doing when you were off? You know you're not Henry David Thoreau. The world won't appreciate a new version of Walden. There are important things on Tumblr you missed! People are upset about a new Disney movie appropriating other cultures. I tried talking about it with one of my clients, but she stared at me like I was crazy. I think she was picturing me naked.*

She responds. *Very likely. I mean, it can be tough with you looking all professional in that suit. You look so suave and accomplished. So respectable. But I'm sure she's motivated. She's probably in love with you. They're all in love with you, aren't they?*

I respond. *A little.*

I can't blame them. If you were holding my hand, fighting to take everything from my awful ex, and looking at me with those big, pretty eyes.

The eyes again?

She replies. *What can I say? They're fucking gorgeous. I get lost in them. And when you smile—forget about it. I think you had me the first time you smiled. I wanted to see that a million more times.*

Even though you were engaged to Ryan?

We both know you were only talking with me to make him jealous.

I reply. *Or maybe I wanted to get a better look at the famous Alyssa Summers.*

Only I'm not famous.

Well, maybe it was because you're so fucking gorgeous. Maybe you turned my stomach inside out and I wanted to take every chance I could to be near you.

She replies. *I'm sure there was some of that. But mostly it was to fuck with him, right?*

Maybe.

I knew it! You little shit! I can't believe you. Actually, I can completely believe you. You do realize that you're completely deranged, don't you?

I reply. *Guilty as charged. It's true. I did talk to you at first to fuck with him. But once I got to know you, hell, after that first conversation, it was all about you.*

Yeah, me too. I'm sorry it took me so long to figure it out.

I should have been more patient. I love you Ally. I miss you.

I miss you too.

Tell me everything about the movie. I don't care if it seems boring. I want to hear it.

She replies. *We shot a lot of scenes in what was supposed to be my character's apartment. It was so cramped, and it was decorated in this awful mix of teal and salmon. You wouldn't believe the clothes wardrobe put me in. In this one scene, I was wearing a petticoat.*

That sounds amazing.

It was kind of amazing. Even if it was light, I enjoyed it. It was nice to have a little more fun with acting. I forgot about that for a little while, getting so stressed out about Model Citizen premiering. I think I'm finally getting back in the swing of things.

I respond. *I'm glad.*

It was good to get out of my head for a little while. To get away from everything.

So you didn't think about things?

Not yet... Can we just talk for now? About anything besides the future?

I respond. *Okay. As long as we'll get to the future eventually.*

We will. How are things? How is Samantha?

I'm awful, but I'm managing. Ryan is driving me crazy. He keeps offering to buy out my half of the business, but I don't want to give it to him.

She replies. *You should. You have plenty of money. You can start over. He can be out of our lives permanently.*

Yeah, but... I'll think about it. I've been reading a little. This cultural studies book about Starbucks's branding.

Really?

I used to read that kind of thing all the time. All these things you wouldn't think end up being true. Like the drinks being expensive is part of what adds to the experience. It makes it feel like a treat.

I'd never consider that.

I reply. *I hate to admit it, but I haven't been doing great without you. I can't stop thinking about you. I don't want to pressure you. I really want you to have as much time and space as you need, but I'm going crazy feeling like I fucked things up. Like everything is ruined.*

It's not, I promise. But can we save that kind of heavy stuff for later? I want to talk to you and remember how happy you can make me.

You should come over. We'll watch Monk and take tequila shots.

So we can argue over which assistant is better?

Yeah, I like arguing with you. You're passionate.

She replies. *I can't believe you don't like The Philadelphia Story.*

I'm sorry, but I don't find jokes about domestic violence humorous.

It's a product of the times.

Still.

You're impossible.

I'll buy you a hundred lattes. With almond milk and honey. I'll buy an apartment over a coffee shop, and pay off a barista to deliver the coffee to us in bed.

What if he walks in on us having sex?

I reply. *We'll make a little "Do Not Disturb" sign for the door.*

That will only encourage him.

So we'll let him watch. It could be part of his payment.

And then we'll make out with nasty coffee breath?

Your breath is never nasty.

I appreciate the lies. But first thing in the morning? Forget about it.

I reply. *Uh-huh. It's still fine. Even after three coffees. There's so much honey in them, that's all you taste like. Honey. I swear, sometimes I can't drink a cup of tea without thinking of you. Because of that faint taste of honey. It's so Alyssa. It's warm and sweet. Really, tea is the second-best thing in the world.*

After Law and Order?

After you, silly.

She replies. *Sorry, but you're third at the very best. A distant third after coffee and tequila.*

Please. You would absolutely rate your Kindle above me. That puts me in fourth at best.

Yeah, I forgot about my Kindle. You're right. Fourth. But you know, tea has been growing on me. I might have to push you back to fifth place.

What about acting? Shouldn't that go before me?

Yeah, I guess it should. But we better stop before you're out of the top 10.

I love you.

I love you too.

Tell me what you need, Ally, and I'll do it. I want to make this right.

You will. I just need more time.

Do you think you want to look for apartments with me? No pressure. I just need a feminine opinion.

Maybe in a little while. Not yet.

Okay. Well, you're welcome in the condo anytime. Even if it's to look through my things without my permission.

Hey, I thought we were over that.

I am. I just... if you need to talk, call. I'll shut my pretty mouth and listen.

God, it is a pretty mouth.

I miss you.

I miss you too.

And our conversation bleeds into my week. Every beep of a new message immediately draws my attention.

Alyssa may not be all mine yet. But she will be soon.

———

IT'S THE MIDDLE OF THE AFTERNOON WHEN ALYSSA CALLS.

"Hey," I answer.

"Can I come over?" Her voice is low, breathy.

Damn. There's no way I'm getting out of my meeting. I'll never hear the end of it from Ryan.

But I can duck out early.

Hell, I don't have much of a choice when she asks like that.

"Of course," I say. "But I packed up most of the house. I'm staying at the condo."

"Do you want to talk about it?"

"No."

She takes a deep breath. "I hate to call you about this. I know it's not fair. I asked for space and I don't want to drag you around." There's fear in her voice.

Something is wrong. "Ally, are you okay?"

"Yeah." She takes a deep breath. "I don't want to talk about it yet. I just want to be around you. To talk about nothing and drink too much coffee and watch some bad TV show."

"Of course."

"I'm going to leave soon. With traffic, I'll probably be there in an hour."

"I have a meeting."

"Go to it. I'll make myself comfortable."

"Comfortable how?"

"Do you mind being used as a distraction?" she asks.

I swallow hard. I like the thought of Alyssa getting comfortable in my bed, sliding off her clothes, draping herself over the sheets. Part of me is satisfied by it.

But I want all of her, not just her admittedly amazing body.

Still. This is what Alyssa wants. And it's tempting. Just imagining her on the couch, a coy smile on her face, her dress trailing up her legs—my blood starts to flow downward.

"Whatever you want," I say.

I hang up.

And just as my head is filling with all sorts of delicious ideas, there's a knock on the door.

Ryan.

He enters with his usual smug look and folds his hands.

"I spoke to Mrs. Pike again," he says.

I shake my head.

I'm not letting Ryan get to me. Not today.

"Yes?"

"She asked me to represent her." He tries to play it cool, like this isn't the best news he's heard all week.

"Sounds like she found what she wanted."

"I'm sorry, Luke. But I'm sure it's not personal."

"Fine. I have someplace to be. Do you think you could —" I motion for him to leave.

But he stays put. "Don't you have a consult in twenty minutes?"

"And I have twenty minutes of work between now and that."

He shakes his head. "If you want to stay in this firm, you need to listen to what your clients want."

"Yes, we established that Mrs. Pike prefers whatever it is that you promised her. If you don't have anything to add, I have things to do."

"I hope you have more planned for this consult than a little flirting."

"I've got it covered."

He plants his palms on my desk like it's his. "I don't want to clean up any more of your messes. And I don't want to have to take any more of your meetings or counsel any of your clients."

I unclench my fists. It would feel great to punch Ryan in his smug face, but I have something much better waiting for me. I offer him my most polite smile. "It sounds like you should agree to dissolving the firm."

Ryan looks at me with pity. "You'll never survive alone. Your charm gets you far, but it's not enough."

"And it won't be your problem anymore."

Ryan looks at me closely. I could swear there's something human about him. Something vulnerable.

"I'd still be happy to buy you out," he says.

I say the unthinkable. "I'll consider it."

It won't kill me to let Ryan win this one time.

Not if I have Alyssa.

Chapter Twenty-Six

Alyssa is reading in the bedroom, of course.

Her dress is hiked up her thigh. The straps are falling off her shoulders. She acts like she doesn't hear me come in, even as she deliberately shrugs her straps completely off her shoulders.

"I didn't realize you loved your Kindle that much," I say.

She smirks, turning to look at me. "We do this kind of thing all the time." She puts it aside, clearing enough space on the bed for me.

She shifts again, her dress sliding down her body, clinging to her.

Fuck, she's not wearing a bra.

I stare at the way the fabric sticks to her skin, creating a perfect outline of her breasts.

Her nipples are already hard.

She nods to a neat pile on the floor—her bra and panties. There's nothing under that dress but Alyssa.

She shifts to her side, trailing her fingers over the curve of her hips.

Her eyes are on fire.

She looks like she wants to devour me, like she's never wanted anything more than she wants me.

"I had an idea," she murmurs. She doesn't break eye contact as she reaches for a jar of honey on the bedside table.

Damn. That's an idea I can get behind.

Any doubts I had are gone.

Right now, I don't need to talk. I need to feel her and taste her and put my mouth on every part of her. I need her in every way I can have her.

A warmth spreads over me as blood flows to my cock.

I'm on fire. I need all of her and I need it now.

I move towards her. But she shakes her head.

"Not yet. I want you to watch first." She bites her lip as she shimmies out of her dress.

It falls to her waist, exposing her perfect tits. She runs her hands over them, her fingers making small indentations in the soft skin.

Closing her eyes, she lets her fingers drift lower.

It's so intimate and vulnerable, like she's inviting me into her world.

A world I definitely want to be in. Her tongue slides over her lips, her fingertips drawing circles over her firm little nipples.

She opens her eyes and looks at me.

It's an invitation.

No more waiting.

I grab her hips and push her onto the bed. Her legs part, and I'm on top of her, pinning her to the bed. She squeezes me with her thighs, and I sink into the sweet pressure of her body enveloping mine.

She holds my gaze for a moment. It's pure want. Pure need.

Then her hands are in my hair, another sweet pressure. She's tugging and pulling my head towards her mouth all at once.

Her mouth hovers over my ear, her breath hot and wet. Shivers run through my body.

I need to rip her clothes off and get my cock inside her.

She whispers. "This is going to be payback for every time you tortured me." She runs her tongue around my ear.

It's so light and soft. My body floods with want.

I grip her tighter, digging my fingers into the soft skin of her hips.

I need to grab those hips and pin her to the bed and fuck her until we come together.

Alyssa wraps her hands around my wrists. She pushes me onto the bed like I'm her toy.

I want to be her fucking toy.

Her teeth scrape against my earlobe. Harder.

She slings her legs over my hips, straddling me. Her crotch is pressed against mine. There's nothing under the dress.

The only thing between us is my slacks, my boxers.

It's still too much. I drag my fingertips along her thighs. She shudders, a soft groan escaping her lips.

But she grabs my wrists and presses them against the bed. "Patience, Luke."

She smirks. Clearly enjoying torturing me the way I always torture her.

She plants her hands next to my shoulders, leans down, and presses her lips to mine. Her kiss is so hot and electric, the agony we've worked up in the last few weeks pouring between us.

She takes my hand and sticks my index finger into the sticky jar of honey. She brings my finger to her mouth and licks around the edges, a low groan passing through her lips. Then her entire mouth is on my finger, and she sucks off every last bit of honey. Her tongue is so soft and wet and it hits every nerve in my innocent fingertip.

Jesus.

She kisses me again, probing gently with her tongue.

Then she dips her finger into the jar. Leans back. And she traces the outline of my lips. Her touch is soft and hot. I need more.

I grab her wrist, slide her finger into my mouth, and suck hard. It's such a sweet mix—the honey and her skin—and she closes her eyes at the feeling.

We lock eyes when she opens hers once more.

I expect her to beg me to release her from the torture, but she says nothing.

She dips my finger back into the jar and brings it to her chest. I run my fingertip over her nipple, spreading the honey over the tight point.

Then I bring my mouth to her.

I lick her slowly. It's sticky and sweet, and I can't stop myself from licking every drop, until it's just my mouth closing in on her firm flesh. It's so luscious, the pressure of her against my mouth as I suck harder and harder.

She tilts her head back in ecstasy, moaning through her teeth.

Mhmm.

I flick my tongue against her again and again, shallow strokes that drive her wild.

She digs her hands into my hair, her body convulsing.

And I do it again—another sweet dab of honey on her nipple. I retrace my finger's motions with my tongue, sucking harder the louder she gets.

When I finally bring my lips back to hers, she kisses me

so hard and fast I can't breathe. It's pure need, pure lust, a *fuck me now* without the hassle of vocalizing the words.

I inhale the feeling of the kiss. Everything inside her is pouring into me, and everything inside of me is pouring into her.

I need her so badly I'm shaking.

I shove her dress to her knees and dig my hands into her hair.

She tugs at my shirt. "Stupid fucking buttons."

She manages to undo most of them and pushes it off my shoulders. Her eyes pass over me slowly, her expression filling with delight.

I love the way she looks at me. Like she wants to consume me. Like I'm the hottest thing she's ever seen.

We kiss again, and it's still hard and fast, but there's something soft and sweet about it too. There's a need, a vulnerability.

We're both lost in this moment.

She shifts back, rubbing her crotch against mine, squeezing me with her thighs. Her eyes connect with mine and she smiles.

It's devilish, a promise.

She presses my shoulders against the bed. I relax.

I'm hers now. I'm not about to deny her whatever she wants.

She drags her fingers across my chest and stomach.

"Mhmm." She undoes my belt and unzips my slacks.

Then it's her hands rubbing me over my boxers. Fuck.

Any remaining blood flees from my brain. I can't think anymore. There's nothing in this moment but Alyssa.

She's on top of me, her dress around her waist, her eyes lit up with lust, her tongue sliding over her lips. She pulls her dress over her head. And then she strokes me.

The ache inside me grows. Warmth floods my body.

Her eyes connect with mine. She shifts off me and pulls my slacks to my knees. Then my boxers.

She reaches for the jar of honey.

She dips her finger in the pot and runs it along my cock. Then she's perched in front of me on all fours, her eyes glued to mine as she slides her tongue over me.

Jesus.

Her tongue is soft and flat, and it sends sparks through my body. An ache builds inside me. It burns deeper and harder as she licks me up and down.

She laps up every last drop of honey and her mouth closes around my cock. She moans, sucking harder and harder. She feels so good, so wet, and there's so much desire in her eyes. I can barely take it. I dig my hands into her hair, run my fingertips over her chest, anything to make her feel as good as I feel.

She moans, sucking harder and harder. I knead her breasts, run my fingers over her nipples. She closes her eyes, groaning again. She drags her nails against my thighs. It's the slightest hint of pain, a sweet, soft hurt.

She shifts off me, wraps one hand around my cock and sinks her teeth into my thigh. Damn. I squeeze her nipples, reveling in her soft groan, in her eyes closing in ecstasy.

She sinks her teeth into my thigh again. Harder. I squeeze her. Harder.

"Fuck." She moans. Her eyes find mine. A *you're going to pay for that* look.

She drags her lips up my thigh, kissing and nibbling, her mouth getting closer and closer to me. Almost... almost...

And then she brings her lips to my cock. It's such a soft and light pressure. The ache builds. She is torturing me. And expertly. It feels so fucking good. I can barely take it.

She grips me hard and flicks her tongue against me. Jesus. She does it again and again. I squeeze her nipples harder.

She groans, vibrating all around me.

"Fuck, Alyssa," I moan.

She envelopes me with her mouth. It's such a sweet pressure. It's almost too much to take. I pinch her nipples, harder and harder, as she sucks harder and harder. That sweet ache builds and builds until I'm nearly at the edge.

I grab her hair and guide her mouth over me.

She moans louder.

With one hand firmly around my cock, she slides her mouth over me. Again and again and again. The tingling in my groin increases. Almost.

She settles on my head, sucking hard, her tongue flat against me.

Her eyes find mine. They're on fire. She sucks again, harder, deeper, and it pushes me over the edge.

"Fuck," I groan. "I'm going to come."

She makes her grip on me firmer, sucking harder and harder and harder. The fullness grows.

I can't take it anymore.

An orgasm rocks through me. I shudder, squeezing her, groaning her name.

She doesn't move off of me until I'm empty. She swallows hard and looks back at me.

I catch my breath as she moves to lie down next to me, wrapping her arms around me.

I lean into her, pulling her close.

My mouth hovers over her ear.

"Remind me to torture you more often."

"Deal."

Chapter Twenty-Seven

The rest of the night is amazing.

I help her make dinner. She's come a long way since her fear of the chef's knife, and I mostly stand back and watch as she slices an onion into tiny pieces. I swear it takes her twenty minutes, but she's so amazingly focused on doing it perfectly. I make fun of her speed, and she furrows her brow, trying to work faster.

I put my hand on hers to stop her. "Don't," I say. "You'll slice off one of those fingers."

She shakes her head, but she moves more carefully.

We eat together. It's a sweet, slow thing. We soak in the silence, the sound of the waves lapping against the marina, the wind blowing through the balcony.

There's something nice about being in the apartment. So much has happened here. It's as much a part of us as the house was.

We can make our home here, or somewhere else. We can make our life together.

She drags me to the couch, draping her body over mine.

Her lips are on my lips. Her hands are on my hips. And then she peels off her layers—a T-shirt and boxers borrowed from my bottom drawer—before getting to work on mine.

Just like the first time, our bodies melt together on the couch. It's only the two of us, our breath, our heartbeats, the moans and groans escaping our lips.

Afterwards we lie together, our limbs a tangled mess. I can feel her heart beating through my chest, and in this moment, I know everything will be okay as long as she's here.

Eventually, she presses her lips into mine. I'm so tempted to ask what this means, if she's done with this awful space, but I wait. I need to prove I can be patient. I need to prove I can let her come to me.

We lie together for a minute. Then she pushes herself off the couch and slips back into her clothes. Well, my clothes, really.

I reach for my boxers but she pushes my hand aside. "You should stay naked. It's a good look for you."

"I will if you will."

She shakes her head. "It's too cold." She moves into the kitchen and looks through the cabinets, picking out a canister of rooibos tea before filling the electric kettle.

She turns back to me, looking me over once again.

It's not like before. It's not base. It's... sweet.

"Come on." She nods to the balcony. She fills two mugs with tea and makes her way to the sliding door, a mug in each hand. "Luke. A little help?"

I play dumb. "Help with what?"

"The door."

"Oh, this door?" I run my fingers over the handle.

"Yes, that door."

I pull it open and she steps outside. "Jerk." She rolls her eyes, but she's smiling.

She sets the glasses on the floor and sits on one of the lounge chairs. She shivers, rubbing her arms with her hands.

I bring out a blanket, and she accepts it with little protest. She looks adorable with the blanket wrapped around every part of her but her head.

There's something bothering her, something she wants to say. But she isn't ready yet.

I sit next to her.

We listen to the wind. There's something so calm and peaceful about it. This could be our life together. It could be this perfect.

After a few minutes she turns to me.

She's still not talking.

I lean closer. "You want to tell me what's wrong?"

She looks out at the water—a giant mess of black bleeding into a dark sky. "I've been taking a lot of meetings. Mostly they were good. The show is doing well, and it looks like it will be a huge boon to my career."

"That's great."

"Yeah, it is." She trails off. Her eyes move to the sky, to the tiny sliver of moon above us. "It's mostly been the same kind of thing. The hot chick, the ex-girlfriend, the bitch. I have to thank Laurie for writing Marie Jane as such a completely awful woman, because everyone thoroughly buys me as awful."

"It suits you."

She laughs but the joy fades quickly. "This one was different though. This guy is in his thirties. He's a writer-director. Shot this tiny micro-budget film that rocked the festival circuit. And now he's looking for a lead for his next feature."

"That's great."

"I thought so. And the character is great. She's dynamic, strong and vulnerable all at once. A bitch sometimes, but still sweet and caring. And she isn't the love interest. She's not the hot babe. She's the star." She squeezes my hand tighter. "It's stupid. It's not a big deal at all, really. I shouldn't be upset."

"What happened?"

"Well." She turns her gaze back to the water. "He talked so much like he was different. He talked about how he wanted to make something real and gritty." She imitates him, hunching over, clutching an invisible cigarette. She brings the invisible cigarette to her lips and inhales deeply. "I see all this fake Hollywood bullshit. Happy endings, pretty people. It's all fake. That's not the world. That's not life." She exhales from her fake cigarette, looking to the sky ever so pretentiously. "Life hurts. And I'm not about to show people sanitized bullshit. Have you ever seen downtown LA in a movie? It looks so clean. So fake." She shifts back to her normal posture. "He went on and on about how real he wanted the movie to be."

"Sounds like a douche bag."

"Yeah, basically." She pulls the blanket tighter. "I liked his passion at first. He had me convinced." She bites a fingernail, her eyes on her knuckles. "I really thought he was different."

"But?"

"He told me I was too fat to play the lead." She pulls her fingernail from her mouth and presses it into her free hand. "Not in those words, of course. But he got the point across."

That fucker.

"Ally, I'm so sorry."

"It shouldn't bother me. This is just how it is for

actresses. We need to look a certain way if we want to fit into roles."

"That's bullshit."

"Sure, but there's nothing I can do about it. And your outrage isn't going to make it any easier."

"If you tell me where he lives, I'll kick his ass."

She cracks a smile, but shakes her head. "That's not necessary."

I move closer to her. "I'm so sorry. I wish you didn't have to go through this."

She bites her lip. "I don't. I don't have to keep acting." The look on her face is grim, like it's a horrible thought she hates considering.

"You love acting."

"Yeah, I know, but... maybe Ryan was right. Maybe I can't handle it."

"Alyssa, don't do this to yourself. Don't let him back into your head."

"I'm not."

"You are." I run my fingers across her cheek, tilting her head so her gaze meets mine. "He convinced you that you're weak. He convinced you that you're useless without him. But he's wrong. You are the strongest person I know."

She shakes her head. "This has been so hard. Especially on my own."

"You don't have to be on your own. I'll always be here."

"Always?"

"Always." I press my lips into her forehead.

"Even if I sleep with Ryan?"

"As long as you help me hide the body."

She laughs. "You know, I'd never..."

"I know."

She looks into my eyes. Her eyes are so bright, but there's a sadness in them. She's still upset. I wish my words were enough to convince her she deserves every bit of happiness in the world.

She continues. "There's going to be a point, one day, where I'm too old to play the hot ex-girlfriend, and I'm going to be miserable, pulling my hair out."

I formulate an argument, but she's right. There aren't exactly a lot of women in film and TV over the age of thirty-five. And they tend to fit into very narrow roles—the mom, the wife, the innocent schoolteacher. There are exceptions, sure, but not enough.

She hugs her chest. I can tell she wants to say more, that it's hard for her to even entertain the thought. "Is that what you want?" I ask.

"No. But... after that meeting, all I wanted to do was inhale two pints of ice cream and throw them up." She pulls the blanket tighter. "I'm so lucky with *Model Citizen*. It's a cheesy show, sure, but the work is interesting. Do you know how rare that is?"

"But you get so excited about acting. You light up when you talk about it. How could you give up something that brings you so much joy?"

"But it brings me just as much pain." She hangs her head. "Maybe I would be happier if I resigned myself to this. Just do *Model Citizen*. Take the occasional film role. It's ridiculous. I'm either the hot chick or the fat chick. It's never anything in-between. No matter what, I'm always defined by the shape of my body. The only way it will change is if I lose fifteen pounds."

"That's not funny."

"I'm not joking," she says. "It would help my career."

I bite my tongue. She can't be thinking of losing weight for her job. Not now, not when she's come so far with her recovery. I want to tell her how wrong she is, that she's perfect, that she shouldn't risk all the progress she's made.

But I hold back. She doesn't want another person who tells her how to live her life.

She brings her gaze back to me. "Maybe it would be better if I had a job that didn't rely on my looks."

"Like what?"

"I don't know," she says. "I've never wanted to do anything but act."

"Then you'll find a way to make it work for you."

She nods, but not like she means it.

"I meant it. You're the strongest person I know. You can do anything."

She holds my gaze for a while. "Maybe."

I nod. "You might not get it perfectly the first time, but you'll figure it out."

She pulls her eyes away, bringing them back to the water. There's still something haunting her.

"I'll be here," I say. "If you start to fall, I'll be here."

She looks back to me, the corners of her lips curving into the tiniest smile. "What if that's not enough?"

"It will be."

"How do you know?"

"I know."

She laughs. "Of course you do." She looks at the water for a while. It feels like forever passes. It's just the two of us on this balcony, in our own sheltered world.

Then Alyssa stands and pulls the blanket around her shoulders like a cape. "Come on. Let's watch a movie."

"Which one?"

"I don't care, as long as it's something you love." She catches herself. "That I'm not in."

"Damn, I almost slipped that one by you."

She smiles. "Something that means a lot to you."

I have just the pick.

Chapter Twenty-Eight

I run my fingers along the smooth edge of the DVD case.

This shouldn't feel like a big deal. It's not like it's a secret movie no one has ever seen. *The African Queen* is on the AFI top one hundred films list. Near the top.

It's not a big deal that I'm going to watch it with Alyssa.

She sees right through me. "What are you thinking?

"I've never watched this with anyone but my mom." I slide the DVD into the player. "It was her favorite."

I still remember sitting with her on the couch, way too young to appreciate anything she watched. My friends forced their parents to watch cartoons or silly action shows for kids, but I didn't want to do that to my mom.

I still remember the way the light of the TV flickered over her face. The way she smiled. The way she was glued to the screen. It was the only time she ever seemed alive. It was the only time she was more than Mrs. Lawrence, more than Luke's mom. She was Emilia, a person.

Most of her life was so dull and gray. Every day she

cooked dinner for my father. She waited for him to come home, and they sat together in silence.

I eavesdropped while I did my homework. He never listened to her. He never cared about any of her wants, her feelings, her dreams.

She was his wife, and it was all she was allowed to be.

But when it was just her and her film collection... she was a different person. She had passion. Joy.

"Luke, your smile is ridiculous."

I shake my head. "It's no big deal."

Alyssa nestles next to me. "What was she like?"

"She was sweet," I say. "She was the sweetest person I've ever known."

"So that's where you get it?"

"I'm not sweet. I'm... normal."

Alyssa shakes her head. She holds me closer.

She's so close to being all mine. All I can do now is lose her.

"She was quiet," I say. "She was always busy thinking about something, but she kept it to herself. I know I was a stupid kid, and I probably wouldn't have understood half the stuff going through her mind. Hell, I probably would have been shocked that my mother was a person with her own inner life, but I wish she would have talked to me. She needed someone."

"You shouldn't have had to take care of her."

"I didn't," I say. "She took great care of me. It was all she had to do—she watched films when I was at school, and when I was home, she took care of me. She coddled me, actually. She'd make me snacks after school. She'd ask about my day. She'd allow me to watch movies with her when I was supposed to do my homework." I smile. "It was the same every day. Mom insisted I wouldn't like a film.

That it wasn't appropriate for someone my age. She kept that line up even when I was sixteen."

"Was she right?"

"Sometimes," I say. "I watched *Apocalypse Now* when I was twelve. I had no idea what was going on."

"It's based on an incredibly dense novel."

I shake my head. "I wish she was still around. She would have loved you. My God, if I told her I was dating a woman who played Ophelia in *Hamlet*."

"Only in high school."

"Still. She would have adored you as much as I do."

Alyssa studies my expression. There's something so sweet about the way she's looking at me.

This is what she wanted, isn't it? To carry some of the weight that has been dragging me down.

"What else?" Alyssa asks.

"By the time I was eight, our movie afternoons were a daily event. Monday through Friday. She picked me up from school. We usually went straight home and watched something from her collection. Of course, my father made her keep all five hundred of her movies in a closet, some place where no one would ever see it. So no one would get the stupid idea that his wife was anything more than a trophy."

"That's awful."

"Yeah. And only a small part of why I hate him so much."

I feel Alyssa's hand on mine. My heart pounds against my chest like it's the first time she ever touched me. I take a deep breath.

This is harder than I thought it would be.

"A few times a week we went to the independent video store across town. She even let me pick out a box of candy, so long as I promised not to tell my father. We had a lot of secrets from him. I knew the pen name she used to write a column for the local paper. I tried to read it, but it was so far over my level. She didn't even have to tell me to keep our movie dates a secret. I knew he would hate it. I knew he didn't want his son to get stupid ideas in his head."

"What kinds of stupid ideas?"

"That caring about film was anything besides a waste of time." I smile. "You should have seen his face when I told him I was going to major in film studies. It was a bluff, but it was the most brilliant bluff. He was so angry he turned beet red."

"Why didn't you?"

"I wanted to. But it was too painful. It made me think about how much I missed her."

Alyssa nods, a nod that says she understands exactly what I mean. But I don't know where it comes from. Who did Alyssa lose?

There's still so much I need to learn about her, so much of her I haven't seen.

But there's time. There has to be.

"Those were the best afternoons," I say. "She explained the movies to me. Not the plot. She would talk about the lyrical cinematography or the canted angles or the score. I was probably the only ten-year-old who could carry on a conversation about *Seven Samurai* and *Some Like it Hot.*"

Alyssa laughs. "So you were a little know-it-all."

"Yes."

"Things never change, huh?" She moves closer to me again. "But *The African Queen* was her favorite?"

"Yes," I say. "It's a cheesy movie. Completely unbeliev-able. Katharine Hepburn plays a proper English woman, a missionary, and Humphrey Bogart plays a working class stiff. War breaks out, the First World War I guess, and they have to flee their village on the old beat-up ship, the

African Queen. They face a lot of silly obstacles. Some terrible special effects. And they fall in love. They're from two different worlds. Their relationship could never work, but they fall in love."

"Do you think she believed it was possible?"

"Maybe. I don't know. She thought it was romantic. At the end... well, I won't spoil it," I say. "But she loved it. Don't get me wrong, she loved lots of other movies, but this one was her favorite."

"And you think it's cheesy?"

"Yes, but I love it. It's like she's here when I watch it."

"You miss her, huh?" she asks, her expression soft.

I nod, feeling that ache. "She had to hide all the parts of herself that mattered. She was like a robot most of the time. Like a Stepford wife. But she was a totally different person when it was the two of us and she could geek out over her film collection. She was so happy poring over classics. She could watch a movie she'd seen a hundred times —literally a hundred times—and still notice something new."

"So that's where you get it."

"Get what?" I ask.

"How many times have you watched *Law and Order*?"

"Not a hundred."

"Uh-huh."

I tap her lightly. She smiles, playful, her face lighting up. There's such a warmth here.

I lean down and kiss her.

For a moment, I feel like I'm floating.

Her eyes flutter open when our lips separate. "Does it still hurt?"

"I don't usually think about it."

Alyssa's eyes bore into mine. She's listening with such rapt attention. She actually wants to hear this.

"Yes," I say. "It hurts whenever I think about it. She never had a chance. She lived her whole life hiding her passion. And she did it all for me, because she didn't want me to grow up in a broken home."

"It's not your fault."

"She was thinking about divorcing my father. I overheard her on the phone with a friend once. But she wouldn't do it. She knew he'd fight for custody, just because he could. After not working for years—at my father's insistence—she'd have no way to support herself. She felt like she had no choice but to stay married to that asshole."

I feel Alyssa's fingertips on my cheeks. Her eyes are back on mine, sympathy in them. "That's why you're a divorce lawyer, isn't it? So you can be the person your mom needed?"

I nod. "I could get her a very generous settlement today."

"Is that why you represent so many women?"

"Yeah. They need someone to look out for them for once. Someone to take care of them for once."

"Did you ever think that maybe you need someone to take care of you for once?"

"I didn't." I bring my hand to Alyssa's and press my fingertips into hers. "But I'm reconsidering."

She smiles briefly.

"What was it like when she died?"

I sigh, thinking back.

It feels like a long time ago. But it also feels like yesterday.

"It hit me... hard. I couldn't function for a long time. I drowned myself in schoolwork. I took every class I could, went to every club I could, tried making friends with every person in the school. I was obnoxious. And, when I finally finished my homework at midnight, I would fall asleep to one of her favorite movies. It hurt so much, thinking about her while the images flashed on screen, but it was a good kind of hurt. Like pressing on a bruise. It was like she was still around."

"I'm so sorry," she whispers.

And I know she means it.

"This is the one I watched the most," I say. "It was her favorite, and I must have fallen asleep to it a hundred nights."

She takes my hand.

"Let's add another watch to your tally."

We settle onto the couch and spend the next two hours wrapped in each other's arms, our attention on the screen.

And, once again, I swear I could float.

It's so fucking perfect.

Chapter Twenty-Nine

Everything is perfect.

Alyssa is here with me, in my apartment. We spend the night tangled up together. When we wake, the sun is shining bright in a cloudless sky. The air is sweet and salty.

She's here. She's mine. We could have this every day.

I fix her coffee. When she sees it, she smiles like she's won the lottery.

She slides her arms around my neck, presses her lips into mine. I close my eyes and soak in the feeling of her.

Her eyes find mine. She looks so comfortable, so damn happy. I want to ask if she's finally done with this space, if she's ready to come back and be mine again, but I hold my tongue.

I don't want to fuck things up now by scaring her off.

She motions to the balcony and sets herself up on one of its lounge chairs. She has everything she needs—her coffee and her Kindle and, in a minute, me.

I fix a cup of tea and sit next to her. It's a warm day, but Alyssa shivers when the breeze passes over her arms.

"You want to borrow a sweater?"

She shakes her head. "Coffee is the only sweater I need."

"Then I guess I won't offer my shirt."

"You should have opened with that."

Our eyes connect and she smiles. There's a lightness to her right now. Like she's finally relaxed.

I take a deep breath. "I've been thinking."

"You look cute thinking."

"Do you still need space?"

She shakes her head. "I don't like being away from you."

The tension in my body releases.

"But I only want to do this if we're going to do it right." She looks down at her coffee and takes a long sip.

I turn my body towards hers. "What does right mean?"

"Well, um." She presses her fingers into the cup. Her eyes are still on the floor.

She's slipping, going somewhere else in her head.

"You know you can tell me anything," I say.

"It's just..." She looks up. Her eyes are heavy. "I'm not sure how I'm going to handle this if you say no."

"What is it?"

She bites her lip. Looks at the ground again. "Did you think about what you want?"

"You know what I want. I want you."

She closes her eyes and takes another sip of her coffee. Then another. She downs most of the cup before her gaze turns to my tea. She looks at me like she's asking permission to take it.

I hand her the mug and she holds it tightly.

"Ally, you're not inspiring confidence."

"Do you know what that means? What I expect that to mean?"

I swallow. It means I banish Samantha from my life. This is a choice, apparently, and I only get to pick one.

Either I abandon my needy friend or I lose my girlfriend.

It's a hell of a choice.

Alyssa means so much more to me than Samantha does. Under any normal circumstance, I'd choose Alyssa every time. Everything I have with her is magic.

And it's not as if Samantha has been a good friend. She can be manipulative and inconsiderate. Hell, she spent our entire romantic relationship lying to my face. Fucking my father behind my back.

She took up all the sadness when he died. Like it was hers. Like she had the right to it. Like I needed to be the one to comfort her.

I know all of this. I know she's been awful at times even though she was so important to me when I was a kid.

Her suicide attempts might just be cries for my attention.

But what if they're not?

Alyssa sighs. She shifts back in her seat, her attention on my cup of tea. "That's what I figured."

"No. It's not."

Her eyes find mine, but there's no hope in them. She's defeated. "So you're ready to end your friendship with her?"

"As soon as she's back on her feet."

Her eyes turn to the sky. "Does she know that?"

"She may have attempted suicide a few weeks ago, even though she denies it. I'm trying to ease her into this."

"I bet." She shakes her head. Shifts back into her seat.

It's a beautiful day, but right now it feels ugly.

Alyssa's voice is harsh. Impatient. "I'll take that as a no."

"Ally..." "You act like her boyfriend."

"That's not true."

She shakes her head. "You like being the person she needs. You're never going to stop. Not as long as you keep feeling needed."

I move towards her. I offer my hand but she ignores it. "Yes, in the past, I've appreciated feeling needed. But that isn't what is happening here."

"Right."

"It's not out of line that I'm worried about her."

Alyssa shifts out of her seat. She moves to the railing. Presses her hands against it. "So what if I step over this railing and say the only thing that will keep me from jumping is if you tell Samantha to get lost... would that do it?"

"It's not like that."

She turns to face me. Her eyes are on fire. Her voice is demanding. "It's exactly like that."

"I trust you not to manipulate me."

"But she can manipulate you all she wants?"

I stand and grab Alyssa's wrists. She gasps, but she doesn't fight me.

I pull her closer, until she's only inches away. Her eyes find mine, scanning them like she'll find some answer.

"She's almost there," I say. "She has a job and a place to live. All I want to do is make sure she has someone she can call if things get bad."

Her eyes narrow. "It's called a therapist."

"Then I'll make sure she has a therapist. But you've been where she is. You know a therapist isn't going to be enough to convince her to get better."

She pushes me away. Hard. "Fuck you. I've never been where she is. She's in some kind of bullshit, made-up problems, manipulation land. I never once tried to use my eating disorder for sympathy. Ever."

"That's not what I meant."

"Is that why you like me? Because I'm your replacement crazy girlfriend?" She shakes me off.

"Don't touch me right now," she orders.

I lower my voice. "You know that isn't true."

"What do I know? Maybe you saw some other wounded bird you needed to nurse back to health and that was all that mattered. You had a mission—to liberate me from Ryan—and you did it well. So good job."

"Don't say that," I say.

"Maybe it's true."

My eyes find hers. "If you believe you're nothing more to me than a cheap replacement, then leave right now."

She holds my gaze. Neither one of us is going to back down from this.

My voice is rough. "And if you believe, for a second, that I don't love you, then leave right now."

She takes a shallow breath. Her eyes are on fire, but she says nothing.

"Is that what you believe?" I ask.

"No. But I'm still not sharing you with Samantha."

"All I'm doing is repaying a debt."

She rolls her eyes.

Anger grows inside me. She understands how this feels. I know she does.

"Don't tell me you've never felt like that," I say.

"So what if I have? I'm still not sharing you with her." She moves to the sliding door and steps into the apartment.

I follow her. "Alyssa."

"You sound like Ryan."

"That isn't some bomb you can drop to destroy a

conversation." I take another step towards her. "I'm not going to give up on this that easily."

"And I'm not sharing you with her. End of story." She moves to the table to collect her bag. "You don't even like her anymore. Hell, you probably hate her. You're still holding a grudge against Ryan. How could you not hate her?"

Her back is to me. Her voice is low. She's already out of here mentally. She's already made up her mind.

"I have a grudge against Ryan because he treated you like shit."

She takes a slow breath. "And it has nothing to do with the fact that he used to fuck me?"

"I doubt it was very good."

She laughs, releasing a bit of the tension. "Always cocky, huh?"

"I wouldn't want to disappoint my number one fan."

I move towards her. She backs into the table. Her eyes turn up to me. There's a desperation in them. A need. I grab her hips and lift her onto the table.

Alyssa's eyes flutter shut. Her teeth sink into her lips. "Luke..." Her legs wrap around my hips. Her nails dig into my shoulders.

I run my fingers over her cheek. "You're not sharing me. I'm yours. All yours."

She shakes her head. Her breath is heavy. She squeezes me tighter.

I want so badly to press her against this table, to show her that I'm all hers and she's all mine.

But not like this. Not when she's about to cry.

She forces her eyes open and stares at me. "What if this is the last time?"

I bring my hands to her waist. "It's not."

Her gaze turns to the floor.

She sighs, unwraps her legs, and scoots back on the table. "You've done so much to help her. You can be done with her now. It's more than she deserves."

"I can't. I'm not going to leave her when she really needs someone."

"So is she going to be able to play that card forever?" Alyssa looks at the table. "What if the only thing that will make her feel better is your cock inside her?"

"That's ridiculous."

"Is it? It could be late one night, and she's miserable, and she promises, just this once Luke. Please. Just one last time, so she'll feel a little less lonely for a while."

"I'd never do that."

"But would she ask?"

I bite my lip. It's possible Samantha would make some kind of play for comfort sex, but it's unlikely.

I bring my gaze back to Alyssa. "I would never do it."

She sighs, shifting off the table. "This isn't you. You don't let people push you around, and certainly not this transparently. You don't even like her!"

"I know." The second the words are out, I can't deny it any more.

I don't like Samantha. I sometimes hate her. She betrayed me and held my life hostage for years.

She's still holding it hostage.

"So why are you helping her?"

"We have history. I have to repay this debt."

Her eyes find mine. "And when will that be enough?"

"When she's better."

Alyssa looks out the window. "I'm trying here, I really am, because I know you mean well. But I can't do this. I can't be with you unless you let go of this."

"But..."

"From everything you tell me, it's clear she has some

kind of serious problem. Maybe depression. Maybe borderline personality disorder. I don't know. I'm not a shrink. And neither are you. Maybe you don't realize this, because you're fortunate enough not to have had any brushes with mental illness, but you can't friendship her out of her sickness. She needs a professional, not a friend, and not a friend acting like a boyfriend."

"I can't just let her... hurt herself."

"You can't stop her," Alyssa says. "If that's what she really wants, you won't be able to stop her."

"Ally..."

She looks right at me. Her eyes are on fire, but there's something so sad about her expression. "I'm sorry, but I love you too much to share you. If we're going to do this, we need to do this all the way."

"Give it another month."

"I can't." She moves into the bedroom. Without a word, she gathers her things and heads for door. "I hope you come to your senses."

And then she's gone. Again.

Fuck.

Chapter Thirty

Work does little to distract me from the overpowering dullness that surrounds me.

I check in with a few clients, finish a few contracts, glare at Ryan's office from behind my closed door.

I take lunch alone. I talk to no one.

But, come my meeting, I turn on the charm. I have another potential client courtesy of Ryan. He claims she requested me. But it's more likely that he is making it impossible for me to make any kind of clean break from this firm.

The more new clients I take on, the more difficult it will be for me to leave.

And he enjoys causing me pain.

Still, I'm going to help Penny.

She's young. Twenty-five maybe. Much younger than most of the women who come here. They've been stuck in bad marriages for their entire adult lives. For years they've been ignored, abandoned, told they don't matter.

But, somehow, Penny came to her senses much sooner. It's usually because of awful men like Ryan, who convince their wives and girlfriends that they are worthless without them. Men like my father, who convinced my mother that leaving would hurt me, that his reputation was more important than her happiness, that her passion was somehow embarrassing.

I hate both the assholes.

Penny has been married for three years, and her husband is already ignoring her. He's given up everything she ever loved about him. And the prenup—a prenup she signed without speaking to a good lawyer, I'm sure—is awful. It's standard. Considered fair by all the other asshole divorce lawyers and their asshole clients.

She's not entitled to much. A one hundred fifty thousand dollar payoff. It's a lot to most people, but it's nothing to her husband. I hate prenups.

I know, I'm in the wrong line of work. But I hate them. Marriage is supposed to be a partnership. It shouldn't be about me keeping what's mine and you getting nothing. About me getting everything after you give up your career for mine.

She arrives early. She's dressed nicely. Perfect hair and makeup. The image of a trophy wife.

But there's something weary about her as we make our introductions. This marriage is destroying her.

"We used to ski," she says. "We would fly to Europe for the weekend for no reason at all. He would take me to French lingerie shops and beg me to model underwear for him. He used to make me feel beautiful. Now... he doesn't even look at me."

It's the same old story. I hear it every day, sometimes once an hour. Where do all these men come from and why do they give up on their wives the second things get difficult?

"He was always busy," she says. "But he made a point of sitting with me when he got home from work. He asked me about school. He offered to help with my career. It was never forced. It was only an offer."

"What do you do?"

"Nothing. I studied psychology. He owns a software company. He offered me a job in marketing—a much higher position than I deserved—but I said no. I didn't want to muddy our relationship."

Penny purses her lips. She's trying to stay composed. Lots of women are like this. They hate when people see them cry.

I offer her a tissue.

She takes it, and nods a thank you. Once she's gathered herself, she continues. "He was always a workaholic. I should have seen the signs. I should have known."

"Love does crazy things to us. I've overlooked far worse."

"Really?" she asks.

I nod. "You wouldn't believe how awful I am with women."

"You're right. I wouldn't believe that."

She smiles, but it's not flirtatious like it is with other women. Penny is still used to men taking an interest in her. She won't fall for a few compliments. She's friendly. Or maybe she's desperate to feel like she's not the only fuck-up in the world.

"It's true," I say. "I had a chance to have everything I wanted, and I didn't take it."

"Why not?"

Why couldn't I take Alyssa up on her offer? She was

right—I'm not getting anything out of this relationship with Samantha. It assuages the uneasy feeling in my gut— the one that reminds me she might leave the world forever if I don't watch her carefully.

Even though I may not like Samantha, I want her to be okay.

But I don't want her in my life. Not really. Even if it eases my guilt.

"Mr. Lawrence?"

"I thought I couldn't agree to the terms, and she completely refused to negotiate."

"Your girlfriend?"

"I'm sorry," I say. "This is completely unprofessional."

"But now you've got me intrigued. What were the terms?"

"I really shouldn't," I say. "Mr. Knight is out for reasons to lecture me."

"I won't tell if you don't." Another smile.

Maybe Penny is flirting with me. No, it's friendly. She did study psychology. Maybe, once upon a time, she wanted to help people.

"She thinks my ex is in love with me," I say.

"Is she?"

I nod. "But it has nothing to do with me. It's only because she has no one else."

"I'm sure it has something to do with you."

"She wasn't very interested when she had me."

Penny smiles. "Well, you know women. We always want what we can't have."

"Maybe."

"I'm sure women fall in love with you all the time. I mean, look at you. I've only known you five minutes and I'm already enamored." She laughs. "Though your girlfriend doesn't have to worry. I'm still mixed up about my husband."

"I'll let her know."

She smiles. "I guess I shouldn't be giving you advice, since I'm here looking for a divorce. Who could be less prepared to give relationship advice than a twenty-five-year-old divorcée-to-be?"

"You learn a lot about relationships from watching them end."

"Then you should be the one giving me advice." She laughs. It's casual, like we're friends.

I already have her hooked. She's going to sign a retainer at the end of this meeting.

This is almost too easy.

Penny leans a little closer. "But I did study psychology and I would so like to feel useful, so here goes. If you really love her, then you can probably find a way to agree to those terms."

"Probably."

"You sure you don't want to tell me a little more?" she asks. "It would be nice to think about someone else's problems for a minute."

"You've been very helpful."

"Yeah? Maybe I'll end up a counselor." She sighs, relaxing. "You know, my soon-to-be ex-husband always thought psychology was bullshit. Just a marketing tool. He thinks people that go to therapy are weak."

"He's too busy working to think."

"Yeah. He used to talk to me, tell me what he was feeling." She looks out the window. "He's probably telling someone else now. It's probably something that obvious. Probably an eighteen-year-old intern."

"Penny, if he needs to trade in his gorgeous twenty-five-year-old wife for a younger model, that's his issue."

She laughs. "No wonder Maribel recommended you. You're an incorrigible flirt, aren't you?"

"I plead the fifth."

"And you say your ex has no reason to be in love with you." She shakes her head. "You know, when I spoke to Mr. Knight on the phone, I was expecting some dry conversation about numbers. He wasn't very confident about the prenup."

"Don't pass this on to Mr. Knight, but he's a coward about these things."

"Yeah?"

I nod. "We can think outside the box here. There's always a way to get what you want, even if you have to resort to manipulation."

"Like blackmail?"

"Not legally. More like reminding him that the details of an affair will become public if you two go to court."

Penny smiles. "Okay." She laughs. "I feel ridiculous giving you advice, but the way you lit up when you mentioned your girlfriend—"

"I did?"

"Definitely. It's charming. If I hadn't sworn off men, I'd be madly jealous. The thing is... the more space that came between me and Alexander, my husband, the harder it got to talk to him. What started as a little distance snowballed. And now I feel like he's a stranger."

"I understand." I lean a little closer, really selling the charm. "But we should get back to your divorce. Your husband expects you to walk away with no struggle because of the prenup. I don't know your background, but I'd understand if you thought it was generous. A hundred and fifty thousand dollars is a lot of money to most people, but it's nothing to him. He agreed to be your partner, and he didn't hold up his end of the bargain. Now he's going to pay for it, and he's going to lose the only thing he cares about—cash."

"Maybe." Penny squeezes the tissue in her hands.

"I'll be honest. Mr. Knight doesn't want me to be so aggressive in these negotiations. He'd prefer that we make a reasonable offer and get this over with. It's not the choice I would make, but I can understand if you'd rather get out of your marriage quickly than get out of your marriage with a boatload of money."

"A boatload?"

I smile. "Yes, a boatload. If you want to be greedy, this is your chance."

"I don't know."

"This is a terrible offer, Penny. He can do better. You can do better."

"But it's not my money."

"I know how you feel. You think you'll be a gold digger if you ask for what you deserve. But that's a lie someone else has sold you. He agreed to support you, and he failed. I'm here to make sure you get what you are legally entitled to."

"And I'm legally entitled to a boatload?" she asks.

"According to his financial statements. You'll never have to work again. Not if you don't want to."

"But what about the prenup?"

"A prenup is only as good as opposing counsel. And trust me, I'm much better than this prenup."

"But won't that take a long time?"

"Yes, but not your time. And, thanks to Mr. Knight, we bill a flat rate."

"So I might as well let you go crazy?"

I nod. "It would be my pleasure."

"Yeah," she says. "Maybe losing a boatload of money will finally get his attention."

"Exactly."

I offer my hand. Penny shakes it.

Thank God she's here. She has options. She's not trapped in an empty relationship like my mom was.

Like Alyssa was.

Chapter Thirty-One

I've had a miserable time sleeping since my mom died.

I spend nights tossing and turning, staring at the TV or working until I drop.

For so long, I've run away from the fear in my belly—that uneasy feeling that promised I'd lose another person I cared about.

I haven't loved Samantha in a long time, but I've been terrified of losing her. I've been terrified that, if I stopped doting on her, helping her, running to her, she'd swallow another bottle of sleeping pills. That my friendship is the only thing standing between her and suicide.

Alyssa was right. I hate Samantha. I've hated her since the moment she told me about Edward. I hated her for fucking someone else behind my back. I hated her for lying to me. But mostly, I hated her for falling in love with him.

She knew how I despised him. I admit, I was vague about the details. I never felt the need to share that part of my past with her.

Truth be told, I doubt she would have cared much. She

was too busy concerning herself with how everything looked to give a damn about how things were.

I've swallowed that hate for so long. I've tried to convince myself I could push aside my anger.

But I can't do it anymore.

She's gone too far. She's not just hurting me anymore. She's hurting Alyssa.

And that's unforgivable.

No. That's not quite right. Samantha isn't the thing standing in the way of my relationship with Alyssa. Not really.

I'm standing in the way.

But not anymore. I don't like Samantha. I'm helping her out of some misguided sense of obligation. But my attempts at help are useless. She's as depressed as she was a year ago.

She's never going to get better like this. She's only going to keep dragging me down.

Maybe I'm actually hurting her too by continuing to act as a crutch.

I shake my head. I never would have realized it without Alyssa. I would have kept living that night over and over again—my mom running out of the house, the hours passing quietly as I pretended to sleep, the cops arriving at the doorstep at the break of dawn.

But my mom is gone and there's nothing I can do to bring her back.

If I don't act now, I'm going to lose the most important person in my life. And I can't have that. I need to get my life back.

———

I meet Samantha to finalize the transfer of the mortgage. We're in the Chase across from the water. It's like every other Chase in existence—tinted windows blocking out the rest of the world, convincing me I'm in some cocoon of dimness rather than the sunniest part of the country.

I stare at the contract. It's a fair deal. Not that I care about the money. I have plenty of money, even if most of it once belonged to my father.

The paper seems more blindingly white than usual. That black ink seems darker, more permanent.

I run my fingers along the smooth plastic of the ball-point pen.

It's only a house. I'll miss it, sure, but it's not worth the fight.

I sign on the dotted line.

Samantha wears the happiness in her eyes, but she tries to play it cool. She offers me a handshake. Then, fuck it, she throws her arms around me in a hug. It's too tight, too close, too intimate.

A few weeks ago I would have denied it meant anything.

But now it's too obvious to ignore.

I may hate Samantha, but I still don't want to destroy her.

"Thanks, Luke," she says.

She squeezes me tighter, even as I pull away.

"Can we talk?"

"After we celebrate."

"I have to get back to work. I should make it quick."

"One drink. Please." She looks at me with need.

Okay. This is the last time I'm giving her what she wants. I might as well do it all the way.

I nod. "Okay." A glass of Cabernet will calm her down. It will make all this go down more easily.

I rack my brain. This won't be easy for her. She needs someone to call, someone who can come and comfort her. Someone else.

"Give me one minute," I say.

I hate to do this to her, but I don't have a better option.

I text her mother. *Can you please call Samantha in half an hour? She's going to need you.*

Her mother isn't the strongest person, but she doesn't share Samantha's father's obsession with appearances.

No. I have to do better than her mother. She had a friend, a friend she always used as an excuse when she was really visiting Edward. I still have her number somewhere.

"Make it two," I say, pointing to the bathroom in the corner. I wait until I'm inside and then I call Delia, Samantha's college roommate. I doubt they're close, but I know Delia is still in L.A.

It rings three times and she answers. "Hello."

"Hey."

"You're shitting me. Is that really you, Luke?"

I laugh. "I was worried I'd have to remind you who I was."

"No. I still remember everything that happened with you and Samantha."

She sounds guilty. So, she still remembers being Samantha's excuse.

"It's okay," I say. "All water under the bridge."

"Thank God. I always liked you. I didn't want to lie. I just..."

"Tell you what—you can make it up to me."

"You sure?" she asks.

"Are you and Samantha still in touch?"

"Here and there."

"Can you get out of work and get to the marina quickly?"

"At this time? Maybe."

"Samantha is going to be at this hotel bar. I forget the name. I hope she's not going to be devastated, but she's probably going to be devastated."

"Why?"

"I'm breaking up with her... well, as a friend."

"Oh," she says. She exhales, thinking it over. "Good for you."

"I'm a little scared, to be honest."

"I think it's for the best. For both of you."

"I'll text you the address. Get there as fast as you can. Take her out. Spend as much as you want. I'll pay you back."

"That's okay. I think I owe you this one." She takes a long breath. "Good luck."

I hang up and check my reflection in the mirror. It's the calm, composed professional. Suit and tie, hair arranged as neatly as possible.

Doubt creeps up on me, but I push it aside.

This has been a long time coming.

Outside, Samantha is waiting with an annoyed look. But she doesn't mention it. She follows me to the hotel around the corner. I make a note of the address and text it to Delia.

"Who are you talking to?" she asks.

"Scheduling a meeting." It's an excuse she won't question.

I look around. The lounge is dark, and the furniture is a strange shade of gold. This won't be the worst place in the world for Samantha to wait, and the bartender seems friendly enough. The type who would listen to a crying woman.

Samantha insists on paying, as if she didn't just transfer all her money into my savings account.

She lifts her glass to toast, her expression all smiles. "To our futures."

I nod. "To our futures."

Our glasses touch with a gentle clink, and she takes a long sip of her wine. "Are you happy for me?"

I nod. There are no more legal ties between us. Nothing that can make a mess or get in the way.

"I'd be so fucked without you," she says.

"You got by okay without me."

She shakes her head. "No. I was such an idiot before. I can't believe I didn't realize what I had." She looks at me, her eyes filling with delight. Then she inches closer.

I know this look.

And then she kisses me. It's quick. A flash. Fast enough it could be two friends saying hello.

But there was more in it than that.

She stares at me, her brown eyes unwavering. I expect an *I'm sorry* or a *that was out of line*, but she says nothing.

"Sam?"

"I was so wrong before. I was stupid. I wouldn't let myself love you. But it's different now. I can now. I can love you so much, Luke. Please... I want to make all this up to you. I want to earn some of your love." She looks at me again. "Please, just kiss me. Hold me. Even if it's only for today. I want to be with you. You're the sweetest guy I've ever known. And I was lying before. You were better than him. The best I ever had."

I'm dizzy again. I knew Samantha wouldn't take this lying down, but Jesus.

"I know you still love her, but you'll move on."

"What is wrong with you?"

She reaches for my hands. "Alyssa isn't like you. She'll

never understand your world. She'll be happier with someone like Ryan."

Anger surges through me. I was going to do this gently, calmly, but all that flies out the window. "Fuck you."

She blinks at me, clearly in shock.

"What? I..."

"You can say what you want about me, but you don't know Alyssa." I shake my head. "You know what? It doesn't matter. I'm not going to be around to hear you speak of anything again."

The color drains from her face.

"Luke, I... You can't."

"I can't? You just asked me to cheat on my girlfriend."

Her eyes narrow. "You did the same thing to her."

"That's different."

"How?"

"Alyssa and I were strangers. You and are I friends. Hell, I come running every time you need me. Would you really throw that all away just to get in my pants?"

"I've never asked you to 'come running.' Never."

"You beg me not to leave."

"I'm sorry," she says. "But I love you. It's your fault, you know. You keep showing up when I need you."

"I don't feel like that about you. I don't feel anything for you anymore."

Now she just looks confused.

"Then why do you... what are you so..."

"What else was I supposed to do?" I ask. "You drop hints that you'll fucking kill yourself if I don't stay."

She stares back at me. She looks like she's about to cry, but she'd never cry in public.

She shakes her head. "You can't do this. You're my best friend. I'm sorry I said stupid things, but I do love you. I've been stupid all this time. I never should have been with Edward. He was nothing compared to you."

"You were in love with him."

"No." She bites her lip, her eyes quivering. "I loved you. Always."

She doesn't believe a word she's saying.

"Love is something you do. And you don't manipulate people you love. You don't spend two years carrying on an affair behind their back."

"I was mixed up. But I always loved you."

"Stop. It doesn't matter if you ever loved me or if you still love me. I'm done."

"Because of Alyssa?"

"Because of me."

She pouts. "She's not worth it. She's never going to give you what I could give you."

"I don't like you, Samantha. Lately, I hate you. You have no qualms about taking advantage of kindness. About manipulating the situation to get your way." I take a step back. "Whatever debt I owed you, it's repaid. You're on your own."

Her voice is low, but desperate. Even now, she's too aware of how things look to really make a scene. "Please, Luke. I'm sorry. I'll change. Just stay with me."

It's not difficult to stand my ground by this point. She's done too much. "No."

"You'll get over Alyssa," she tries, her eyes a little too intense.

"I won't. And I don't want to."

Samantha straightens. She runs a hand through her hair, trying and failing to look composed.

She grips my wrist, her hold too tight. "Think about this. She's not the faithful type. And she's not interested in guys like you. She'll be hooking up with her co-stars by her next birthday."

Does she really think she has room to talk about faithfulness?

I bite my tongue. Samantha doesn't mean this. She's just angry. And I'm not going to cause a scene. "I'm trying to give you a chance to walk away with dignity."

Samantha blinks back a tear. She looks like she's about to scream, but she keeps her voice even. Quiet. "Are you really this blinded by some L.A. bimbo because she's got a nice rack?"

"Is that the best you've got?" I shake my head. "Fuck off."

Her face twists into an ugly expression.

She doesn't look like the girl I once knew.

"You're just like your father. You think you want someone young and pretty, but—"

"Jesus, Sam. Get a grip. She's only four years younger than you are. And it's got nothing to do with how she looks. Hell, you just called yourself pretty."

"I thought you were better than this."

I shake my head. "I love her. I love her in a way I never loved you. In a way I never will love you. You could be the most beautiful woman on the planet, and I still wouldn't love you, because you're ugly inside. You're selfish and manipulative."

She changes tactics, clearly realizing she's not getting anywhere.

"Luke, please... You're wrong. I'm trying to help you. She's probably after your money."

"Really?"

Alyssa clearly isn't hurting for money.

Her eyes turn to the floor. "It's possible."

Even she doesn't believe it.

"You're making a fool of yourself." I bite my tongue. I could walk out now. But I can't yet. Not until Samantha understands how wrong she is. "I know it hurts, but you have to accept that you're wrong. I love her and she loves me. It has nothing to do with her looks or my money. Or my looks for that matter."

She shakes her head, still not giving up.

"I loved you. I know you. We went through so much together. She'll never understand you like I do."

"No. You'll never understand me. Because you're self-ish. You'll never know how it feels to really love someone." Even now, I can see she's just thinking of what this means for her. And isn't that just sad? "I feel sorry for you. It's lonely when everyone else is just some pawn for you to manipulate. But you know what? That's not going to be me. Not anymore."

"Luke, please..." She clutches her purse, her eyes filling with tears she refuses to let drop.

Appearances are important after all.

"We're both better off this way. I hope you can see that at some point." I step away.

She calls out to me, but I don't turn back.

That chapter of my life is over.

Chapter Thirty-Two

The rest of the day drags by.

It takes all the willpower I have not to pull out my phone and call Alyssa. But I have to wait until I'm sure. She won't take another false start.

By the evening I'm lost in work. It's comfortable. Easy.

And then Ryan decides to interrupt my zen.

He calls me into his office. No—like the dick he is, he has Janine, our assistant, ask me to go to his office.

He's sitting at his desk, his hands folded, his expression calm. He nods for me to sit.

I don't.

His neutral expression fades. "You shouldn't discuss personal matters with clients."

I smirk. "I have my methods and you have yours."

"It's not professional."

"So, dissolve the firm. You can be as professional as you want."

He moves towards a filing cabinet and pulls out some legal document. "Sell me your half." He hands me the document.

It's a contract to sell the firm.

Everyone is trying to buy half of what's mine today.

"You know I won't sell," I say. "There's a non-compete clause in our partnership agreement."

"I won't enforce it."

"No."

He narrows his eyes. "I'm not going to dissolve. The only way out of this impasse is you selling your half of the firm."

"No."

He offers me a look of pity. "I can manage my feelings, but it's clear that you're not able to stay professional while working with me."

Fucker. "Is that so?"

"Yes," he returns with confidence. "We've had our disagreements, but I do respect... your way with clients. I'm not holding on to what happened with Alyssa."

Bullshit.

"It's not happening."

He scoffs, rolling his eyes. "You're not as hard to replace as you think you are. There are plenty of attractive men in Los Angeles. Plenty who are more dependable."

I bite my tongue. He's trying to get a rise out of me. I won't give it to him.

His brow furrows. "If you're going to be here, you need to be here. Not taking off without notice."

"That won't happen again."

"Really?"

"Yes. Really."

He smirks. "Did Samantha finally get rid of you once and for all?"

I throw him a fake smile. "You could put it like that."

"Good for you."

"Thanks." I slam the paper onto his desk. "Is that all?"

He offers me another pitying look. "Is there any way you can be convinced?"

"No."

He taps his fingers against the desk. " The non-compete is only for L.A. County."

"Funny, that's where I live."

"Come on, Luke. You may be romantic, but you aren't this naive. Alyssa isn't going to stick around."

"Mind your own business."

"That's rich, coming from you."

Not so unaffected after all.

I bite my lip to keep from smiling.

He narrows his eyes. "I'm sure the passion is intoxicating. Lust always is. But we both know you and Alyssa aren't going to last."

"Do we?"

"Yes, we do." He picks up the offer and places it in my hands. "So sell, move somewhere else, and get on with your life."

I set the paper on the desk. "It's not happening."

He smiles. "You know, I saw her this morning."

My fingers curl into fists. He's got such a smug look on his face. He thinks he knows what Alyssa wants.

He thinks he can come between us.

"She was rushing out of the condo," he says. "And she looked upset."

"If you touched her, I swear—"

"You don't have the moral ground to swear on that."

He is so fucking calm. How can he always be so calm when he's talking about me stealing his fiancée?

Does he really even feel anything?

His voice is even. "What if I did touch her? What if I brought her back to my place and I fucked her all morning?"

I dig my nails into my palms. There's no way Alyssa would fuck Ryan. She's been done with him for a long time.

"What would you do if she decided she wanted to go back to me?" he asks.

"You're dreaming."

"Even so." He smirks. "I've made her come more times than you can count."

I swallow hard.

"She used to beg me for it. You know what she's like, when she's on her knees, pawing at your slacks, desperate for a taste."

"Fuck off."

"With you two fighting, I bet she'd love a distraction."

He's fucking with me. She wants nothing to do with him.

Still, the thought flashes across my mind like a bolt of lightning.

It's such a sickening image—him on top of her, thrusting away in missionary while she lies there bored out of her mind.

I shake my head. Ryan isn't worth the fight.

"She has better taste than that."

He shakes his head. "Do you have any clue how many times she begged me to touch her? How she would look at me with those big, blue eyes and plead. Please, Ryan, just tonight. Please."

A tension builds in my chest. "Shut the fuck up."

He just pushes harder. Like the dam has burst.

"Do you have any clue how badly she needed me by the time I fucked her? How loudly she'd scream my name?"

I suck the air between my teeth. He's not going to get a rise out of me.

"I can't say I've considered it."

He laughs. "You know, for a charming guy, you really are pathetic. You think you're the first good-looking guy Alyssa has used for sex?"

My fists curl into tight balls. "Do you?"

" She's about due to get bored with you and throw you away like the garbage you are."

"And what does that make you?"

He shakes his head.

"You don't know her like I do. I've been her friend for ten years now. I've been the person she can count on. You really think three months of sex is enough to make her love you? You really think she'd stay with you after you abandoned her to take care of Samantha?"

I press my nails harder into my palms, hard enough that I wouldn't be surprised if I find blood there later.

I can stay calm here. I can be the bigger person.

"You filled a void. That's it. I'm sure by now she wants to go back to someone who knows how to take care of her."

"Like you?"

"Maybe. But certainly not someone like you," he scoffs.

I try to push this anger down, but it won't budge. This is all his fault. He hurt her so much... if he hadn't scarred her...

"She loves me."

"Do you do anything besides fuck and talk about me?"

I feel my control give, a silent, almost gentle snap.

I lunge towards him, grabbing his collar and shaking him. "She loves me."

Ryan doesn't move. He doesn't blink. "Believe whatever helps you sleep at night. Though we both know you aren't capable of that either."

I pull my arm back and drive it into his face. It lands with a thud, a crack of bones and flesh.

He's going to hurt as much as I do.

He pushes me back and throws a punch of his own. Pathetic, as usual.

I pull my arm back and unload again, driving my fist into his stupid face over and over. Until everything around me is a blur of flailing limbs and all I feel is the smack of my knuckles against his bones.

"I'M SORRY."

It's Janine, in the lobby, talking to someone else.

It went so fast—Janine screaming, her hands curling around my biceps as she tried to pull me off Ryan. The stupid look in his eyes—like he was glad, like this proved he's better than I am once and for all.

"Should I call the police?"

"No. It won't look good. Even if it would help get rid of him. Besides, I don't want to waste the time pressing charges."

"But Mr. Knight! He attacked you. You shouldn't allow him to hurt you like that."

"It's nothing. Barely a scratch." I almost laugh at that. "Just take him to his office and give him these. He'll calm down. Maybe for once he'll regain his senses."

He handed her a bottle of pills. A prescription with Alyssa's name on it. Some anti-anxiety medication.

Something he used to keep her drugged, so she'd better fit the role he wanted for her.

Did he really think he had that kind of control over me? I shrugged Janine off. "If you're going to kiss his ass, you might as well just offer to fuck him."

She gasped, pretending she was scandalized. But her eyes flashed with delight. She'd been thinking about it for ages. "Mr. Lawrence. I would never..."

"I'll leave when I'm finished with my paperwork."

"Should I call Marcus?"

My law school friend who lives in New York. My supposed emergency contact. I see him occasionally, but there's nothing he could do now.

"Don't call anyone. I'm an adult. I can take care of myself."

She looked at me with pity. A look she learned from Ryan, no doubt. She shook her head, tsk tsking like a teacher scolding her second-grade student.

We settle our disagreements with words, not fists.

But she lost interest as soon as I closed the door. Probably skittered back to Ryan's office to suck up again.

Poor girl has no idea he'd never date his secretary. Wouldn't look right. Wouldn't appear professional.

He deserved this.

But that doesn't matter anymore.

Yes, Ryan is an asshole.

But I am an adult.

However awful he is, however much I hate him, however good it might feel, it does me no good to hit him.

Yes, Alyssa would have been mine so much sooner if he hadn't fucked with her so royally.

But she's also not mine right now. And Ryan had nothing to do with it.

I have to take responsibility for my decisions and my mistakes.

This time, I was the one who hurt Alyssa.

But I'm not going to wallow. I'm going to make it up to her.

"I didn't know who else to call. Mr. Lawrence sometimes has lunch with a college friend—a Mark—but he lives in New York."

"It's okay."

My heart thuds in my chest. It's Alyssa.

Fuck. She isn't going to like this. She's got some silly idea that I'm holding on to the past.

Ridiculous, I know.

The door to the office opens. Even now, even though we're separated, she's still a beam of light in my gray existence.

She has pity in her eyes. And a good dose of irritation. This really wasn't for her. It was for me—because I hate that fucker and his stupid face. It's not just because he hurt her, but because he rubbed me raw, because I had to see his ugly face every day for three years. Because I have to see every asshole he represents—another fucker who ruined his wife's life, who took away everything that ever mattered to her and tried to take away her kids and house too.

I hate him because he is my asshole father, only thirty years younger and infinitely less charismatic. I've held on to that pain too long, until it festered inside me. It hasn't done me a bit of good.

There's no sense in holding on to anything that isn't Alyssa.

She looks me over, shaking her head.

"I thought I was the one with issues." "I was defending your honor."

"Uh-huh."

Clearly not buying it. She eyes me almost clinically. "Did he at least start it?"

"It depends on your definition of 'start it.'"

She sighs. "What the hell am I going to do with you?"

"Kiss me."

"Ha!" She gives me a look. "Come on—let's get out of here you idiot." I hold her gaze. "I love you."

"I know." She rolls her eyes. "But I really don't know what I'm going to do with you."

"I don't care about anything but being with you."

"Your black eye disagrees," she points out.

"My fist cares about smashing Ryan's face. But you can hardly blame me for that."

She laughs. Grudgingly, but she does.

"Come on," she repeats, turning around and walking out of my office. "I'll take you home."

Chapter Thirty-Three

Alyssa shoves me onto the kitchen counter. I have no clue what's going through her head—if she hates me, if she's convinced I don't deserve a second chance—but she's here in my apartment.

It's something. She scans my freezer. "How is it possible you don't own a single bag of peas?"

"I outgrew peas almost twenty years ago."

She gives me side eye.

"You should have planned this better. Kept an ice pack on hand at the least."

"There's always next time."

She looks at me like I'm ridiculous. Then she slips back into her stoic facade.

She settles on a bag of frozen blueberries and moves towards me.

"He looks worse, right?" I ask.

"How old are you?"

"Twenty-six."

"That's what I thought, but I figured I must have it

wrong. Because there's no way a twenty-six-year-old man, a lawyer, would get into a fistfight at his office."

"You'd be surprised."

"Clearly."

She presses the bag of blueberries to my eyes. It stings, but it's nothing compared to the hole in my gut from her being away.

"He was insulting you," I say.

She shakes her head. "Uh-huh."

"Implying that you're some kind of harlot."

"Some really current slang there."

"He called you a slut," I try.

"I've been called worse."

"Maybe. But he went on about how you were using me. How you were already bored of me."

She raises a brow at that.

"And you believed him?"

"No. But the thought stung a lot worse than this black eye does."

She gives me a disbelieving look. "God, what the hell am I going to do with you? You hit him because he called your girlfriend a slut?"

"I hit him because he deserved it," I say. "And maybe I hate that he ever mattered to you."

She runs her fingers along my neck, sighing. "Not like you do."

"But really, he looked awful, right?"

"He looked worse than I'd expect."

"Excuse you?"

She smirks. "He's obsessive about going to the gym."

"I go to the gym," I retort. "I'm very fit."

"I've experienced your level of fitness firsthand. Your stamina is very impressive. And your cardiovascular conditioning... I have no doubt you could outlast him."

"Continue."

She shakes her head. "In your dreams."

"Maybe I need to take you to the bedroom and remind you."

If her eyes roll any harder, they'll pop out of her head. "I remember just fine. But he lifts. You don't."

"I do tabata."

"Of course you do. What the hell is tabata?"

"Tactical body weight exercises."

"I'm pretty sure you made that up." She doesn't sound impressed as she rearranges the bag of blueberries and takes a long look at me. "Sit still."

She takes a wet paper towel and wipes my forehead. Her touch is still soft and gentle.

I look into her eyes. "Samantha bought me out of my half of the mortgage today."

"Oh." She frowns.

"And after... we had a talk. I told her that we can't be friends anymore."

She stills.

"Why is that?"

"Really?"

She nods. "Really. Why did you end your friendship? She's your friend, isn't she?"

"She was."

She slides the paper towel over my cheek. "So you must have had a reason."

"Isn't that what you wanted?"

She nods. "But what did you want?"

"Ally... the only thing I want is you."

She gives me a long look.

"Last time we were here, having this conversation, you phrased things a little differently."

"I know." I look up at her. She's still a beam of light.

She's still everything I ever wanted. "I didn't think she'd be okay without me."

"What changed your mind?"

"What you said. Of course. How can you be so fucking smart?"

She smiles, but it's guarded. "It's a curse."

"You were right. I've been trying so hard to be there for her that I forgot how much I fucking hated her."

"You hate everyone."

I nod. "Not you."

"Lucky me." She runs her fingers through my hair.

Her eyes are locked on mine.

"You don't think you're lucky?" I ask.

"Smug asshole." Her lips curl into a smile. She's relenting. "What did Ryan say?"

"He said you were only using me for sex. That you were done with me."

"That's awfully progressive for Ryan," she remarks.

"And I wouldn't blame you if you were. I mean, look at me."

"I think we've established that you're sexy as hell."

I feel her fingers on my skin. There's such a warmth to it. A softness.

She pulls away the frozen fruit and locks eyes with me. "That was your offer—to be my revenge fuck?"

I shake my head.

"I could not have handled that. I would have gone crazy thinking about you."

"This isn't crazy?" She nods to my black eye. Runs her fingers over my bruised knuckles.

"This is inevitable. I've been daydreaming about punching Ryan since he called you a whore."

"And it has nothing to do with you?"

I shake my head. "Oh no, it was ninety percent me.

He's been a condescending asshole for years. Did you know he always acts like he's my boss?"

She stares at me like I'm hopeless. She's right, in some ways.

But I won't give up on her, or on us. And I don't think she'll give up on me.

"How would you have gone crazy?"

"Honestly, Ally, you had me hooked from the minute I met you and shamelessly flirted with you to make Ryan jealous."

She narrows her eyes at me. "I knew it."

"I would have said anything to keep you in my apartment that night. I had convinced myself it was better than nothing. Maybe it would have been."

Her cheeks flush. "You can't distract me with memories of sex."

"It would have killed me to see you stay with Ryan. It did kill me."

She's here, in my apartment, cleaning me up.

She could have dropped me off and left. But she didn't.

She's in this for the long haul.

I don't know how I got so lucky, but she loves me. She loves me enough to stick around even when I punch out my business partner.

I brush the hair from her eyes. "I've been thinking."

"Rare for you."

I nod. "If he won't dissolve the business, I'll sell. He's not as aggressive as I am—"

"Your black eye disagrees."

I laugh. "In court." I take her hand. "But I have to admit, he's a decent lawyer. He'll manage my old clients okay." I look down at Alyssa. She's here, with me, and that's all that matters. "It's not ideal, but I'd rather he be out of our lives."

There's such a sweetness in her eyes. Maybe all this time I've been the one that needs her, instead of the other way around.

She smiles. "I'm proud of you."

"Really?"

"This requires great maturity."

"I'm trying to learn."

I run my fingertips along her cheek. She melts into the gesture, nestling into my hand. I'm tempted to stay quiet, to soak in this moment.

But I don't have the patience for it.

"Please tell me this space is over. Tell me you'll be mine forever."

"Forever is a long time." She holds my gaze.

"You're torturing me on purpose."

She nods, her teeth sinking into her lip. "You had to know your torturing would come back to haunt you."

"It's worth it." I slide off the counter and move closer to her.

With my hands on her waist, I bring our bodies together. Until we're only inches apart.

"I love you, Alyssa."

She searches my eyes. I know she'll find only sincerity.

"I love you too."

I reach for her hand and squeeze it tight. "I know things aren't perfect yet. I know we have a lot more kinks to work out. But I want to work them out with you. I'll go anywhere you go."

She smiles, a small smile.

But her heart is in it.

"Me too."

She closes her eyes as I kiss her again.

I feel things click back into place.

My world is finally back to what it should be.

Thank God.

———

IT'S A SUNNY DAY. BUT THEN AGAIN IT'S ALWAYS SUNNY here.

I didn't tell Alyssa where we were going—only that it was important to me—but I'm sure she guessed by the time the 405 merged into the 5.

The bouquet of flowers was probably a dead giveaway.

Neither of us is wearing black. But this isn't a somber occasion.

She follows me out of the car, walking slowly on the grass. She's wearing a brandnew pair of hot pink sneakers and she wants to keep them clean.

"I'll buy you a new pair," I offer.

She shakes her head. The grass is wet from the sprinklers and there are small patches of mud everywhere.

Alyssa takes huge leaps to avoid them. She lands on her tiptoes like some kind of ballerina.

"Come here," I say. I slide my hands under her ass and lift her into my arms.

She raises her brows.

"You know I'm not going to fuck you in a cemetery."

I kiss her nose.

"There's always after."

She shakes her head, but she's smiling. She likes the idea.

Hell, her cheeks are red. She's probably envisioning it right now.

"Mr. Lawrence, this is a family establishment. You shouldn't discuss such topics."

"Uh-huh."

I let her down on a safe spot and she latches on to my

shoulders. She stares straight through my eyes. It's like she's looking into my soul, like she can see everything inside of me.

She brushes her lips against mine. It's soft and sweet enough to make me melt.

"Come on." She takes my hand and squeezes tight.

I lead her through the cemetery. I still remember the way—ten rows from the back, three columns from the left.

And there they are.

Two slate gray tombstones. Emilia Lawrence and Edward Lawrence.

I run my thumb over her fingers. "I've never been here with anyone else."

She laces her fingers with mine.

"Thanks for bringing me."

"I never came here much. I always felt bad about it, like I was disappointing her again." I stare at the writing, like it could actually tell me something. "They were fighting over me. If it hadn't been for me, she would never have run out of the house. She would have never gotten into the accident."

"It was an accident. There's nothing you could have done about it."

"I know, but... it's been so long now—ten years almost —and nothing has ever taken away that uneasy feeling in my gut. Nothing but being with you."

She leans against me.

"I get the feeling it would be horribly inappropriate to kiss you the way I want to."

I smile slightly.

"It would be much worse if you tore off my clothes and fucked me senseless, but I wouldn't complain."

She shakes her head. "You aren't that irresistible."

"Now that's a bald-faced lie."

Her lips curl into a smile. "Maybe. But I've gained a lot of self-control." She rises onto her tiptoes and presses her lips to mine. "I'm sorry you hurt so much."

"Everyone hurts."

She nods. "But you've been through so much, and you've done most of life on your own."

I bring her hand to my lips, kissing it softly. "I don't want to do it on my own anymore. After my mom died, I couldn't shake the idea that it was my fault. If she hadn't been taking such good care of me, defending me against my dad, it never would have happened." I press my fingers into the bouquet. "I know, intellectually, that it was an accident. That it was because of weather and some other driver's mistake. But it still felt like it was my fault. I convinced myself that I could survive without ever needing someone again, that things would be easier that way. Less risky."

Her eyes fill with sympathy.

"Everyone needs helps sometimes."

I nod, glad she's here with me. Kneeling, I place the bouquet on my mom's grave.

"I miss her," I murmur. "She was the greatest mom in the world. She wasn't perfect, but she was always there for me."

"I'm so sorry, Luke."

She moves closer to me. Until I can feel her heart beating.

"I always blamed my dad," I continue, staring at the small cracks in the stone. "I started hating him the day she died, and I never stopped. I still haven't stopped. At first it was for hurting Mom. Then it was for hurting Samantha. I was always angry at him... but never sad. And even though I hated him... he was my dad. I still remember our family trips to the park, playing catch, him trying desperately to convince me not to watch movies with my mom. He had good intentions. She did show me the most horribly violent movies. They were completely inappropriate for me."

The sun is high in the sky, bringing out the vivid hues of the grass, the flowers, even the tombstones.

"He was awful too. But it still hurt to lose him," I say.

"You've carried a lot on your shoulders."

I turn to Alyssa, meeting her eyes. "I'm not saying I'm going to be perfect, or that we're going to be perfect. But I want to do things right, Ally. I want to be there for you. It's hard to admit it, but I want you to be there for me too. I know we have problems. But I also know I can take on anything if it's with you."

She smiles. "I want to be there." She moves closer to me, wrapping her body around mine. "I love you. No matter what happens, I love you."

"I love you too."

I press my lips to hers. And I know that everything is going to be okay.

———

Want more?

Come to Me, the last book in the trilogy, <u>is now available</u>. Keep scrolling for a sneak peek!

Come to Me - Special Preview

ALYSSA

Get *Come To Me* Now

Luke's face lights up when I step into the restaurant.

"I missed you so much," he murmurs in a low voice.

God, I missed him too.

I missed him holding me while we watch television, I missed arguing with him about the stupidest little things, I missed having him there while I drink my morning cup of coffee.

I missed the way he looks at me with those dark eyes.

Like he wants me so badly he can't wait to be alone. And might not.

It's been barely any time at all. Five days. One week of shooting on location, far, far away from Los Angeles.

But it feels like forever.

He wraps his arms tight around me, secure and warm. My body hums from the proximity.

It's as good as the first time he touched me.

"I missed you too," I whisper.

I bury myself deeper in his chest, inhaling him. He

smells good. He always does. Like soap and Luke and my shampoo.

The obscenely girly honey scented shampoo I buy at Lush.

He brushes his cheek against mine; the beginning of stubble rasping against me lightly.

My whole body feels light, like I'm floating. It really does feel like it's been an eternity since I've been in his arms, since I've felt his skin against mine.

"How did you bribe Laurie into releasing you early?" he asks, his voice rumbling in his chest.

"I'm the star. I get to make all kinds of ridiculous demands," I half joke.

"Hmm. I'll make sure I use that to my advantage in the future."

I smile, breathing him in again, letting the feeling of being back in Luke's arms soak in.

"You're using my shampoo."

"And your conditioner." He squeezes me tighter then pulls back to look at me, his eyes soft. "It smells like you."

My heart squeezes in my chest.

"Barely. I only wash my hair once a week."

"It's close enough." He offers his hand, his palm flat like he's Prince Charming asking me to dance. I brush my fingers against it.

"I promised her a sleep over," I explain.

He raises a brow.

"She's a little old for that."

"Ah, but she's also incredibly abusive of her power. Reminds me of someone else I know."

"I do no such thing," he counters with mock affront.

"Then why is your assistant always booking my appointments?" I point out.

He raises a brow. "What's the point of having an

assistant if she isn't assisting?" He sighs dreamily. "And thanks for reminding me I have my very own assistant."

Luke used to work with my ex, Ryan. They were partners in a tiny, two-man law firm. About six months ago, Luke sold his half of the practice to Ryan. He wanted to cut any ties with him forever.

Thank God.

Now, Luke works independently as a divorce lawyer. He really adores his job. He loves discussing the virtues of dissolving toxic marriages.

I bite my lip to keep from laughing at his expression. "You certainly didn't forget how to gloat in the last few days."

"It's a skill I'd never let die," he says seriously. Shifting his attention, he squeezes my hand and points me to the staircase. "Miss Summers, I'd love to stand here talking shit about your boss all night, but our reservation is for 7:00."

"Is that so?"

He nodes gravely.

"Yes, and I'd hate to be late to my anniversary dinner. It would be dreadfully embarrassing."

"So it would," I agree, smiling slightly.

He leans down and brushes his lips against mine.

They're so soft and sweet. Kissing him feels like home.

I'm so glad to be back.

I follow Luke upstairs.

He tried to convince me we should celebrate our anniversary at the restaurant where we shared our first meal, but I nixed the idea. Ryan still works across the street, and I don't want to ruin a year of bliss by running into my bitter ex-boyfriend.

Instead, we're at a secluded restaurant on the other side of the marina. It's close to the water, close enough that we should have a gorgeous view of the sunset.

It's popular for that reason.

But today... it's quiet. Unusually quiet.

I frown, just then noticing it.

I was too busy taking Luke in before.

But I'm not in suspense for long.

When I get to the top floor, I see why.

There's space for 100 people.

But no one is here.

Light streams through the windows, bouncing off the clean hard-wood floors and the mostly empty room.

There's only one table set up.

One.

My jaw drops at the sight. It's so... perfect.

Luke knew I was dreading potential interruptions. Between *Model Citizen* taking off and my last film winning an Independent Spirit Award, I'm recognizable. Every few days, someone stops me to offer a compliment or, if I'm really lucky, a criticism of the show.

But not tonight.

Tonight it's only us.

Luke grins at my reaction. "I promised you'd like it."

I shake my head.

"I never doubted you."

The light from the windows falls over him. He looks so sharp in his black suit and royal blue tie, his dark hair falling in soft waves.

He had to wear a suit for work, but he doesn't usually go all out. I know it's for me.

"Stop objectifying me," he teases.

I sigh.

"But you look so good."

His eyes pass over my body. "You're not so bad your-self." He leans closer, his fingers on my upper back, his breath on my ear. "You know that's my favorite dress."

"Oh, this old thing?" I ask with mock coyness. It's a very sexy dress--smooth blue silk that clings to my curves.

Especially my chest.

"God damn, Alyssa. You are going to pay for wearing that."

I suppress a shiver at the heat in his eyes.

No one has ever made me feel sexier.

My response is more than a little breathy.

"I'm looking forward to it."

He pulls my chair out for me and sits across from me. There's a candle in the middle of the table, casting a soft light.

"I can't believe it's been a year," he marvels, his expression wondering.

"Me either."

It feels like the time flew right by.

"It's been the best year of my life."

"Me too," I agree. He's just... the best. So much more than I could have expected. "I just wish we didn't have to spend so much time apart."

"Yes." He offers his hand, and I take it. "I hate it too." He leans in closer. "I fantasize about just coming with you when you leave."

"You have a business to run," I murmur, wishing he could.

He shrugs.

"Sure. But it would be so much more fun to just say 'fuck it'. To quit and spend my life traveling the world with you."

"You'd get bored," I try next, my smile wider.

"Never," he scoffs. "I could never get bored with you."

"You love your job."

"Yes." He leans in close. "But I love you more."

I feel my cheeks flush.

I know it must be true--we've been together for a year.

A year ago, I dumped Ryan's sorry ass to be with Luke. We've been through a lot together. But it's been fucking amazing.

I was never a romantic person. I'm still not, not really. But, being with him... I finally get it. I understand pop songs, greeting cards, proposals written in the sky.

He's so damn sweet. He's smarter than anyone I know, driven, funny. So sexy I sometimes can't stand it.

He's also an insufferable tease and there are moments in the middle of an argument where I want to just scream.

I wouldn't change him for anything.

He's perfect.

"What are you thinking, Ally?" He searches my face.

I shake my head. "It's nothing."

He tilts his head, giving me a look.

"It looked like something."

"Just that I love you," I say. "That's all."

His face lights up with a smile.

God, that was it. The first time I saw his face light up like that, I was hooked.

"Go on."

I laugh, rolling my eyes.

"In your dreams. Your head is already too big."

He shakes said head, a wicked glint in his eye. "No. My dreams of you are never that tame."

My temperature goes up a couple of degrees.

"Mr. Lawrence," I whisper, making a show of looking around. "This is a family restaurant."

"So it is."

"But... I wouldn't necessarily ask you to stop."

His eyes darken.

I feel my heartbeat quicken.

I know that look.

"Would you ever ask me to stop?"

I bite my lip. We've been so busy--I've had early call times and he's been home late--that we've barely touched each other in the last two weeks.

Tonight can't come soon enough.

"We'll see," I say.

This time, his smile is too sharp, too hungry to be at all innocent.

I can't look away.

"Ally... you're going to be in agony tonight." His finger traces a line across my palm, oh so lightly. I feel that small touch... everywhere. His gaze is knowing as he continues. He knows exactly how he affects me. "In the most delightful agony. You're going to beg me to do anything to release you from it." He brings my hand up to his mouth, kissing my palm softly. "And... I just might."

I still haven't fully caught my breath when the waiter arrives.

———

Dinner is an amazing, three course affair-- a fresh salad with plump tomatoes, seared sea bass with braised kale and roasted yams, and a plate of chocolate dipped strawberries.

Yum.

The sun sets, until the only light is from the stars outside and the candle flickering between us. I tell Luke about all the irrelevant details of my trip--the oppressive sunshine in Arizona, getting dragged to townie bars by the other cast members, Laurie scolding the director of the week for getting too invested in his shots.

It's exactly what I didn't know I wanted.

After dinner, Luke insists on driving. "It's a surprise," he tells me.

I don't know what to expect, anticipation building.

My heart melts when I see where we end up.

The bookstore. The place where we had our first real date.

Just like the first time, we walk around the aisles, our fingers lingering on the crisp paper. We find a corner upstairs, in the non-fiction section, and steal a long, deep kiss.

It's been so long, and there's so much need pouring from both of us. His hands brush against my thighs, all the way to the edges of my dress. I moan into his mouth.

"Not here," I say hoarsely.

"Of course not here," he agrees. He nods to the movie theater across the street. "Not when I have a chance to repeat one of my favorite-"

"We're not going to luck into an empty theater tonight."

He draws back, feigning offense.

"Miss Summers. What do you take me for--some kind of pervert?"

His eyes twinkle mischievously.

"What do you have planned?" I ask, suspicious of that look.

He just smiles, squeezes my hand, and leads me to the theater.

Inside, the theater is the same as it was before--fluorescent and almost empty. That's not a huge surprise--there's a new, cool movie theater across the street. One that serves dinner and drinks and has couches that beg you to push the limits of decency laws.

Of course, I don't need any extra motivation.

My body has been flooding with want since I first felt Luke's arms around me.

He was right. This is already painful.

But I'm not shying away from more. It's going to be such delicious agony.

We buy tickets to a film that started five minutes ago. The usher assures us that the trailers are still rolling, that the theater is nearly empty. He looks at us like he knows what we have planned. Are we really that obvious?

I whisper in Luke's ear. "Are you sure this is wise? What if someone recognizes me?"

His hand slides over my waist, until his fingers are pressed against my bare back.

Jesus. My skin tingles with an electric current.

There's no way I can sit through a two-hour movie before getting his hands on me.

He brings his mouth to my ear, his breath hot and heavy. "I am dying to make you come."

I must have a stupid look on my face, because he's grinning again. It's that confident look of his, the one that says *I know how much you want me. I know how good I am at filling you with desperate, achy need. And I'm going to do it. Then, I'm going to release you in a torrent of ecstasy. But not until you're begging and pleading.*

"But we could always go home. Traffic has cleared by now," he offers.

But there's no doubt in his voice. He knows we aren't going anywhere.

He knows I need him now.

I shake my head. "No. I like that other plan."

He presses his lips into my neck. I already feel it--the rush of want between my legs. "Good," he whispers. "I've been daydreaming about it all damn week."

His lips are on my neck again, a harder kiss. We're in the middle of the lobby. The surly teenager at the concession stand is staring at us, but I don't care.

I close my eyes and lean into his kiss.

He takes my hand and leads me into the empty theater.

It's dark, but I can just make out a few people in the back-middle rows. The very back corner is empty. Is it the same corner, the same theater where we...

"It is," he responds to my thoughts. "But I don't want you thinking about that day when you scream my name. I want you so filled with pleasure that you're practically incoherent."

Jesus.

I nod. "I'm... on board."

His hands skim my waist as he follows me into the row. I sit next to the wall. It's the farthest corner of the theater. If anyone looked, they would be sure we were doing something...

Just like last time.

My heart pounds in my chest. Someone might see us, but I don't care. I almost want someone to see us, to see how damn good he is at delivering on his promises.

Luke lifts the arm rest and presses his lips into mine. It's soft at first. He moves slowly. His fingertips circle my knees and slide up my thighs, inching closer and closer to the edge of my dress. His kiss intensifies as his hand slides under my dress.

I clench my thighs, soaking in the feel of his skin on mine. God. He's about to... Almost... It's been so long.

This is already torture.

His tongue plunges into my mouth as he presses his hand against my panties. Every sense in my body turns on all at once.

I can hear his soft, heavy breath, even with the air conditioning on full blast and the movie launching into some loud action sequence.

He keeps his hand flat against my panties, another one

of his horrible, wonderful teases. I flood with want, squirming in my seat, kissing him harder and harder.

Then, he runs his fingers over my panties. It's so light and gentle I can barely stand it. "Luke," I groan. "Touch me."

But he keeps at it, his touch still light and slow and soft.

"You look too damn beautiful like this," he growls. He kisses me, as hard as I was kissing him. His tongue swirls around mine as he slides his hands under the fabric of my panties.

Jesus Christ. My body burns from his touch.

It's been too long.

I kiss him back even harder as he rubs me with long, slow strokes. His hand is so soft and hard all at once, and I arch to meet his touch.

But I need more.

I pull my dress to my waist, pull my panties out of the way. I don't care that someone could see. All I care about is him touching me, him delivering on his promise.

Get *Come To Me* Now

Stay in Touch

Thanks for reading *Come Apart*!

If you enjoyed the story, please help other readers find it by leaving an honest review on Amazon or Goodreads.

If you love to review and want to get books before anyone else, join the Crystal Kaswell ARC team.

Want to talk books? Awesome! I love hearing from my readers. Like my page on Facebook, join my fangroup, follow me on Instagram, follow me on Twitter, or friend me on Facebook.

Also by Crystal Kaswell

Come Undone Trilogy

Come Undone

Come Apart

Come To Me

Dirty Rich

Dirty Deal - Blake

Dirty Boss - Nick

Dirty Husband - Shep

Dirty Desires - Ian

Dirty Wedding - Ty

Dirty Secret - Cam

Pierce Family

Broken Beast - Adam

Playboy Prince - Liam

Ruthless Rival - Simon - coming soon

Inked Hearts

Tempting - Brendon

Hooking Up - Walker

Pretend You're Mine - Ryan

Hating You, Loving You - Dean

Breaking the Rules - Hunter

Sign up for the Crystal Kaswell mailing list

Printed in Great Britain
by Amazon

10199946R00192